## 'I have yet to agree to your romantic proposal.'

'You will.'

'You're so sure?'

'You have no other options.'

She looked at the dirty cloth in her hands, picking off one loose thread around the frayed edge before she faced him again. 'You're right. I have no other options. However, you could present your case in a less businesslike tone, with a little civility and charm.'

'You don't strike me as a woman ruled by romantic notions.'

'No, but I'm still a woman, and I would like to be wooed just a touch.'

For the second time that day he wanted to smile, but didn't. Instead he stepped closer, admiring her spirit. She didn't just surrender to him—sign her name on the contract, as it were—but demanded his respect...not his money or anything else. Once again his instinct for business had proved correct.

'Miss Townsend, will you do me the honour of accepting me as your husband?'

D0184810

# AUTHOR NOTE

When Philip Rathbone first introduced himself to me as a character in *Rescued from Ruin,* he caught my attention. He was supposed to appear in one scene, say his lines and then disappear. However, he wouldn't go so easily. I was intrigued by this young man who let nothing fluster him, and wondered what it was in his past that had forced him to be so stoic. Once I got to know Philip and his tragic backstory it was a challenge finding the right woman to help break down the walls he'd built around his heart.

Laura is the perfect woman to help Philip overcome his past. She too has suffered tragedy, but her resilience has kept her from withdrawing from the world. Instead she is determined to surmount obstacles—one of which becomes winning Philip's heart.

A challenge for me in writing *A Debt Paid in Marriage* was developing Philip and Laura's world. Researching the private lives of a moneylender and a draper's daughter meant digging deep into first-hand accounts from the Regency. Moneylenders weren't portrayed in the best light, and merchants didn't leave many written records of their day-to-day existence. To explore Laura's world I looked to books on the history of textiles, and examined the records of other merchants of her class. To get a sense of Philip's life I had to study the world of money and credit. It was a challenge, but a fun one, that helped me make both the characters and their stories richer.

I hope you enjoy reading Philip and Laura's story as much as I enjoyed writing it.

# A DEBT PAID
# IN MARRIAGE

Georgie Lee

MILLS & BOON

All rights reserved including the right of reproduction in whole
or in part in any form. This edition is published by arrangement with
Harlequin Books S.A.

This is a work of fiction. Names, characters, places, locations and
incidents are purely fictional and bear no relationship to any real
life individuals, living or dead, or to any actual places, business
establishments, locations, events or incidents. Any resemblance is
entirely coincidental.

This book is sold subject to the condition that it shall not, by way of
trade or otherwise, be lent, resold, hired out or otherwise circulated
without the prior consent of the publisher in any form of binding or
cover other than that in which it is published and without a similar
condition including this condition being imposed on the subsequent
purchaser.

® and TM are trademarks owned and used by the trademark owner
and/or its licensee. Trademarks marked with ® are registered with the
United Kingdom Patent Office and/or the Office for Harmonisation in
the Internal Market and in other countries.

Published in Great Britain 2015
by Mills & Boon, an imprint of Harlequin (UK) Limited,
Eton House, 18-24 Paradise Road, Richmond, Surrey, TW9 1SR

© 2015 Georgie Reinstein

ISBN: 978-0-263-24769-5

Harlequin (UK) Limited's policy is to use papers that are natural,
renewable and recyclable products and made from wood grown in
sustainable forests. The logging and manufacturing processes conform
to the legal environmental regulations of the country of origin.

Printed and bound in Spain
by CPI, Barcelona

A lifelong history buff, **Georgie Lee** hasn't given up hope that she will one day inherit a title and a manor house. Until then she fulfils her dreams of lords, ladies and a Season in London through her stories. When not writing, she can be found reading non-fiction history or watching any film with a costume and an accent.

Please visit www.georgie-lee.com to learn more about Georgie and her books.

**Visit the author profile page at millsandboon.co.uk**

A special thanks to RWASD
for your inspiration and motivation.

# *Chapter One*

*London—spring 1817*

'**W**hat exactly do you think you are doing?' Mr Rathbone demanded, his deep-blue eyes fixing on her through the wisps of steam rising from the copper bathtub. Dark-brown hair lay damp over his forehead. One drop escaped the thickness of it, sliding down his face, then tracing the edge of his jaw before dropping into the tub.

Laura slid her finger away from the trigger, afraid of accidentally sending a ball through the moneylender's sturdy, wet and very bare torso. She had no intention of killing him, only frightening him into giving back the inventory he'd seized from her uncle Robert. Judging by the hard eyes he fixed on her, he wasn't a man to scare easily.

'Well?' he demanded and she jumped, her nerves as taut as the fabric over the back of a chair.

When she'd slipped into the house determined to face him, she'd expected to find him hunched over his desk counting piles of coins or whatever else it was a moneylender did at night. She hadn't expected to surprise him in his bath with a film of soapy water the only thing standing between her and his modesty. What had seemed like a good plan in the pathetic rooms she shared with her uncle and her mother, when hunger gnawed at her stomach and cold crept in through the broken window, now seemed horrible.

Laura settled her shoulders, shoring up the courage faltering under his steady stare. Beyond this humid room was nothing but ruin and poverty. She had no choice but to continue. 'I demand you return to me the fabric you seized from my uncle.'

The moneylender raised his arms out of the water, disturbing the calm suds, and she caught sight of his flat stomach before the soapy water settled back over it. His hands rested on the curved sides of the tub. They were long but sturdy, like those of the delivery men who used to haul the bolts of cloth off the cart and into her father's draper shop. Mr Rathbone's were smooth and free of calluses, however, and, except for the red of an old cut snaking along one knuckle, the hands of a gentleman.

She took a step back, expecting him to rise from the water and rush at her. He did nothing except study her, as though appraising her market value. 'And who exactly is your uncle?'

Laura swallowed hard. Yes, this was important information to impart if one was to make demands of a naked man. 'Robert Townsend.'

'The gambling draper.' Neither shock nor surprise broke his piercing stare. 'He came to me six months ago in need of a loan to pay a large debt accrued at Mrs Topp's, among many other establishments. In return for my money, he put up the inventory of the draper business as collateral. When he defaulted, I seized the goods, as was my right pursuant to our contract.'

The floor shifted beneath her. Uncle Robert had lost the business. In the past, he'd stolen merchandise from the storeroom, a bolt of silk or a cord of tassel, and sold it to fund his gambling. They were losses to the business, but not the whole business.

It couldn't be gone, not after everything she'd done to hold on to it after her father's death.

Anger overcame her shock and she gripped Uncle Robert's old pistol tighter, her sweating palms making the wood handle stick to her skin. 'I don't believe you. I know how men of your ilk operate, taking advantage of desperate people with high interest rates until they have no choice but to turn everything they own over to your grasping hands.'

Mr Rathbone's eyes narrowed a touch. What the gun and the element of surprise had failed to do, her smear of his character managed to achieve—a reaction.

'If it's proof you require, I'm most happy to oblige.' He pushed up against the edge of the tub and rose.

'Sir!' Laura gasped and shuffled back until the edge of a table caught her hip. She clutched the pistol tighter, unable to tear her eyes away as fat drops poured down his slender body, catching in the ripples of his stomach before falling into the sloshing water of the tub. The drops were not thick enough to offer any semblance of modesty and she struggled to keep her gaze from wandering from his handsome face to the long length of chest, stomach and everything else beneath. Her heart pounded harder than when she'd crept into the house through the open terrace door, then pressed herself deep into the shadows of an alcove beneath the stairs when a maid had passed by.

He lifted one long leg, then the other over the copper tub and stepped dripping on to the small towel on the floor next to it. Over a nearby chair lay a brown banyan of fine silk—French, she guessed, by the subtle pattern in the weave. She expected him to take it up and pull it on over the long expanse of him, but he didn't. Instead he strode past her, through the wide double doors adjoining the dressing-and-bathing room to his bedroom without so much as a second look, as though she were not standing there threatening his life and he was not stark naked and leaving a trail of wet footprints on the wood floor. He headed to the small desk in the opposite corner of the bedroom, near the windows and across from the tall, four-poster bed hung with expensive embroidered curtains. Behind the desk, he opened one of the drawers. Neither the neat stack of papers on top nor the oil lamp on the corner did anything to prevent her from seeing him as Eve must have seen Adam after they'd tasted the apple. Laura could feel her own judgement coming. What she wouldn't give for a lightning bolt from above, or at the very least a large fig leaf.

'Here is the contract we drew up the day he

came to see me.' Mr Rathbone came around the desk, holding out the paper.

Laura forced her eyes to meet his. 'Would you please get dressed?'

'This is my house. You broke into it and threatened me. I may stand as I like. Now here is your proof.' The paper fluttered at the end of one stiff, outstretched arm.

In the flickering candlelight she read the list of her uncle's debts laid out in points in the centre of the page. There were more names than just Mrs Topp's. Most were unfamiliar, but a few she recognised from snatches of conversation she'd caught in the hallways of their ramshackle building. Below the terms were Mr Rathbone's signature and that of a witness, a Mr Justin Connor. Next to them sat Uncle Robert's uneven letters, the wide way he wrote his R and T clear.

It wasn't so much his signing away the shop that shocked her, it was the document he'd put his name to. 'Where did you get this paper?'

'Mr Townsend brought it to me the night he came here seeking a loan.'

'This is mine. I wrote this, it was my plan to save our business.'

'It was an excellent one and, combined with the collateral he possessed to secure the loan, the reason I extended him the sum. He could have succeeded, if he hadn't gambled the money away.' He laid the document on the desk. 'Are you quite satisfied?'

'I am.' *And we're ruined.*

'Good, then you won't need this.' Mr Rathbone grabbed the barrel of the pistol and wrenched it from her hands.

'No,' she cried, as naked as him without the weapon.

'The gun would have done you no good. It was improperly loaded.' He pulled the flint from the hammer and tossed the now-useless weapon on the desk along with the contract. 'Had you fired it, you would have blown your pretty face off.'

She looked to where the weapon lay on the blotter, as useless as her hope and her foolish plans. This morning she had thought her situation couldn't sink any lower. It seemed she had yet to reach the bottom, but all she could think of was her mother. Laura's botched attempt to save them would no doubt land her in gaol. How would her mother survive without her and what would Uncle Robert do to her? 'You should have let me fire it and finish myself.'

He strode past her back to the bathroom. 'You'd have ruined the carpet.'

Anger overcame her sense of loss and she whirled on him. Without concern, he took up the banyan from the chair and slid his strong arms into the sleeves, pulling it shut over his nakedness. Laura's anger flickered, nearly blown out by the sight of his skin caressed by the dark silk, before it flared again. 'I can see all you care about is money.'

He pulled the banyan ties tight across his slim middle. 'I'm a businessman, Miss Townsend. Men interested in financial backing for ventures come to me, as well as those seeking to shore up a struggling business. I offer them finance to be repaid with interest, or, if they default, as your uncle did, I seize their goods and sell them to cover my losses. I have a family and employees whose welfare I must ensure. I am not a charity.'

'No, of course not.' She looked down at the carpet he was so worried about, moving one toe of her worn-out half-boot to trace the swirling curve of a vine. In the brief time she'd spent plotting this ridiculous scheme, she'd failed to work out exactly how she might extricate herself from it without landing in the Old Bailey, or worse. She only hoped the generous nature he spoke of with his family and employees might extend to a very foolish young lady.

'Mr Rathbone, please forgive me for intruding on your privacy and for trying to blacken your good name. I was not in possession of all the facts before I decided to confront you. It seems I was not in possession of my reason either.' She smiled, trying to look the way she imagined a senseless young lady might look, in the hope of saving both her dignity and her freedom. It failed to soften the hard set of Mr Rathbone's mouth.

'Don't play the fool. It's not becoming of a woman of your ingenuity.'

She dropped the smile but not her hope, unwilling to concede defeat. She couldn't, not with her mother shivering at home. 'Then let me offer you a proposal, one that speaks to you as a businessman.'

Mr Rathbone stood silent and she couldn't discern if he planned to listen or to summon a footman to fetch the constable. She didn't give him a chance to answer, hoping her words might at least make him consider her offer and postpone for some time whatever fate he had in mind for her. 'Among the contents of the inventory you seized was a large bolt of cotton woven into a very fine cloth. It's from a special variety, grown in Egypt. It can be rendered, like the Indian kind, into a very fine, almost transparent cloth, but it costs less to produce. I plan to introduce it through Madame Pillet, a modiste to many fashionable and influential ladies. Their orders for the fabric alone could bring in hundreds of pounds. With the profits, I can import more and establish a fine trade. If you return the inventory to me, I'll pay you a portion of the profits until the original debt is settled.'

'I'm afraid I can't entertain your proposal,' he answered without consideration. 'The contents of the draper shop were sold to settle Mr Townsend's debts. I no longer have the bolt of cotton to which you are referring.'

'But you know who has it. You could get it back and we could still reach an arrangement.'

'I cannot.'

'You're leaving us to starve,' she blurted out as even this slim hope dissolved. There was no chance of reviving the business, or doing anything other than sinking into even more degrading poverty.

No sign of sympathy or regret marred the smoothness of his face. 'Your plan has merit, but will not succeed. If the cotton becomes fashionable, those with better connections and more money will race to import it before you can secure more, flooding the market with it and lessening its value.'

'But before then?' she protested meekly.

'I can't afford to gamble my money on the whims of the *ton*. Nor can you.'

'I can't rely on my uncle Robert if that's what you're thinking. He's got everything out of us he wanted, my father's business and what was left of the money,' she scoffed. 'It won't be long before we see the backside of him. Then what will happen to me and my mother?'

'You must have other family?'

She shook her head. 'No.'

'Friends?'

'Uncle Robert saw to it that they were driven away when he borrowed money from them and never repaid it.' She dropped her hands to her sides in imitation of Mr Rathbone, trying to appear as confident and sure as he did. 'I know what I did tonight was foolish and I never meant to hurt you, I only wanted the merchandise back because I couldn't see the business fail. It took my father years to build and my uncle Robert less than a year to destroy.'

If Philip had passed Miss Townsend on the street, he'd have overlooked her. Forced to stare down the end of a barrel at her, he couldn't miss the stunning light of determination in her round hazel eyes. It was undiminished by the faint circles darkening the smooth skin underneath them or the slight hollow beneath the high cheekbones. Loose waves of auburn hair hung on either side of her face and down to the shoulders of her worn-out dress. The sad garment hung loose on her. Regular meals would bring back the fullness of her cheeks and the softness of her waist. Her skin was pale, like Arabella's had been, but where illness had faded his late wife's bloom, only hardship dampened the lustre of the lady before him. 'In business, it's always best to keep facts and emotions separate so one does not cloud the other.'

'I'll remember that when I'm starving,' she spat.

'You won't starve. You're too smart.' There was something of life and fight in Miss Townsend, a trait Arabella had not possessed. Despite his annoyance at being disturbed tonight, he admired it too much to see it snuffed out by gaol fever. He swept the pistol from the desk and held it out to her. 'Thank you for an interesting evening, Miss Townsend.'

Hope flooded her cheeks with a wash of pink. 'You're letting me go?'

'Would you prefer I call the constable and have you hauled before the magistrate?'

'No.'

He moved aside and waved his hand at the door. 'Then go.'

In a flutter of threadbare bombazine, she was gone.

'You there, stop.' Justin's voice sounded through the downstairs hall before the thud of the back door hitting the wall and the squeak of the garden gate let Philip know Miss Townsend was away.

A second later Justin came running in, his pistol drawn. 'Are you all right?'

'Quite.' Philip sat down in his chair, rubbing his still-damp chin with his fingers. Miss Townsend had stirred something inside him— not pity, or even lust, though she was pretty. No, it was curiosity, like the first time he'd seen Arabella sitting across his desk next to her father, Dr Hale. Philip hadn't been able to focus on anything but her while Dr Hale had laid out his plans for a small medical school. The school had failed and Dr Hale had lost both his and Philip's money. It was the only time Philip had allowed emotion to guide a business decision.

'Leave it to you to be so cavalier about an

intruder threatening you.' Justin lowered the hammer on the pistol.

'She was never a threat.' Philip curled one finger to rub it along his ring finger still missing the plain wedding band he'd buried with Arabella. No, this was nothing like the day he'd met his wife. There was no emotion to touch his love for Arabella, especially not in the guise of this stranger, no matter how intriguing she might appear.

'You look like the devil.' Justin slid the pistol in the holster under his coat.

'It's been a trying day.' He'd thought the headaches of it were over when he'd sunk down into the hot water. He couldn't have been more wrong.

He stared past Justin to the copper bathtub and the thin tendrils of steam still rising from it. Nothing but problems had plagued him today. A cobbler had called to secure a loan to increase his business. The cobbler's endless words of reassurance and lack of collateral had warned Philip off the venture. The man hadn't reacted kindly to Philip's refusal. He'd only just been ejected from the house when Justin had arrived with news of an import company with an outstanding loan having been declared bankrupt. It'd been a scramble to seize the goods stored in the warehouse before the importer moved them and left Philip with the loss.

With business matters secured, household ones had rushed in to consume the remainder of the day. His sister, Jane, had tried his patience with yet another demand for an expensive dress too mature for a budding young woman of thirteen. She'd railed at him with their grandmother's temper before stomping away after Philip threatened to cut off her dress allowance. On the heels of Jane's tantrum came the news that Mrs Marston, his son Thomas's nurse, was moving to Bath to take care of her grandson, leaving Philip with only a month to engage a replacement. Jane was too young to be of assistance and Mrs Palmer, despite running his house with the efficiency of a factory, was not up to the task of mothering his sister and son or finding a suitable replacement for Mrs Marston.

What Philip needed was a wife, someone to deal with these domestic matters.

Justin plucked a small chair from the wall, turned it around in front of the desk, then straddled it, leaning his elbows on the polished back. 'So, who was the woman?'

'The niece of Robert Townsend.' Philip

smoothed his hands over his wet hair. 'She wanted her collateral back.'

'Don't they all.' Justin snorted, propping his chin in his palm. 'I left two extra men to guard the importer's stock until you can sell it.'

'We'll see to it tomorrow,' Philip said vaguely, his thoughts consumed with something other than business.

Justin raised one curious eyebrow. 'What did she do to you?'

Philip straightened a pen on the blotter. 'What do you mean?'

'Never seen you this cavalier about a full warehouse. Usually you're all plans until I'm up all night and engaged through most of tomorrow seeing to it, but not tonight. Why?'

Philip studied his old friend and partner. Justin had stood beside him at his wedding and at Arabella's funeral. He balled his hand into a fist. His wife should have had the chance to raise their son and attend to their house. Now, it fell to the people Philip paid to assist him. Not the most ideal of situations and one he would soon correct.

Straightening in the chair, he laced his fingers over his stomach. It wasn't Miss Townsend's disturbance which troubled him now, as much as the opportunity she presented.

His father had trained him to assess a client in a matter of seconds. He'd measured up Miss Townsend and, despite the ridiculousness of her attempted threat, found her useful qualities continued to tip the scales in her favour.

It was madness and he knew it. He should recommend her and the mother to Halcyon House, his charitable organisation, and be done with them both, not continue to entertain the plan developing in his mind. He'd chosen Arabella with his heart, ignoring her frailty, believing it wouldn't come between them. He'd been a fool and in the end their love had killed her.

Small footsteps pattered down the long hallway outside his bedroom door before steady, larger ones followed. In a moment, he'd help Mrs Marston get Thomas back to sleep, but first there was business to discuss.

'I have another plan in mind, Justin.' He picked up Robert Townsend's contract. It was sheer luck he'd decided to bring it upstairs with the others, as was his habit, to review before bed or if he was restless in the middle of the night. He handed it to his friend. 'Find out everything you can about his niece.'

'I knew I wouldn't get off so easy tonight.' He rose from the chair and set it back by the wall, then plucked the paper from Philip's hand.

'Speak to anyone who might know her from her lodgings and from the neighbourhood where the draper shop used to be, I'm sure you can discover its location.'

'You know I can.' He folded the contract and slid it into his pocket.

'Get a sense of her reputation, character and situation. Find out any and every detail you can and bring it to me as soon as possible.'

'Is she going to become a client?'

Philip rose, eager to see to his son. 'No. She might become my wife.'

## Chapter Two

Laura stared at the worn and splintered door, frozen where she stood, her uncle's dirty tankard in one hand, a cleaning rag in the other.

Someone had knocked. No one ever knocked here. It couldn't be good.

She jumped again as the wood rattled beneath the fist of whoever was on the other side. She set the tankard down and hurried to the door, eager to silence the person for fear they'd wake her mother.

'Who is it?' she hissed through a crack near the centre.

'Mr Rathbone.'

She jolted away from the wood. It'd been two days since she'd fled from his house and there was nothing he could want from her, unless he'd changed his mind about seeing her gaoled. The constable might be outside with him now.

She twisted the rag around one hand, then let go. No, the constable would have announced himself. She'd heard him banging on enough doors in the building to know. Mr Rathbone must want something else, but what? The cotton. Maybe he'd finally seen the sense in her offer, found a way to buy back the bolt and was here to discuss an arrangement.

She pulled open the door to find him standing on the other side. Unlike the few others who came here, he didn't clutch a scented handkerchief to his face or look around as though expecting a rat to pounce. He stood exactly as he had two nights ago, businesslike, determined, a dark-blue redingote falling straight from his shoulders to cover his lithe but sturdy body. Her eyes trailed the length of him, from the low hat covering his almost black hair to the tips of his polished boots. Taking in this groomed and dressed moneylender, she tried not to imagine him without his clothes. If she hadn't seen him in such a fashion, she would be more terrified of him now, not mesmerised by the way his high white collar traced the angle of his jaw to where it narrowed to his chin.

'May I come in?' His crisp but polite words snapped her out of her musing.

'Yes, of course.' She waved him in with the rag, closing the door behind him.

In four steps he reached the centre of the room. The faint, citrus scent of his bergamot cologne struck Laura harder than the stench of the street coming in through the window. The richness of the scent reminded her of the perfume shop situated next to her family's old shop and for a moment took her away from the filth permeating her life.

Mr Rathbone glanced down at the table where the dirty tankard sat, then turned to face her, his scrutiny pulling her back into the mire. 'Miss Townsend.'

'Shh…' Laura gestured to silence him, then caught sight of her dirty fingernails and lowered her hand as fast as she'd raised it. 'I must ask you to speak quietly. My mother is resting. She slept poorly last night and every night before.'

He nodded and removed his hat, holding it against his left side. 'Miss Townsend, I've come to speak to you about a business proposal.'

She twisted the rag tight between her hands. 'You've come to accept my offer? You found a way to retrieve the cotton bolt and return it to me?'

'No. As I told you, it is no longer in my possession.'

'But—'

He raised a silencing hand. 'Mr Townsend knew the consequences when he took my money and he will pay them. He is no longer my concern or yours.'

She perched one fist on her hip. 'Then what is our concern?'

He shifted the hat to his other hand so it rested against his right thigh instead of his left. If she thought the man capable of emotion, she might say he was nervous. 'You managed your father's draper business before Mr Townsend assumed control?'

'Before my uncle stole it from us,' she corrected, more curious than cautious.

'You kept accounts, inventory, credit?'

'I did.' She didn't hide her pride. 'My father thought it better for me to learn the business than attend a lady's school.'

'I know by the speed at which you comprehended the agreement that you can read and understand contracts and your business plan indicates you can write.'

'A fine hand.' She wondered where this line of questioning was leading. Maybe he'd taken pity on her and come to offer work. She smoothed one hand over her hair, wishing he'd given her some notice and a chance to make herself more presentable.

'And you are well, your mother's illness does not extend to you?'

'I am very hearty, thank you. My mother broke her leg a few years ago and, though it healed, she's afflicted with rheumatism. It's nothing food and heat wouldn't ease, but since we have neither, she suffers.'

His eyes dropped down, covering the length of her in a heartbeat before his head rose a touch as though appraising her collateral. She couldn't imagine what he saw since she wore no jewellery and her dress was too old to be of much value to even a secondhand-clothes merchant. 'There is no one, apart from your mother and Mr Townsend, to make a claim on you?'

Worry coiled inside her, fuelled by the memory of him parading before her naked without shame. 'If you've come to make an immodest proposal, you can leave.'

'There's nothing untoward in what I'm about to suggest, Miss Townsend. After a great deal of thought, I have another venture which might interest you.'

From the next room, her mother coughed and Laura tensed, waiting to see if she settled back to sleep or awoke. Hopefully she'd sleep. She needed the rest as much as she needed a decent meal and a proper pelisse to keep out the cold. Eyeing the moneylender, her dread increased. Even if he made her an indecent offer, she couldn't afford to refuse it. With the business lost, there were only more horrors waiting for her and her mother out on the street. 'I'm listening, Mr Rathbone.'

Philip shifted his hat to his other hand. From somewhere outside he heard the cry of an infant. It sounded too much like the way Thomas had wailed in the nurse's arms while Philip had held Arabella in his, clutching her to him as her life had slipped away.

He set the hat down on the table. This transaction had nothing to do with the past, but the more pressing needs of the present. 'A year ago, I lost my wife in childbirth. I'm in need of the services of a woman with your skills.'

Her brow scrunched down over her straight nose. 'You mean as a nurse?'

'No, as a wife.'

'A wife?' Her jaw dropped open before she pulled it closed, her eyes wider than when he'd snatched the pistol from her.

'I assume you're not already married.'

'No, but—'

'And you have no suitors?'

'Unless you consider the drunk who sits in the doorway and pesters me whenever I come and go, no.'

'Good. At present, I employ a capable nurse for my son, but she is leaving at the end of the month. I think it preferable for family to see to the welfare of a child. My sister is thirteen and too young for such things. She is also in need of a guiding hand. She will soon be faced with suitors and I don't have aunts or cousins on whom I may call to assist her.'

'And my mother?'

'I will see to her welfare and care.'

'By placing her in a home with some ill-mannered nurse?'

'She will have a suitable room in my house and a proper maid to attend her. You will learn my business and help me manage it.'

She continued to stare at him as if he'd suggested she be presented to the king. 'I nearly killed you and you wish to trust me with your son and business?'

Her reservations needled him. He'd reviewed the facts last night and they made sense. There was no room for doubt. He pressed on. 'You were never a threat to me.'

A tiny curve appeared at the corner of her mouth and he couldn't tell if she was going to smile or frown. 'How do you know I won't steal from you and run off?'

'Not likely with your mother residing under my roof.'

'There is truth in that.' She uncrossed her arms, the crease beside her lips growing deeper as she silently considered the merits of his offer as any wise client might contemplate the terms of a loan. 'Why me? Why marriage?'

'In my experience, a wife is a better business partner than any other as her interests are my interests. As to why you, you seem a quick wit, except where firearms are concerned.' Her crease deepened into a disapproving frown but he didn't let it deter or distract him. 'Your brazen act the other night demonstrated a degree of courage and strength.'

'Some might call it rash and reckless.'

'It was, but your plans for the fabric demonstrated an innate sensibility and intelligence. Your prior experience in your father's shop is an asset. Your reason for breaking into my house was to protect your mother. That demonstrates a proper degree of concern for those in your care. I have no doubt you can transfer such regard to my sister and son.'

Her brow rose a touch in surprise. 'I have never heard my attributes stated in such a plain way. I'm not sure if I should thank you or chide you for insulting me.'

'I meant it as a compliment.'

She nodded her thanks. 'You may find me a poor partner. I know nothing of moneylending.'

'You will learn so that if anything happens to me, you will know how to successfully carry on until our son reaches an age where he is able to assume control of the business.'

'Our son?'

'He will soon be as much yours as mine, and others will follow. I assume your courses are as they should be.'

She crossed her arms again. 'I beg your pardon.'

'We're making a bargain and, in such deals, we must be frank with one another.'

'They are as they should be.' No blush spread over her pale skin as her eyes dipped down the length of him, pausing near his hips before rising again to meet his gaze. 'Is everything as it should be with you?'

The girl possessed pluck and for the first time in almost a year, he felt the twitch of a smile tug up the corner of his lips before he squashed it. 'It is, as you will discover.'

'I have yet to agree to your romantic proposal.'

'You will.'

'You're so sure?'

'You have no other options.'

She looked at the dirty cloth in her hands, picking off one loose thread around the frayed edge before she faced him again. 'You're right, I have no other options. However, you could present your case in a less businesslike tone, with a little civility and charm.'

'You don't strike me as a woman ruled by romantic notions.'

'No, but I'm still a woman and would like to be wooed just a touch.'

For the second time today he wanted to smile but didn't. Instead, he stepped closer, admiring her spirit. She didn't just surrender to him, sign her name on the contract as it were, but demanded his respect, not his money or anything else. Once again, his instinct for business had proven correct. 'Miss Townsend, will you do me the honour of accepting me as your husband?'

Laura stared up at the stranger who stood only an arm's length from her, thankful he hadn't taken her hand or dropped to one knee.

She might have demanded a modicum of romance, but with her head still swimming from this unexpected proposal and a lack of food, she wasn't sure she could handle the shock of his touch. Her parents had raised her to be sensible and she was, but it didn't mean she didn't have dreams. All her life she'd wanted the same happiness she'd seen between her parents, to have a shop and a family with a man she loved and respected. Uncle Robert had destroyed such dreams when he'd ground the shop and their reputations into the dirt. Whatever hope she possessed of reviving them now lay with this gentleman.

Mr Rathbone watched her and she studied him, trying to gauge something of the real person beneath the stiff businessman, but she could see very little. He'd not offered one ounce of warmth since he'd opened his distracting blue eyes in the tub, nor even a brief flicker of sympathy for her plight, yet now he wished to make her his wife and take care of both her and her mother. It defied all reason, except his argument made perfect, rational sense to the practical side of her.

It was the physical realities of marriage which nearly made her sensible side flee. He expected children and there was only one way to get them. The image of him naked in front of her seared her mind and she swallowed hard. After leaving his home, she'd hurried back here and slipped into bed beside her mother, trying and failing to sleep. Mr Rathbone's was the first male body she'd ever seen undressed and the memory of it had insisted on teasing her.

She touched the loose bun at the nape of her neck, the skin beneath suddenly damp with perspiration. Seeing him naked hadn't been an unpleasant experience. If she accepted him, she would see him again in such a state and he would see her, but what would their more intimate moments be like? Her fingers fumbled with the loose strands of hair she gathered up to tuck back in with the others. She'd heard the fallen women cackling together in the hallways. They clearly enjoyed congress with the men they ran after. However, late at night, through the cracked and thin walls of their tumbledown rooms, she often heard the couple next door and the indignities a cruel husband could inflict on his wife. She wasn't sure whether it would be pain or pleasure she'd face with Mr Rathbone, if he would be tender or approach the matter with stiff efficiency. Whatever might pass between them, if she refused his offer, a hundred more degrading things from many strange men most likely awaited her. Their situation was already growing desperate and she knew what happened to desperate women in Seven Dials. There was as much uncertainty with Mr Rathbone as there was without him. At least with him, Laura knew they would be warm and well fed. 'Yes, Mr Rathbone, I accept your proposal.'

'Good. My men are waiting with a cart in the street.' He strode to the window and waved to someone below. 'Ready your things, we leave at once.'

'You were so sure I'd accept.' The man was unbelievable.

He faced her as he had in his room, his confidence as mesmerising as it was irksome. 'I'm always sure when it comes to matters of business.'

Not a second later, the door opened and another young man in a tan coat entered. 'Philip, you kept us waiting so long, you had me worried.'

'Mr Connor, allow me to introduce Miss Townsend, my intended. Miss Townsend, this is my friend and associate, Mr Justin Connor.'

Mr Connor swept off his hat and made a low bow. He was shorter than Mr Rathbone and broader through the hips and chest. His hair was light brown like his eyes, which revealed his amusement as much as his smile. 'A pleasure, Miss Townsend. It seems you've made quite an impression on my friend.'

Finally, someone with some sense of humour. 'Yes, he was just telling me how much my beauty and charm have enthralled him.'

'Spirited, too. I think it'll be a successful match.' He directed the comment as much to Mr Rathbone as to her.

If Mr Rathbone was needled by his associate's wit, he gave no indication, his countenance the same as when she'd surprised him in his bath. She wondered if he possessed any other expression.

Behind Mr Connor, four burly men in coarse but clean jackets filed into the room. Laura shifted on her feet at the notable tension coursing between them as they took up positions along the wall and near the door. From their thick belts hung clubs like the ones the night watchmen used to carry in Cheapside, where the draper shop was situated. The old watchmen didn't dare wander through these parts after dark. It was a wonder Laura had made it home unmolested after leaving Mr Rathbone's. It seemed whatever luck had led her into his house and out again without landing her in the

Old Bailey had followed her home. Hopefully, it would continue to walk with her down the aisle.

'Mr Rathbone, is there some reason for the weapons?' If he was to be her husband, there was no point being shy with him. 'Are my mother and I to be made prisoners?'

Mr Rathbone moved closer, his eyes stern and serious. 'Mr Townsend has proven himself selfish and uncaring. I assume he has held on to you and your mother for this long because he thinks there's still something to gain from you. He won't take kindly to my removing you from his control.'

Laura sank a little, sickened by how accurate a sketch Mr Rathbone drew of her uncle. 'I don't know what he could hope to gain from us. Everything we had, he took.'

'Not everything.' The words were softer than before, just like his eyes. Concern lingered behind his stiff countenance, faint like the subtle weave in a silk pattern, something one could only see if it were held the correct way in the right light. It dissolved some of her fear and made her wonder what other hidden depths existed beneath his stoic exterior.

Mr Connor's watch case clicked closed. 'Philip, we should hurry, he could return.'

The prodding snipped the faint connection

between them like scissors against a fine silk thread.

Mr Rathbone's eyes swept the room and, it seemed, deliberately avoided hers. 'Now, Miss Townsend, what should we remove?'

Laura looked over the sad furniture, happy to break his gaze and the odd line of reasoning it created. The setting sun cut through the room and she wished there were curtains to close, anything to hide the mouldering walls announcing the extent of her poverty. Despite how far they'd fallen since her father's death, the indignity of it all still burned. Most of the furniture was her uncle's, from his time with the army in India, where he'd made even less of a success of himself than he had in London. It was all in a sorry state, chipped and scratched. A couple of pieces belonged to her and her mother, the remnants of happier days in the rooms above the draper shop.

'We'll take the portrait of Father.' She motioned to the painting hanging over the sagging mantel. The varnish had turned dark around the edges, but those hazel eyes, so similar to Laura's, still watched over them with the same clarity as they had in life. It was the one aspect of her father the artist had rendered perfectly.

One of Mr Rathbone's men reached up and

removed it from its nail, exposing the stained and faded wallpaper beneath it.

'And this?' Mr Rathbone tapped the tip of his walking stick against a locked trunk beside the bedroom door.

'It belongs to my uncle.' She rolled her wrist—the memory of the bruises she'd received when her uncle had caught her trying to pick the lock one night still stung. Whatever was in there, be it valuables or the body of a wife from India, he hadn't wanted her to see it. At this moment, she didn't care. He could have the trunk and whatever comfort he drew from the contents. 'The desk was my grandmother's. My mother will want it.'

Two men took up positions on either side of the desk, heaving it up and shuffling past the door to her mother's room just as she tugged it open.

'What's going on here?' she demanded, her thin frame barely filling the tilted and sagging jamb. She snapped up her walking stick, laying it across the chest of the closest burly man and stopping both cold. 'Are we being evicted?'

Laura rushed to her mother, gently lowered the walking stick and took her by the arm to steady her. 'No, we're moving. Now, this moment.'

'Moving? Where?' She looked past Laura to the men behind her.

'Mother, allow me to introduce Mr Rathbone.'

Mr Rathbone bowed with respect, not mockery, but it failed to ease the suspicion hardening her mother's pale-brown eyes.

'Yes, I know who he is.' Her mother eyed the moneylender down the length of her straight nose like she used to do with ragamuffins intent on swiping a ribbon from the shop. The fierce look would send them scurrying off in search of easier pickings. Mr Rathbone wasn't so easily cowed. He met her stern glare as he had met almost everything else which had transpired between them, with no emotion.

'He and I are to be married and we are to live with him,' Laura announced. There was no other way to break the startling news.

'Was this the price of Robert's loan?' Her mother banged her walking stick against the floor. 'If so, I won't let you do it. I won't let you sell yourself to pay off one of Robert's debts. Your uncle isn't worth it. I deny my permission for this marriage.'

Laura stiffened. At three and twenty, she was two years past the age when such consent was necessary. However, she could feel her mother's strong will rising, a will which illness, misfortune and widowhood had sapped from her this past year. It gave Laura hope for her future.

'You have every right to object,' Mr Rathbone agreed, his features taking on a more civil countenance. 'As Miss Townsend's mother, I should have consulted you on the matter before making the proposal. I apologise for my breach of manners, but the circumstances of our betrothal are most unusual and allowed no time for a more formal courtship. May we discuss the matter now, in private?'

He moved forward and held out his arm. Beneath the stern set of her mother's expression, Laura caught the subtle arch of a raised eyebrow. He'd won her with his manners, hopefully whatever he intended to say to her would win her favour for the match.

'Yes, for I wish to know how my daughter has so suddenly transfixed you.' Mrs Townsend laid her hand on his arm and allowed him to lead her back into the cramped bedroom and help her to sit on the edge of the broken-down bed.

Laura pulled the door closed on them, not envying Mr Rathbone. It'd been a long time since she'd experienced her mother's chastising scrutiny. It was formidable, but she felt the moneylender equal to the challenge.

In the tiny sitting room, she tossed a weak smile to the two remaining men flanking the door. They nodded in return before Mr Connor came to stand beside her.

'You're a very fortunate lady, Miss Townsend.' There was a hint of teasing in the compliment.

'Am I?'

'Yes, the widowed Mrs Templeton has been trying to capture Philip's attention for many months now. If I'd known aiming a pistol at him would do the trick, I'd have advised her to try it.' He threw back his head and laughed, filling the room with the merriest sound that had been heard there for ages.

Laura let out a long breath, his humour allowing her to smile. 'You are Mr Rathbone's business partner then?'

'We're friends. Grew up together. My father worked for his father, seeing to the more practical aspects of the business.' He nodded at the men by the door. 'Just as I do. Though not for much longer. I intend to establish myself in a business, once I decide which is the best to pursue.'

'Then I wish you the greatest success.'

'As I do you.' He threw her a wide sideways

smile she couldn't fail to meet with one of her own.

'Tell me, is Mr Rathbone always so businesslike?'

'Oh, he's almost jovial today. You should see how stern he is with clients.'

'Apparently, I will.'

The door to her mother's room opened and she and Mr Rathbone stepped through it. His face revealed nothing of their conversation. Her mother, however, beamed, striding in on his arm as though a duchess in Hyde Park. Laura gaped at them, wondering if there would be any end to the surprises in store for her today. She wasn't sure she could handle too many more.

'You have nothing to worry about, my dear.' Her mother patted her shoulder. 'Now, let's be off. I see they've taken the painting and the desk.' She looked up at Mr Rathbone. 'Would you please ask your men to fetch our trunk from the bedroom? Everything else Robert can have.'

'It would be my pleasure.' Mr Rathbone motioned to the two remaining men. They hurried past Laura into the bedroom, emerging a moment later with the sad trunk holding what remained of Laura's and her mother's possessions.

They were not a foot into the room when

another figure staggered into the doorway, the stench of pipe smoke and cheap ale swirling around him.

Uncle Robert.

The air thickened with tension as Mr Rathbone's men slowly set down the trunk and straightened, dropping their hands to the clubs hanging from their belts. Mr Connor stood behind her uncle, his laughter gone as he shifted back his redingote to reveal the smooth handle of the pistol fastened at his waist. Laura's hand tightened on her mother's arm, Mr Rathbone's warning rushing back to her along with a cutting fear.

'What's all this then?' Robert Townsend demanded, struggling through his stupor to pronounce each word. His eyes fixed on the two men carrying the trunk and his sallow face scrunched with confusion before his bleary look fell on Mr Rathbone. At once, his red-rimmed eyes ignited with anger and he advanced on the moneylender. 'What's the meaning of this? I paid my debt to you. I owe you nothing.'

'My business here today doesn't concern you, Mr Townsend.' Philip crossed the room to the older man, preventing him from advancing any further. They were matched in height, but Robert Townsend was wider in the shoulders with a barrel chest made thicker by his large coat. 'Your niece has agreed to marry me. She and Mrs Townsend are removing to my house.'

'My business wasn't enough for you, was it? You had to have everything, you greedy pig.' Her uncle swayed forward on his feet. 'Do you know what Moll Topp pays for a virgin like her? It would have cleared all my debts.'

Her mother's hand tightened in Laura's the way it used to do when she was small and they would cross a busy street. Laura knew her uncle held no love for them, but she hadn't thought he'd sink to such sickening depths to save himself. She trembled as the shadow of another possible fate passed over her.

Only the stretching of Philip's leather glove as his hand tightened at his side revealed his disgust. 'I ask you to remember we are in the presence of ladies.'

'Don't pretend you're my better.' Robert stuck one thick and dirty finger in Mr Rathbone's face. 'I know your kind, feeding off the backs of men like me until you've gained every last shilling from us, then crushing us under your boot heels. Well, I won't be crushed, not by a coward like you.'

Robert pulled back his arm and rammed it forward. Mr Rathbone dipped, dodging the blow, then he came up fast, his fist catching Robert under the chin. The larger man stumbled back across the room, slamming into a small chair, his weight crushing it beneath him. He sat for a moment, stunned sober, and Laura wanted to rush over and add a few kicks of her own in retribution for all he'd done to her parents. There was no time, as Robert hauled himself to his feet, ready to rush at Mr Rathbone.

Mr Rathbone's men stepped up behind him, sticks clasped in their hands. Mr Connor pulled out his pistol and levelled it at the drunk man.

'I wouldn't do that, sir,' he warned.

Laura drew her mother back, ready to flee into the bedroom and bar the door, but no one moved. She barely dared to breathe.

Through the thin walls came the muffled voice of the man next door cursing at his wife.

Robert met Laura's eyes over Mr Rathbone's shoulder, hate twisting his lips into a sneer and drawing tight the red bruise forming beneath the grey stubble on his chin. 'You think you've got the better of me, ya little wench, but ya haven't. Neither have you, Mr Rathbone. Your men won't always be around to protect you. Some day you'll be alone and I'll be there.'

He spat at Mr Rathbone's feet.

Mr Rathbone plucked the hat from the table and settled it over his hair. 'Good day, Mr Townsend.'

He took Mrs Townsend by the arm and escorted both her and Laura around Robert. Laura eyed the old man acidly. Behind them, Mr Rathbone's men filed out, two carrying the trunk while the other two stood guard. Mr Connor was the last to leave, still brandishing the pistol.

Her mother leaned heavily on Mr Rathbone as they picked their way slowly down the stairs. It took all Laura's energy not to sag against the railings as fear pressed down hard on her. As she reached the bottom and stepped out into the chill evening air, she willed herself not to think of her uncle or how horribly true Mr Rathbone's assessment of him had proven. It no longer mattered.

Mr Rathbone settled her mother in the landau and Laura joined her. The hood was open and with the sun dipping, the air had taken on a chill. She drew the blanket over their knees as Mr Rathbone climbed in across from them.

Laura took one last look at the rickety building as the vehicle started to roll away. Robert stood at the filthy window, his obvious hate as searing as if the spring sun were reflecting off the panes. Laura swallowed hard. She might never see this rotting pile of beams again, but she felt certain this wasn't the last she'd see of her uncle.

## Chapter Three

If events had proceeded with stunning rapidity in their rented rooms, it was a marvel to see how they moved once they arrived at Mr Rathbone's house. Business pulled him and Mr Connor away, leaving Laura and her mother in the capable hands of his housekeeper, Mrs Palmer. She proved as efficient as her employer, though much more talkative. In a flash she had them fed, their few things arranged in their separate but adjoining rooms, baths drawn and the clean nightclothes Mr Rathbone had procured from a client laid out on the bed.

While Mrs Palmer assisted Laura's mother, her coarse laugh carrying through the walls at various intervals and joined by her mother's higher one, Laura pulled on the cotton chemise. She sighed at the sweep of clean linen against her damp skin, revelling in it too much to be irritated by Mr Rathbone's presumption she would accept his strange suit. When she pulled on the silk banyan lying next to it, she nearly burst into tears. She'd parted with her French one, a Christmas gift from her father, long ago to buy food. She never thought she'd enjoy such a simple luxury again.

If the chemise and banyan felt heavenly, she could only imagine how the clean sheets on the high bed would feel. She touched the turned-back covers, eager to slide between them and give in to the exhaustion heightened by the warm bath, a full stomach and the comfortable night-dress, when the door whispered open behind her.

She turned, expecting to see a maid coming to empty the hip bath. Instead it was a young lady draped in a pale-pink gown, the first small curves of a woman's body just beginning to fill out the lines of it. Her face was round with the slight fullness of youth, but her chin was well defined and her eyes the same deep blue as Mr Rathbone's.

'Good evening, Miss Townsend. I'm Miss Jane Rathbone, Philip's sister.' She dipped a curtsy, pulling out the sides of her simple cotton gown before straightening, arms at her sides just as her brother held himself. 'Philip told me to look in on you and make sure you have everything you need. He also asked me to inform you that you needn't worry about what time you rise tomorrow.'

The girl spoke like her brother, too, but in a childish voice with the hint of a lisp.

'Did he?'

She nodded, her dark curls bobbing around her face and neck. 'You must enjoy it because it will probably be the last time. Philip likes everyone to keep to a schedule.'

'I don't doubt he does.' Nor did she mind. Her parents, with a business to run, had rarely let her dawdle about without purpose. There was always something to do. 'He's very practical.'

'You must be, too, if you agreed to marry him.'

Laura rubbed the soft banyan strings between her thumb and forefinger. 'In this instance, I've proven myself as sensible as your brother.'

'Then it will be a good match.'

*I hope so*, she thought, though any future now was better than the one her uncle had planned for her.

'In the morning, I'll see to it Mrs Townsend is dressed and has her breakfast. We were speaking earlier and she is eager for me to show her the garden, especially the roses.'

The girl's efficiency was surprising, yet not wholly unexpected. Laura wondered what her mother made of the strange creature. She wasn't quite sure what to make of her herself. 'Thank you, she is very fond of roses.'

'It's time for bed now, Jane.' Mr Rathbone appeared in the doorway behind his sister, his reminder more a firm request than the stern demand of a guardian.

Laura tightened the banyan a touch more about her neck. The chemise beneath stuck to her damp skin, pressing against it with an uncomfortable warmth and making her keenly aware of her undress beneath the silk. It brought to mind how he looked beneath his clothes.

His redingote was gone, revealing a dark jacket woven with a subtle checked pattern paired with tan breeches. Without the bulk of the wool, he seemed leaner, tighter. The well-tailored clothes emphasised his coiled strength, giving a hint of the lithe power he'd revealed when he'd avoided her uncle to land a stunning blow on his chin. Laura hadn't expected Mr Rathbone to be so physical and she struggled to keep herself steady as his masculinity pounced on her.

'Goodnight, Miss Townsend.' Jane hurried out, pausing to rise up on her toes and press a small kiss against her brother's cheek. He bent forward so she could reach him, straightening as she disappeared down the hall.

'Your sister is very charming.' Laura adjusted the banyan, trying to relieve some of the heat beneath it without the garment sliding open and making her appear a slatternly hoyden.

'Don't let her deceive you. She can be very stubborn when she wants to be.'

Laura smiled up at him. 'A family trait, I suspect.'

'Indeed.' He motioned to the room. 'May I?'

*No!*

'Of course.' Laura stepped back a touch as he entered, wondering at the awkwardness coming over her. The door was open and he maintained a respectful distance. Even his eyes had not wandered away from hers. Laura tried to match his fortitude, forcing her arms to stay at her sides instead of crossing over her chest. Though there was no point in covering herself entirely. In the very near future, he'd see more than her dressing gown.

'I won't keep you from your rest for long. I

need to know if you'd prefer the banns to be read or if I should secure a common licence.'

'Do you truly want my opinion on the matter or should I acquiesce to your wishes?' She winced a little at her unsubtle question, but exhaustion, his presence in the room and the uncomfortable weight of the banyan were making her tetchy. She craved sleep and wanted to leave everything else until tomorrow.

If he minded she couldn't tell, his steady countenance not changing, even when he spoke. 'You'll find, Miss Townsend, as my wife, I'll often consult you on many things, this being only the first.'

'Of course. I'm sorry, it's been a long day, a long year in fact.'

'I understand, the past year has been a trying one for me as well.' His hard-set jaw softened and Laura remembered the only other time she had seen this happen, when he'd mentioned his wife. A grief she knew well from losing her father had washed over his face and the same expression crossed it again now. Whatever tragedy had brought him to the position of needing help under such unusual circumstances, it'd marked him as hard as all the trials of the past year had stamped her.

She was about to suggest the ease of the

banns, eager to gain the three or four weeks it would take before the wedding to settle in and get to know something of the man she was about to share her life with, when an interrupting cough drew their attention to the door. From further away, Laura heard the wail of a small child.

A thin, middle-aged woman wearing a dark dress stepped into the room. 'Excuse me, Mr Rathbone, I didn't mean to disturb you in the middle of business.'

The woman's gaze jumped back and forth between Laura and Mr Rathbone.

Laura pulled the silk closer to her chin. She could only imagine what the woman must think she'd walked in on.

'Miss Marston, please meet my intended, Miss Townsend,' Mr Rathbone intervened, the stiff mask of business descending over Philip's face and covering the faint hint of emotion Laura had caught. 'Miss Marston is Thomas's nurse.'

'Oh, Miss Townsend, it's a pleasure to meet you.' Mrs Marston's smile was more surprised than relieved. Laura suspected she'd encounter many similar reactions in the days to come. 'Mr Rathbone, Thomas awoke crying and nothing I do will calm him. You always have such a way with him. I thought you might come to the nursery for a moment.'

'Yes, I will.' He started for the door, then paused. 'Miss Townsend, come and meet the gentleman who is part of our arrangement.'

His command given, he didn't wait for her. Mrs Marston wasn't at all surprised by the abruptness and followed her employer out of the room.

Laura walked behind them, the cries of a very young child growing louder as they stepped into the hallway. Mr Rathbone and Mrs Marston made steady strides for the door at the far end, but Laura's progress was slower. When she at last reached the room, the sight inside amazed her. Mr Rathbone stood with the small child in his arms, a little face pressed against his coat, the tears soaking into the wool. One chubby hand clutched his lapel, wrinkling the perfectly pressed crease.

'What's wrong, Thomas? Did you have a bad dream?' Mr Rathbone's steady voice filled the quiet as he shifted back and forth on the toes of his boots. 'You have nothing to worry about. I'm here.'

His deep voice conjured up memories of her father holding her and wiping away her tears after a nightmare. It seemed like such a long

time since she'd felt so safe and loved. His
words curled around her insides, soothing her
as they did the boy until she wanted to lay her
head on Mr Rathbone's shoulder and cry away
all her frustrations and fears from the past year.

'He has such a way with the boy,' Mrs Marston murmured from beside her.

'Yes, he does.'

Whatever reasons she'd had for wanting to
wait a month for the wedding disappeared. Too
many things might happen in four weeks. He
could change his mind and Laura didn't want
to go back to the stinking Seven Dials and the
cold, lonely desperation which crept like the
damp through those wretched rooms. Even if
she never knew the same affection he showed
his son, just being in the presence of such love
eased the hopelessness and despair she'd suffered for far too long. She didn't want to lose
that.

Mr Rathbone buried his face in the child's
soft blond curls, lowering his voice, but never
stopping his soothing words. The boy sniffed,
his eyes growing heavy as his father continued to rock him and stroke his little back. Soon
the child's stuffy-nosed breaths gave way to
steady, quiet snores. Mr Rathbone kissed his
head, then gently laid Thomas back down in

his bed. He pulled the blanket up under his chin, then brushed the soft curls with his hand before relinquishing his place next to the bed to Mrs Marston.

'Come,' he whispered to Laura, his entreaty for her to join him as soft as his soothing words to his son. 'We mustn't disturb him.'

In the hallway, with the door closed behind them, he faced her. A circle of wet from his son's tears broke the smooth weave of his coat, but he didn't brush at it or curse the spot. The caring father stood over her, the man of business gone as his eyes swept her face.

Then the look faded and he began to turn and walk away, but she wasn't ready to see him go.

'Mr Rathbone.' She reached out and took his hand.

He whirled, eyes wide, just as stunned as she was by the gesture, but he didn't pull away. A slight connection jumped between them like a cricket hops between two slender blades of grass, bending but not breaking them. One by one his fingertips pressed against the back of her hand and words deserted her as his breath whispered across her forehead. She didn't know if the strange catch in her chest was from the excitement of the move, watching her uncle receive a well-deserved beating or the whirlwind of going from pauper to the expected wife of a well-to-do gentleman in the space of two days.

Swallowing hard, she recovered her wits enough to finally speak. 'I'd prefer the common licence.'

With his son's tears soaking through the wool to wet the linen underneath, Philip could deny Miss Townsend nothing, not even his hand. 'Whatever you wish.'

Something whispered between them, subtle as the faint scent of lavender soap surrounding Laura. This was the first time they'd touched, but it was as comforting as if it were the hundredth. It soothed the panic the unexpected intimacy had sent shooting through him.

'Thank you for all you did for us today.' Her fingers tightened with her gratitude, digging into the bruises colouring his knuckles.

He winced and her grip eased. It was his chance to pull away, but he didn't. He couldn't.

'You hurt your hand.' The sleeve of her banyan slid back as she traced the dark marks on his knuckles, revealing the soft skin and the hint of her chemise beneath.

'It wasn't the first time.' He forced the words through his lips. She stood so close he could

see the wet curls at the nape of her neck clinging to her skin. Heat rushed in hard beneath
his stomach, making it difficult to stand still,
or concentrate on anything beside the green
and gold in her eyes. 'Mr Connor and I train
with a pugilist. It's imperative my people and
I know how to protect ourselves.'

'Will I learn to box?' A playful smile danced
along the corners of her full lips.

The sharp twitch of old emotions he'd buried with his wife struck him, as hard as Laura's
pulse against his skin.

'No, but you'll learn to properly load and
fire a pistol.' He slid his hand out of hers, careful not to jerk away as he struggled to distance
himself from her and the memories scratching
at his heart. 'Goodnight, Miss Townsend.'

She dropped her hands to cross them in front
of her, letting him go. 'Goodnight, Mr Rathbone.'

In the confines of the stairwell, out of her
sight, Philip paused. Opening and closing
his fist, he tried to shake off the heat of her fingers. There was only one other time in his life
when he'd experienced a connection so powerful with a stranger. The first time he'd touched
Arabella.

He jerked up straight and descended the stairs. This was nothing like what he'd experienced with Arabella. This was a business deal, a venture plain and simple. He'd researched the lady, spent hours pondering both the good and bad aspects of the union. Yet in the end, it hadn't been the tally sheet which had tilted Philip towards her. It was intuition.

Fear nearly choked the breath from him.

Intuition had failed him before where marriage was concerned. What if it was failing him again?

'If I didn't know you better, I'd say you needed a drink,' Justin chided as Philip stepped down into the hall.

'I need exercise.' Anything to clear the uncertainty pummelling him.


An hour later, Justin swung at Philip, who ducked and came up behind him. The skin over Philip's bruised knuckles smarted as he curled his fingers into a tighter fist.

'Not like you to be so sloppy.' Justin danced around the ring out of Philip's reach. 'What's gnawing at you?'

A bolt of pain raced along Philip's arm as he jabbed at Justin and missed. They'd been sparring for over half an hour and neither the exertion nor the sweat trickling down the sides of his face had snuffed out the faint spark smouldering in the back of Philip's mind, the spark ignited by Laura's hand. The spark he feared was distracting him from noticing a potential mistake. 'Nothing.'

'You mean nothing as in your soon-to-be wife?' They circled one another, fists raised. The sounds of other men fighting nearby and the pugilists calling out orders to them rang through the high-ceilinged hall. Though not as elegant or well fitted as Gentleman Joe Jackson's establishment, the lessons here were for men like Philip and Justin who needed their skills to defend themselves, not simply dance around their opponents for show. 'You know, if you have needs, I could arrange something less taxing than a wife.'

Justin stepped in to make a hit, but Philip side-stepped out of the way. 'My needs have no bearing on the situation.'

His needs had nearly risen up in the hallway outside Thomas's room to embarrass him and quite possibly her.

'Liar.' Justin circled Philip, whose raw knuckles itched to knock the smug grin off his friend's face. 'She's the most attractive woman yet to appear on your doorstep, demanding her assets.'

Philip swung, his fist brushing Justin's arm as he turned out of the way. 'She wasn't on my step, she was in my bedroom.'

'And she will be again, many times with the way you've arranged it,' Justin taunted, as unguarded with his words as Philip was guarded with his thoughts. 'I still can't believe you're doing this.'

'Why?' Philip jabbed at Justin. 'My son needs a mother, my sister a chaperon and my house a proper steward.'

The tally sheet he'd compiled on Miss Townsend rushed back to him. What was he failing to see? Why was he doubting himself?

'You think it'll be so simple, but mark my words, it won't.' Justin swung at him, but Philip didn't turn fast enough and his shoulder burned from the hit. 'It never is where women are concerned.'

Philip shook out his arm, the pain dull compared to his concern. Justin was right, it wasn't so simple, nothing in life ever was. He'd loved Arabella and she'd loved him. They'd courted and married and she'd fallen pregnant with his child. Simple. The complications had begun with her pains. Then everything had turned into a nightmare.

'We've sparred enough today.' Philip snatched a towel from the hook on the wall and scraped the coarse linen over his face. It wasn't too late to end the venture. He could send Miss Townsend to the safety of Halcyon House or provide her with a few pounds to start another draper business.

He ran the towel over the back of his neck, studying the mix of footprints in the sand on the floor. He couldn't send her away any more than he could leave Thomas to cry in his bed. He'd seen her lodgings, heard Mr Townsend's nasty words. He knew what waited for her beyond the protection of his home and name. He'd made her an offer and she'd accepted the terms of the deal. This would not become the first time he reneged on a contract.

His determination failed to erase his unease. 'What if I'm wrong about Miss Townsend, the way I was with the silversmith I loaned money to all those years ago?'

'Oh, you're wrong. But not in the way you think.' Justin rocked back on his heels and Philip nearly struck him in the gut. 'You think you can keep Miss Townsend in your house, share her bed and still remain the aloof man of business?'

A bachelor with a taste for numerous women wasn't a man to look to for marital advice, no matter how deep their friendship. 'She understands the terms of our arrangement.'

'Perhaps, but you don't.' He smacked Philip on the arm. 'Now come and get cleaned up. You have tomorrow to face. Tonight, I have a very pleasurable venture of my own to see to.'

Justin turned and made for the dressing rooms.

Philip wrapped the towel behind his neck and gripped both ends. Justin was mistaken if he thought there was more to this contract than convenience. Miss Townsend was as practical as Philip, if not a little rash. She understood their arrangement. Or did she?

The idea Justin might be right about Miss Townsend wanting more nagged. He wasn't stone enough not to feel something for her. She was too determined and strong not to admire. In many ways she reminded him of himself, still struggling to find her feet after a reeling loss. As his wife, she deserved his respect and he would give it. He refused to surrender his heart. Doing so was not a part of their bargain.

He strode to the dressing room, flinging the damp towel at the boy attendant near the door.

He'd made the mistake of writing his emotions into a marriage contract once before and had been made to regret it. He wouldn't do it again.

## *Chapter Four*

The steady chirping of birds broke through the haze of Laura's fading dream. First one warbled, then another, until a chorus seemed to sit outside her window. Over the sharp tweets, Laura strained to hear the bell and her father's voice through the floorboards as he greeted customers in the shop below her room. The only thing she heard was the click of the bedroom-door handle and the soft swish of shoes over the carpet. Laura snuggled deeper into the thick pillow, knowing it was her mother coming to chide her for sleeping late. She clutched the clean sheet up around her chin, trying to snatch a few more precious seconds of rest.

'Miss Townsend, are you awake?' Mrs Palmer asked.

Laura sat up, sweet memories of her old room, of her father alive and her mother well vanishing along with the feeling of warmth and love. The loss burned a hole through her chest.

'Yes, I am.'

A fire crackled in the grate. Laura wondered how she'd managed to sleep through the maid coming in to light it. Perhaps it was the fact she'd slept at all which had allowed her to remain so soundly in her dreams. In Seven Dials, with all the noise from the other tenants and Uncle Robert's drunken mutterings, it'd always been so difficult to sleep. 'I'm sorry I'm still in bed. I should be up.'

'You have nothing to be sorry about.' Mrs Palmer laid a simple blue-cotton dress across the foot of the bed. 'Mr Rathbone had Mrs Fairley, Miss Jane's modiste, send this over. I'm to tell you, you have an appointment with Mrs Fairley at her shop this afternoon. She has a few other dresses from an unpaid order and will alter them to tide you over until a new wardrobe can be made.'

New dresses. Excitement crowded in beneath Laura's lingering sense of loss. The idea of wearing a dress which wasn't practically threadbare proved as irresistible as waking in a clean bed with no sign of rats having traipsed across the floor during the night. Laura picked up the sleeve of the dress and examined the fine stitching. 'I've never had a modiste make my dresses. Mother always did it.'

'You'll like Mrs Fairley. She does good work and is quite nice, too. Came to Mr Rathbone about two years ago seeking a loan to improve her business and has done quite well for herself since. Mr Rathbone prides himself on patronising those he helps who make a go of things instead of wasting the money.'

Laura didn't have to ask what happened to those who wasted Philip's money. She already knew.

She laid the sleeve of the dress down, running her hand over the length of it to press it flat. The dress was sewn from a sturdy but soft cotton, Indian most likely, more utilitarian than silk, but with a few ribbons or the right bonnet it would suit as well for an afternoon at home as it would for attending a small tea. A fond smile tugged at her lips. She could practically hear her father's words in her own thoughts, see the fabric from the bolt draped over his arm as he explained the weave and quality to a prospective lady buyer. Laura's hands stilled and the smile faded. That was all gone now. A visit from the modiste would be the closest she'd ever come to experiencing it again.

'Is something wrong, miss?' Mrs Palmer pressed.

'I'm all right, only a little overwhelmed.' Truth be told, her head was still spinning from everything and it was all she could do to focus. How she would make it through the myriad other, sure to be surprising things which might happen this week, she didn't know. However, if the most troubling thing facing her today was the shock of a new dress, then she really had no troubles at all. After all, she'd dealt with worse problems during the past year, much worse.

Mrs Palmer slid Laura's old black dress from the top of the chair where Laura had draped it last night. If Mrs Palmer was concerned about the tatty dress staining the fine silk upholstery, she didn't reveal it. Her face was all kindness and concern, reminding Laura of the baker's wife who used to give her leftover biscuits from time to time until her husband had found out and put a stop to it.

'I know it all must seem so strange, Mr Rathbone making up his mind so quick about you, but I assure you, Miss Townsend, you couldn't have asked for a better man.'

It seemed Mrs Palmer was as enamoured of Mr Rathbone as Laura's mother. If only she could be so certain about her decision. However, it was a comfort to see the older woman so eager for Laura to like Mr Rathbone as much as she obviously did. It was better than her trying to secretly warn her off him.

Mrs Palmer's ruddy smile returned to her full cheeks. 'Here's me gabbing with the day getting away from us both. There's breakfast waiting for you in the dining room when you're ready. I'll send Mary up to help you dress.'

'I can manage.'

'I don't doubt you can, but Mr Rathbone wants her to assist you. If you need anything, you be sure to let me know.'

Mrs Palmer dipped a curtsy then left as quietly as she'd entered, the nearly frayed edge of Laura's old dress fluttering behind her and almost catching in the closing door. The dress would probably be tossed in the kitchen fire the moment she reached it. Laura was glad to see it go. It was an ugly reminder of how much she and her mother had lost during the past year.

What would the next year bring? She still couldn't say.

Laura flung back the covers and slipped out of bed, determined not to complain or worry, but to face whatever was coming with optimism. At least her uncle had fallen in debt to a young, handsome moneylender and not to one of the many crooked, gap-toothed men she'd seen haunting the rookery in search of payment. It was the only thing of value he'd ever done for her.

A soft knock at the door was followed by the entrance of a young woman with a snub nose and brown hair peeking out from beneath a white cap. 'I'm Mary. I'm here to dress you.'

The girl said little as she helped Laura dress, lacing Laura's worn stays over the crisp white chemise. Holding still so the maid could work gave Laura the chance to take her first real look at the room. It was smaller than Mr Rathbone's, but well appointed with solid, simple pieces of furniture. She wondered if they'd been made by one of the upholsterers who used to frequent the shop. She studied the faint white line running through the flowing silk of the bed curtains, thinking it a familiar pattern, when the image of another room suddenly came to mind.

She wondered how many more mornings she'd wake up here before she found herself in Mr Rathbone's bed.

She breathed hard against the tightening stays, fear and anticipation pressing against her chest. She should have asked for the banns instead of insisting on the common licence. She wasn't ready for such intimacy, not yet, not with everything, especially their future together, so unsure.

Mary tied off the stays then picked up the dress, opening it so Laura could slip inside. She held up her arms and let the blue cotton flow down over her shoulders and body. The soft material made her sigh with delight and eased some of her fears. A man who was so loving and tender with his son wouldn't be cruel to her.

Mary did up the row of buttons at the back, but the dress was too large in the bust. Even Laura's well-formed breasts weren't ample enough to keep the front from billowing and gaping open. While Mary pinned the dress to make it fit better, Laura opened and closed her hand. The shock of Mr Rathbone's touch had remained with her long after she'd blown out her candle and settled into the clean sheets last night. It wasn't his hand in hers which had remained with her the longest, but the conflict she'd noticed coursing beneath his calm exterior. More than once he'd begun to withdraw from her before his palm had settled again, surrendering to her hold. It was as if he both wanted and didn't want to draw close to her. It seemed strange for a man who seemed so determined about everything to be confused about something as simple as touching his intended.

Although it wasn't as simple as she wanted to believe.

At Mary's urging, Laura seated herself in the chair before the dressing table and let the young maid arrange her hair. She barely noticed the tugging and combing as she remembered Mr Rathbone's eyes upon hers. There'd been more in the joining of their hands than conveying her desire to wed quickly. There was something she hadn't allowed herself to consider possible when she'd accepted his proposal yesterday—a deeper concern for her than business.

The faint hint of it made her eager to be done with the dressing table and be in front of him again.

With her hair arranged into a simple jumble of curls at the back of her head, Laura made her way downstairs. She felt guilty leaving Mary behind to see to the room. She'd tried to assist her, perfectly capable of making her own bed, but the maid had insisted it was her duty to straighten it and Laura had reluctantly left her to it.

Laura took in the house as she moved slowly down the hallway. Last night, with the myriad arrangements and settling in, there hadn't been time to explore. Her first time here, she'd been too occupied trying not to be seen to admire anything more than the direct route from the back door, down the hall, to the stairs.

The upstairs hall was plain, the length of it punctuated by doors to the various bedrooms and landscapes in gilded frames. The staircase at the far end made one turn before opening into the entrance hall below. It wasn't overly high, but wider than those she'd seen in the few merchants' houses she'd visited with her father when she was a child. Stone covered the floor, leading to a solid door flanked by two glass windows. Through them she could see people passing by in a steady stream along the pavement lining Bride Lane. Some of them entered the churchyard of St Bride's across the street, the rest hurried on to nearby Fleet Street.

Making for the dining room at the back of the house, Laura noted the rich panelling lining the downstairs hall seemed less dark and foreboding in the bright morning light, though it still made her a touch uneasy to be striding so boldly through the house. It was nearly incomprehensible to think she would soon be mistress of it.

She passed the study, the masculine mahogany desk, neatly ordered shelves and solid chairs inside indicating this must be where Mr Rathbone managed his affairs. He wasn't

there and she ventured inside. The neatness and
fine taste of the appointments matched his attire. Where the back room behind the draper
shop had always been cluttered with account
books and fabrics, not a speck of dirt or an out-
of-place ledger marred the clean lines of this
room. Though Laura was by no means slovenly,
she wondered how she would be able to keep
pace with such a man.

The French doors on the far wall leading to
the garden drew her to them. Outside, the sky
was clear, with a few wispy clouds floating
past the sun. They were only a mile or so from
Seven Dials, but it might have been halfway
around the world for how different everything
appeared here. The air seemed cleaner, the
buildings solid stone instead of sagging wood.
The whole garden was green, punctuated by the
white and red of blooming roses, their bright-
ness a welcome sight after the grime and dirt
of Laura's former lodgings.

The moneylender's fortune must be larger
than she'd thought for him to possess the luxury of such a garden, one surrounded by a tall,
fine wall. Just beyond it, through the iron gate,
the one she'd crept through the other night, she
noticed a horse staring out from the mews.

In the centre of the garden, Jane escorted

Laura's mother around a raised brick bed filled with rosebushes. Excitement lightened each muffled word as Jane pointed out flower after flower, motioning to them with the pride of a silversmith displaying her finest wares.

As they made a turn, her mother caught sight of Laura. She raised a hand in greeting, her simple gesture joined by Jane's more eager wave. Jane's enthusiasm eased the stiffness in her posture and made her look more like a young girl rather than a female copy of her brother.

Whatever changes Laura's mother had wrought in Jane, the young lady's effect on the older woman was tenfold. Laura's mother wore a dress of dark-blue muslin. It needed to be altered to fit properly, but the clean lines and fine material lent her a measure of dignity which showed itself in the new straightness in her posture. She didn't lean as heavily on her walking stick as before and for the first time in over a year, she appeared rested and happy. Whatever Laura's concerns about herself, they were eased by the smile gracing her mother's thin face.

Laura's stomach growled and she left the window and the room to search out the food Mrs Palmer had promised. The dining room sat across the hall from the study, a shining table with ball-and-claw feet dominating the centre. The panelling didn't extend in here, but gave way to a pale-blue paper on the walls overseen by the portrait of a matronly woman in the dress and cap of a few decades ago.

A footman stood beside a heavy sideboard laden with silver dishes full of eggs, ham and bread. Laura gasped at the plenty of it. During all the weak suppers in Seven Dials, she never thought she'd ever see or enjoy such abundance again.

Taking the plate offered by the footman, she selected a little food from each silver server, then sat down at the table. She savoured every bite, glad to be alone so she could relish the simple food without the humiliation of revealing the depths of her previous deprivation. After using her toast to wipe up the last bits of her second helping, she rose to get another serving when Chesterton, the butler, stepped into the room.

'Miss Townsend.' Her name sounded so imperious and important in his deep voice. 'Mr Rathbone would like you to join him in the sitting room.'

'Of course.' Laura slid the plate down on to the buffet, suddenly feeling like a thief for indulging so much. The fork scraped and clanked across the porcelain and she winced, wondering when she'd become such a scared mouse. She straightened the knife and fork on the plate, then stood straight, clasping her hands in a businesslike manner in front of her. 'Would you please show me the way?'

'It would be my pleasure.' He almost smiled and Laura caught something of Mrs Palmer's tenderness around his eyes. With everyone silently encouraging her rather than sneering, laughing or pitying her behind her back, it made the idea of easing into her new place as their mistress a great deal easier.

As she followed Chesterton out of the dining room and across the hall, she thought it strange to have so many people thinking well of her presence here and her the only one in doubt.

Jane came bounding down the stairs, carrying a book and Laura's mother's dark shawl, looking more like a thirteen-year-old than she had last night. Spying Laura, she halted and took the last few stairs with the elegance of a woman far beyond her years. 'Good morning, Miss Townsend.'

'Please, call me Laura.' She smiled warmly, trying to put the girl at ease, disliking such seriousness in one so young.

The stiff set of Jane's body eased with Laura's invitation. 'And you may call me Jane.'

'I see you and my mother are getting along well.'

'Very well.' A proud smile spread over her stern lips, bringing back the youthful light which had illuminated her face as she'd come down the stairs. 'We are to visit Mrs Fairley together tomorrow. She was too tired to go today, but you mustn't worry about her. I'll see she gets enough rest.'

'Thank you. It means a great deal to me to have someone keeping her company while I'm occupied.'

'It's my pleasure. I'm going to read to her now. Where are you going?'

'The sitting room.'

'Philip summoned you?'

Laura choked back a laugh. 'In a manner of speaking.'

The girl moved closer as if she possessed something urgent to impart. 'Touch his hand again like you did last night. Miss Lavinia does it in *The Wanderer* and it drives Mr Welton absolutely mad.'

Laura crossed her arms, mimicking the way her mother used to stare at her whenever she'd offered unasked-for advice or stuck her nose in where it was unwanted. 'Jane, were you spying on us?'

'No, not at all.' Jane possessed too much of her brother's confidence to be cowed by Laura's stern look. 'I peeked out my door and saw you. You two looked just how I imagined Viscount Rapine and Miss Anne must look in *The Lothario.*'

'You're reading *The Lothario*?' Her brother couldn't possibly approve of such a choice.

Apparently he didn't, for Jane clapped her hand over her mouth as if she'd mistakenly revealed a great secret. Her eyes darted to the butler standing a polite distance away, then back to Laura. 'You won't tell Philip, will you? If he finds out I'm reading romantic novels, he might end my subscription to the lending library.'

Laura dropped her stern look and all pretence at reprimanding. 'As long as you reserve your employment of their knowledge to dispensing advice and nothing else, I won't tell your brother and I won't object.'

Jane sighed with relief. 'Good, because Mrs Townsend would be very disappointed. We're going to start reading *Glenarvon* this afternoon and I can't wait.'

'You and my mother are going to read *Glen-*

*arvon*?' She never would have been allowed to read such a salacious book. With the exception of the few novels Laura had managed to borrow from friends and sneak into her room, her reading had been comprised of business tracts and the stock pages. While she was grateful for the education, especially now, she wondered when her mother had grown so soft.

'Yes.' Jane moved a touch closer, whispering with Laura in collusion. 'I hear it's quite scandalous.'

'I've heard so, too.' Laura dropped her voice, encouraging the youthful confidence between them. It was a treat to see Jane acting more like a young lady than a stiff governess. 'When you're done with it, I'd like to read it. I might learn a trick or two.'

Jane gaped at Laura. Then a smile broke the line of her lips and she laughed, a good genuine girlish one which brightened the hall. 'I shall be happy to pass it on to you. Now, I must return to Mrs Townsend. I've kept her waiting long enough and she needs her shawl.'

'And I must answer your brother's summons.'

Jane sobered, laying a hand on Laura's arm. 'Don't worry, Philip isn't as stern as he likes everyone to think.'

'I'll keep it in mind.' And she would, for if his sister believed it, it was most likely true.

With a squeeze of her hand, Jane let go and hurried off down the hall, allowing the door at the back of the house leading to the garden to bang shut behind her.

Laura wished she could follow. After a year of looking after her mother, it felt odd to relinquish her duties to someone else, but at least Jane's attention meant her mother wasn't left alone in a strange place while Laura attended to business.

'Here you are, Miss Townsend.' Chesterton stopped at the sitting-room door at the front of the house.

Laura gave him a smile of gratitude and stepped inside.

Mr Rathbone stood near the fireplace, reviewing papers. Through the sheer curtains behind him passed the shadows of people moving on the pavement outside. Laura barely noticed them. The only thing she could concentrate on was the soft light coming through the delicate fabric and spreading over Mr Rathbone's profile. It lightened his dark hair and caressed the strong line of his nose. A fine, camel-coloured jacket draped his shoulders, emphasising the solidity of the long arms arched gracefully in front of him as he reviewed papers. He appeared to her like one of the Greek statues she'd seen in the British Museum. She'd gone there before she'd sold her last decent dress to view the Elgin Marbles and distract herself from her troubles. Like the statues, Mr Rathbone was elegant and refined, yet the memory of his sudden, lethal movements facing her uncle made her shiver. There was an edge of danger beneath his calm facade, one she hoped he reserved only for the worst clients.

'Good morning, Mr Rathbone.' She tugged down the overlarge bodice, which kept rising up as she moved deeper into the room. She wished she looked as fine and well put together as him, instead of unkempt and thin in her second-hand clothes. 'You summoned me?'

He didn't look up from his papers. 'My sister's choice of words, I assume.'

'She has a very interesting sense of humour.'

'She's a hoyden.' He reached up and removed the dagger mounted on two brass hooks to a wood plaque hanging over the mantel. Behind it lay a small safe set into the wall. 'However, Jane is smart and minds herself well enough for someone her age. She shouldn't give you trouble. If she does, speak to me about it at once.'

She wouldn't speak to him. No, she would

handle it in her own way and see to it there was more of the spirited young lady on the stairs and less of the dour miss. 'Yes, Mr Rathbone.'

Resting the mounted dagger on the floor, he finally met her eyes. 'Please, call me Philip.'

His gaze was intense, but not stern, inviting her to explore more deeply the slight bond weaving them together like embroidery over fine netting.

'Yes, of course, Philip.' The name was as awkward on her tongue as a button held with her teeth while she was sewing. It would take practice getting used to such intimacy with this stranger. Except he wasn't a stranger, but her husband-to-be.

'And you may call me Laura.' She adjusted the dress again, then dropped her hands, determined to face him with dignity. Her attire was only temporary and, with the modiste's help, she'd soon appear respectable again.

Her confidence wavered. Whatever respectability she regained today, it would be thanks to his coin and effort, not hers. Something in her rankled. She'd struggled so hard to save the business, herself and her mother and in the end she could only do it by falling under this man's protection. She tried to recall her mother's encouraging words, or even Mrs Palmer's sim-

ple observation about Philip, but none of them
came back to her with enough force to push
away the strange regret of not having achieved
her own salvation, or the nasty idea she was
selling herself.

Philip broke from her gaze to open the safe
and slide the papers inside.

'Are you sure you can trust your sister's behaviour to a woman who sneaks into men's
houses and threatens them in the night?' It was
a flippant question with an edge of seriousness.
He was certainly trusting her now by revealing the safe and the key on the small ring in
his pocket which opened it. There was nothing
to stop her from stealing the key, emptying the
safe and sneaking away with her mother while
he slept. She would never do such a deceitful
thing, but he couldn't know this.

'You aren't a thief.' He swung the safe door
closed and locked it.

Apparently, he did know she wasn't capable
of robbing him.

She tugged at the dress, wishing she possessed the same unshakeable confidence in herself and her decision to marry as he did in her
and his own decisions.

He returned the mounted dagger to the
hooks. The silver cufflinks holding the crisp

ends of his sleeves together over his strong wrists flashed with the morning sunlight. Only the yellowing bruises along his knuckles kept his appearance from being perfect.

He'd received those bruises for defending her. It was ungrateful of her to stand here lamenting his help because it hadn't come from her own effort, yet she still hated the idea of needing his charity.

His papers secure, this pleasant morning repartee came to an end. 'I asked you to join me because a gentleman is here in need of a loan. It's the perfect opportunity to begin your training.'

'So soon?' The eggs threatened to revolt in her stomach. Perhaps she shouldn't have enjoyed a second serving.

'The prospective client is a cloth importer and your expertise might be beneficial to the transaction. Before I decide whether or not to invest in his business, I need to know if his proposal has merit.'

'My uncle's plan had merit,' she challenged.

'Because it was yours,' he answered flatly.

'But you didn't know that then.'

'I do now.'

'Yet you still lent to my uncle. Why?' she persisted, her unease making her quarrelsome.

'As I said before, he possessed the collateral

to secure the loan. If he'd rebuilt the business, he wouldn't have been the first unlikely client to exceed my expectations.'

She had the distinct impression the remark was directed at her, but it didn't ease the way his past dealing with her uncle Robert continued to chafe. 'Did you know about me and my mother?'

'He failed to reveal your presence when he initially approached me, but in my research—'

'Your research?' Curse it, he was so methodical.

'I research all my clients before extending a loan. I discovered your and Mrs Townsend's presence.'

'And you were still willing to let him ruin us?'

'No.' His expression remained impassive, but the force and sincerity behind the single word was strong enough to wilt her anger.

It didn't stop her from gaping at him in disbelief, not knowing what to think. 'But—'

'I'll explain all to you in good time. Now, we must see to Mr Williams.' He motioned to the door instead of offering her his arm. 'Shall we?'

'Of course.' It was better to face whatever waited for her in his study than to linger here and pick a fight. Being irritable would get her nowhere and it was a poor way to thank him for all he was doing for her and her mother.

She moved past Philip and he stepped back, as if deliberately maintaining his distance. She was tempted to grasp his hand to see if she could reclaim a little of the connection they'd experienced last night. Instead she strode past him and out of the sitting room, afraid of rattling him with her boldness. With her first taste of this business looming at the other end of the hall, she didn't want him out of sorts. She was anxious enough about facing a man in need of money without disturbing Philip's calm.

Outside the room, he fell in step beside her.

'What should I do?' she asked.

'Listen. If you hear something alarming, speak up at once.'

How strange this all seemed when all her life she'd imagined herself behind a shop counter. It was another item to add to the growing list of things to which she must become accustomed, or perhaps resign herself. 'Do you think him a good candidate for a loan?'

'I don't want to prejudice you.'

His answer was strangely flattering, suggesting he valued her opinion. Hopefully, she wouldn't disappoint him.

Laura followed him into the study. Inside,

Mr Connor straightened from where he'd been slouching against the wall next to the French doors. She eyed Mr Connor's dark coat, trying to catch the outline of the pistol she suspected was hidden beneath. How often did he need a weapon here in Philip's home?

The importer who occupied one of the two chairs in front of the desk rose to greet Laura and Philip. He studied her from under bushy black-and-grey brows, his scrutiny unsettling as she took the chair beside Philip's. Something about the rotund man seemed familiar, but Laura couldn't place his face. He appeared to regard her with the same dilemma before giving up and focusing on Philip.

Outside, her mother's muffled voice carried in from where she sat with Jane while the girl read aloud. For the second time that morning, Laura envied Jane, wishing she could pass a leisurely hour engrossed in a story, rather than learning how to lend money.

'Mr Williams, this is Miss Townsend, she will be assisting us today,' Philip announced to the importer as he settled himself behind the desk.

'Don't see why we need a woman here,' Mr Williams said huffily.

'I find her opinions necessary.' Philip rested his hands coolly on the arms of the chair.

'Have it your way.' Mr Williams shrugged and stretched his legs out in front of him as though settling in for an evening beside the fire.

His attitude struck Laura as false. He wanted to look at ease, but the way his foot kept moving back and forth betrayed his nervousness. The small but constant fidgeting reminded her of how Uncle Robert used to face her whenever she'd cornered him about missing inventory.

'Mr Rathbone, I'll come to the point,' Mr Williams began. 'There's a new cotton out of Georgia with a strand so strong it can be woven in half the time and at greater speed than even the cotton coming from Hispaniola. I don't have the money to import it, which is why I've come to you.'

Laura shifted in her chair. She'd heard about men trying to develop such a strand, but she'd never heard of them succeeding. The weak strands of such cotton seemed better suited to making paper than weaving cloth. She looked to Mr William's foot. It moved faster back and forth on the heel. He'd need a cobbler soon if he kept up such fidgeting.

'And your collateral?' Philip asked.

'My shares in a shipping business.' He

withdrew a paper from his coat and laid it on the desk.

Philip picked up the certificate, briefly flashing the yellowing bruises on his hand before he settled the document low in front of him to review. Laura studied him as he read, trying to gauge if he saw what she did. Was it only her lack of knowledge about this business and her own discomfort at sitting in a hodgepodge dress in the middle of such an orderly office that was making her uneasy?

At last, Philip folded the paper and laid it in the centre of the clean blotter. She couldn't tell if he approved or disapproved of it. Neither could Mr Williams, judging by the increased pace of his rocking foot.

'And your personal situation? Do you have a wife and children?' Philip asked.

'Haven't much seen the need of tying myself to an interfering woman.' He slid Laura a hard look which she matched with a steady one of her own. 'Though I don't see what difference it makes to a sound investment like this one.'

Laura glanced back and forth between Philip and Mr Williams, wondering if she should say something about the cotton before Philip agreed to the loan. There was nothing sound about his proposal. Philip had asked her to speak out if she had reservations, but what he'd said in the quiet of the hallway and what he wanted from her now with the client staring him down like an overeager bulldog might be a very different thing.

'It makes a great deal of difference to me since it's my money you're seeking to fund your endeavour,' Philip countered. 'If you fail, I'll be the one bearing the brunt of the loss.'

'I won't fail and you'll get back three times the amount I'm asking for.'

Philip paused and Laura shifted in her chair, unsure whether he was preparing to let the man down or accept his offer. 'When would I see the dividends?'

'There's a ship out of Portsmouth ready to sail within the week if I can raise the money. In six months' time it could be back here, the cotton sold and a tidy sum in your pocket.'

Philip paused again and Laura couldn't stay silent any longer.

'You won't see a farthing of what he's promising.'

'This doesn't concern you, woman,' Mr Williams snapped, struggling to twist his large self around in the chair and glare her into silence.

'Miss Townsend, you have reservations

about Mr Williams's proposal?' Philip coaxed, unruffled by the importer's outburst.

'Don't matter what she thinks of it,' Mr Williams scoffed. 'You're the man. It's up to you.'

'As the man, I'm eager to hear the lady's opinion.'

Laura swallowed hard, wishing she possessed Philip's composure, but now was no time to lose her wits. 'What he's suggesting won't work. The new cotton from Georgia isn't strong enough to take the pressure of the new water-powered looms. Mr Williams may import the cotton, but he won't be able to weave it as he's indicated and it won't be worth even half of what he's going to pay to buy and ship it.'

'You don't know anything, girlie, except what your dressmaker tells you. Judging by your frock, even she don't know two whiskers about cloth.' The man snorted.

'My father was John Townsend, a draper in Wood Street, Cheapside. I worked with him in his shop my whole life. I know more about cloth, cotton, silk and muslin than you can imagine.'

Philip exchanged a quick look with Mr Connor. Laura wasn't sure if it was admiration or worry.

Mr Williams wasn't as enamoured of her

pluck; recognition spread across his face. 'I knew you was familiar. I remember your father. He was a good man, God rest him. What would he think to see you here, meddling with the likes of 'im?'

He jerked his thick thumb at Philip.

'Our business is concluded, Mr Williams,' Philip announced in a low voice as he rose slowly from the chair to stare down at the man. 'I can be of no help to you in this matter. Mr Connor will see you out.'

'You're damned right our business is concluded.' Mr Williams struggled with his large stomach to stand. 'I wouldn't take your money if you offered it to me on a velvet pillow.'

He snatched the shipping share from the desk and shoved it in his pocket before turning a squinted eye to Laura. 'Your father would turn in his grave if he knew his only daughter was now some moneylender's wh—'

'Out, now.' Philip's voice cracked over Mr Williams, stunning the importer silent.

'Come on then.' Mr Connor took Mr Williams by the arm and tugged him towards the door.

Mr Williams jerked free and left of his own accord, a trail of mumbled curses following him.

Philip rounded the desk and closed the door. 'I apologise for what just happened.'

'One would think I'd be used to bullying men after enduring my uncle.' Laura opened her hand, her fingers tight from where she'd gripped the arm of the chair. 'He used to fly into a rage whenever I questioned him about missing money or unpaid bills.'

She studied a deep scratch in the wood floor, following it from where it met the leg of Mr Williams's chair to where it snaked under Philip's desk. The pride she'd experienced when she'd spoken about her father's shop faded like the scratch thinned beneath the desk.

She'd been a fool to think it would be so easy accepting a stranger as her husband. It had been even more simple-minded to imagine they'd touch a few times and it would be as if they were in love and well known to one another. That wasn't how it would be at all. She was going to marry a stranger, live in a strange house and learn a business she wanted nothing to do with. Why? Because she was so desperate, she was willing to sell herself for safety, just as Mr Williams had been about to accuse her of doing before Philip had cut him off.

*I'm not selling myself.* She closed her eyes and took a deep breath, repeating the truth over and over. It still didn't shift the weight sitting hard on her chest. *I'm trying to make a secure life for me and my mother.*

'Laura?' The sound of her name was soothing, like the sound of Thomas's name on Philip's lips last night. She opened her eyes, expecting to revel in the same softness, but Philip's eyes were firm as he studied her.

'In time, you'll learn to disregard such people.' He took up the stack of papers resting on the corner of the desk and shook them into a neat pile. 'Men like Mr Williams often resort to personal attacks when questioned about their business or finances.'

'I know. People who owed my father and couldn't pay often reacted the same way when pressed.' It wasn't so very different and yet it was. They hadn't looked down on her the way Mr Williams had just done. If they had done, her father would send them off and then remind her afterwards of her worth. What was her worth now? Certainly not what she'd once imagined, back when she'd dreamed of a loving husband standing with her behind the counter of their own shop, greeting clients together the way her parents had used to.

'Many people come here when they're desperate.' Philip laid the papers back on the corner of the desk. 'It affects their better sense.'

Laura wondered if she'd lost hers. Whatever comfort she'd taken in the clean clothes, comfortable bed and good food vanished. She eyed the neat stack of papers, wanting to knock it to the floor, scatter the sheets across the wood and cover the scratch. She'd been desperate enough to come here and turn over the only asset she still possessed to Philip, just as her uncle had been willing to relinquish the business, and Mr Williams the shipping shares. Unlike those men, Laura had been forced by others to part with what little she had left, just as she'd been forced to teach Uncle Robert the business when her father had brought him in, despite her and her mother's protests. Then she'd been forced to watch while he'd taken everything away piece by awful piece. 'I wish you hadn't asked me to join you.'

'I needed your assistance and experience. I knew the shipping shares were worthless. The company refuses to invest in steam engines which I and many others believe are the future, and their fleet is outdated. It was your expertise in cloth I needed.'

She sucked in a deep breath at the blunt statement, struggling to push back the tears pricking the corners of her eyes. She straightened her spine and looked at him. If he could stand so impassively in front of her, she would do so, too, and not dissolve into some blubbering girl. 'Surely there are other people you could have called on.'

'There are, but I need to know if you can see through what a man says to find the truth of his situation, to gauge his suitability in case there comes a time when you must act alone.' He pressed his fingers into the stack of papers, making them dip in the middle, something of unease in the simple motion. So he wasn't infallible after all and he knew it. It was encouraging to know. It made him at last seem mortal, though no less irritating. 'Your instincts proved correct, as I suspected they would.'

'And what of my feelings?' She swept the stack of papers off the desk, sending them fluttering to the floor, her anger fuelled as much by Mr Williams as all the frustrations and humiliations of the past year. 'Did you ever take those into consideration, or how being bullied and brought low by a man like Mr Williams might hurt me?'

The papers settled over the floor like snow. Philip watched, emotionless, as a contract balanced on the edge of the seat cushion before sliding off to cover the scratch on the wood.

Outside, her mother and Jane passed by the window as they made their way inside.

Horror rushed in to blot out her anger. What had she done? This was Philip's house, his business and she was here at his whim. His generosity could be withdrawn at any moment and she and her mother would be back in Seven Dials shivering and starving.

'I'm sorry, I didn't mean to act so childishly.' She dropped to her knees and snatched up the papers. The edges flapped with her trembling hands as she tried to force them into a neat pile, but they wouldn't cooperate. The more her hands shook, the more the helplessness widened to consume her. 'It won't happen again, I promise. I don't know what came over me.'

He came around the desk and lowered himself on to one knee across from her. Taking the uneven stack out of her hands, he laid it on the floor beside him. Then he gently caught her chin with his fingers and tilted her face up to his. 'Forgive me. I should have waited to introduce you to the business.'

Concern softened his blue eyes. He was sorry, genuinely so, with no trace of the false, self-serving contrition her uncle used to offer her father. The same faint bond which had slipped between them last night encircled them again. Philip cared for her and wanted her to be happy. The realisation drained the anger from her, but it couldn't erase the hurt, worries, helplessness and humiliations she'd suffered so many times. They pressed down on her and not even Philip's reassuring touch could drive them away.

'I invited you here because you're too strong to be bullied by such a man,' Philip explained.

'I wish I was.' She rocked back on her heels and away from his fingers, then fled the room.

The hall and stairway blurred as her eyes filled with tears. They streaked steadily down her cheeks as she made for her mother's room and pushed open the door without knocking. Thankfully, Jane wasn't with her. Her mother looked up from the chair by the window, her smile vanishing at the sight of Laura's expression. Without a word, she held out her arms and Laura flung herself into them, burying her face in her chest to cry.

Philip lowered his hand, the warmth of Laura's skin still lingering on his fingertips. It didn't dispel the cold sitting hard in his chest. None of the insults hurled at him by any defaulting client had pierced him as hard as the realisation he'd allowed a client to hurt someone in his care.

He dragged the last few contracts out from under the desk and shoved them down on top of the pile on the floor. He should have followed his instincts and waited to introduce her to someone like Mr Williams. Instead, he'd dismissed his doubts and convinced himself she was fit to face the ugly man. He should have known better. She was strong, but she'd suffered a great deal and, like him, needed time. It was a mistake, one he should have known better than to make.

'I said you didn't understand the terms of the contract and I was right.' Justin slid into the room and settled into his favourite chair by the cold fireplace. 'You can't treat her like a client.'

Philip hauled himself and the contracts off the floor. 'It was never my intention to.'

'Yes, it was.' He reached over to the side table next to him and plucked a crystal glass and decanter of Scotch from it. 'Thankfully, she's no shrinking violet which is good if she's going to marry you.'

'Perhaps I was short-sighted in my assumptions about our arrangement.' And its simplicity. Justin was right, it wasn't going to be as easy as he'd first believed. 'Assuming, after this morning, our agreement still stands.'

'Oh, don't worry, she'll marry you.' Justin poured out a measure of Scotch, then returned the decanter to the table. 'Now you must ask yourself, why do you really want to marry her? And I want the real reason, not your drivel about needing a housekeeper.'

Philip traced the scratch in the floor with his boot. The memory of Laura scrambling about for the papers, as lost and frightened as he'd been the morning Arabella had died, tore at him. That cold morning, he'd come to this room and nearly ripped it all to pieces, gouging the floorboards in a fruitless effort to overturn the desk. If Justin hadn't found him, he might have destroyed the room and himself.

'I lost something when Arabella died; it was as if I buried my humanity with her.' Every day he felt the hardness creeping in where warmth and happiness used to be. It hurt to admit it, even to his closest friend. 'My father always said it was the one thing we must hold on to in this business because it's too easy to lose, as evidenced by so many others in our profession.'

'You've hardly become like them. You never will.'

'I'm not so sure.' After Arabella's death,

Philip had shut himself off from his emotions just to move through the day without crumbling. As time passed it was growing more difficult to draw them out again.

'You think Miss Townsend can help you reclaim your humanity?'

Philip didn't respond, but studied the snaking scratch marking the wood. When the workmen had repaired the room, he'd refused to let them sand it away. It was a reminder of his loss of control. Something he'd never let happen again. 'Miss Townsend and Mrs Townsend's influence will do Jane good. I heard her laugh with Miss Townsend earlier.'

'It's about time.' Justin swirled the last sip of his Scotch before downing it. 'She's too serious for a girl her age.'

Philip strode to the table and plucked up a glass. 'I'm to blame.'

'Hardly. Seriousness is a family trait. Your mother was the only one who could enjoy a good joke.'

'She tempered my father.' He removed the crystal stopper from the decanter and rolled it in his palm. 'I worry how my nature might affect Thomas.'

Thomas's happy squeal carried in from outside. Philip set the glass and stopper down and went to the French doors leading to the garden. He opened them and inhaled the pungent scent of roses and earth fighting with the thicker stench of horses and smoke from the streets beyond. 'Arabella should have had time with Thomas. She should have seen him grow.'

'But that's not the way it happened,' Justin gently reminded him.

No, it wasn't. The finality of it was too much like standing at Arabella's grave again, the sun too bright off the green grass surrounding the dim hole in the earth.

Thomas toddled around a square half-pillar supporting an urn. He peeked out from one side of it, and then the other, squealing with laughter as Mrs Marston met him with a playful boo. The sun caught his light hair, making the subtle orange strands shine the way Arabella's used to whenever she'd strolled here.

Philip had used to look up from his accounts to watch her, wanting to join her, but he'd dismissed the urge in favour of the many other things commanding his attention. If he'd known their days together were limited, he would have tossed aside his work and rushed to be with her. If he'd known their love would kill her, he never would have opened his heart to her in Dr Hale's sitting room.

A dull ache settled in behind his eyes, heightened by the bright day. There'd never been a choice between loving or not loving Arabella. He'd loved her from the first moment she'd entered his office looking as unsure as Laura had today. During the first days of their courtship there'd been an unspoken accord between them, as if they understood one another without ever having to speak.

When Laura had reached out to him last night, and when he'd touched her today, something of the understanding and comfort that had so long been missing had passed between them and shaken him to the core.

'Miss Townsend's presence will benefit Thomas,' Philip observed, pulling himself off the unsettling road his thoughts were travelling. His relationship with Laura was nothing like his relationship with Arabella.

'Her presence will benefit you, too.' Justin came to his side and cocked a knowing eyebrow at him. 'Often and quite pleasurably.'

If he wasn't Philip's greatest friend, he would have dismissed him. 'Your experience with women has muddled your impression of relationships.'

'Actually, it's heightened them, which is why I can see matters with Miss Townsend so clearly and you cannot.' He dropped a comforting hand on Philip's shoulder. 'If you let her, Miss Townsend will temper you and more. Just don't resist her when she tries.'

With a hard squeeze, he left.

Philip stepped outside into the shadows of the eaves, watching Thomas without the boy noticing. Thomas hurried around the fountain on unsteady legs, clapping and laughing whenever Mrs Marston surprised him. It touched him to see his son so happy. Philip had forgotten what joy was like.

He looked in the direction of Laura's room, but the portico roof obscured the view. Justin was right, Philip needed Laura to temper him and she possessed the will to do it. He might have misjudged her strength today, but he didn't doubt its existence. When she felt safe, when her life settled into a steady rhythm, she'd find her feet again and he was sure to witness more moments of strength. He looked forward to them.

What he didn't look forward to were the deeper implications of her presence.

In the past year, he'd closed his heart to almost everyone except Thomas and Jane. He wasn't about to open it again and allow anyone to see the hardness which had grown there, or to leave himself vulnerable to having it crushed again. It would be a difficult thing to manage, but he had no choice. There could be no relationship between them without friendship or the most basic of understandings, but he couldn't allow Laura's sweetness to lull him into forgetting the wrenching torment that caring too much for someone could cause. Laura demanded his respect and affection and he would give it, but he would not surrender his heart. He couldn't.

Mother handed Laura her old threadbare handkerchief.

'I'm surprised you still have this old thing, what with Mr Rathbone providing us with all our needs.' Laura rubbed her wet cheeks, widening the hole in the centre of the ragged linen.

'My dear, Mr Rathbone is an excellent organiser, but even he is not capable of remembering everything, much less such a small detail like a new handkerchief.' She smoothed Laura's hair off her face, then caressed her damp cheek.

'At least this isn't his like everything else, like I will be.' Laura leaned back against the wall, worn out from crying. 'It's like being with Uncle Robert again and us helpless to do anything.'

'Mr Rathbone is nothing like Robert,' Mother gently corrected. 'He's willing to share what he has with us and to make you a partner in his life. It speaks to his generosity. And you aren't helpless.'

'Aren't I?' She was a woman with no money, no prospects and almost no family. A proposal from a moneylender was the best she could hope for, even if it made her feel like a purchased bolt of silk. Laura crumpled the damp handkerchief, then threw it to the floor, ashamed again of her foolishness. Better to be a man's wife than to sink to becoming a whore. 'I'm sorry I lost my head.'

'I'm surprised you haven't done it sooner.' She slid her arm around Laura's waist and drew her up from the bed. 'No one can keep their chin up all the time, not even you.'

Her mother guided her to one of the two stuffed chairs in front of the window, Laura leaning as much for support on her mother as her mother leaned on her. Outside, Thomas's happy laughter carried up from the garden. Through the window, Laura caught sight of his cranberry-coloured skeleton suit darting back and forth between the boxwoods as Mrs Marston chased him.

'Now rest.' Mother pressed her down into the chair. 'I think you need it more than me.'

Laura gladly sank against the well-padded back with a sigh, so weary from everything. 'I don't know if I can do it. I don't know if I can go through with the wedding.'

Yesterday, when standing in the middle of the mouldering room in her worn-out gown, it'd been too easy to accept Philip and the life he offered. Today, it seemed too hard. She wasn't certain she could spend her life without love. It seemed a silly, girlish thing to hold on to when everything else was being laid at her feet, but she couldn't let it go. However, if she rejected Philip, she'd be giving up the comfort and safety of his home, along with her mother's health. 'I'm sorry, I shouldn't be so selfish. Only, I never thought it would all turn out like this. I thought we could save the shop, I believed it until the end. I was wrong.'

'You're not selfish, Laura. You've taken on so much over the past year, things you never should have had to deal with. Now you've taken on this. It's unfair and I wish I could have done more to help you realise some of the dreams you believe are ending with this betrothal. But, Laura, I never would have allowed you to accept Mr Rathbone's proposal if I didn't believe he was a good man.'

'Why? What did he tell you yesterday?' Everyone seemed to believe in him. Why couldn't she?

'He was very honest with me and told me of losing his wife and his hopes for Jane and Thomas. It was like hearing myself speak of you and how it felt to lose your father. Look at him,' she entreated, gently turning Laura's face to the window. From the shadows of the house, Philip emerged into the sun. Light shone in the streaks of red in his dark hair and seemed to widen over the light-coloured coat. He approached Thomas, not with the purpose he'd shown last night, but more slowly, as though weighed down by grief. He knelt and threw open his arms to embrace his giggling son, burying his face in the boy's neck as if he were afraid of losing him. 'He's hurting, Laura, but he isn't without love.'

Jane came out from the house, snapped a rose off one slender branch and tapped her brother on the shoulder. He stood and steadied Thomas on his slender hip as Jane held up the flower to the boy's button nose.

'You can see it in how much he loves his child and Jane. For all the girl's peculiarities, when I speak with her, it's obvious she knows he cares for her.'

Laura remembered the juvenile kiss Philip had received from Jane last night.

'Yes, he loves her, but what am I to him? A contract? A convenient solution to myriad problems?'

'If he truly wanted an easy solution, he would have hired another nurse and expanded Mrs Palmer's responsibilities. He asked you to marry him because he saw something in you, something he isn't completely aware of himself. It's as if, deep down, he feels you can help him.'

'He doesn't want help. He wants someone to run his house and warm his bed.'

Her mother's shoulders rose with a sigh as they watched Philip set Thomas on the ground. He took one of the boy's hands and Jane took the other and together they led the child to the far wall where a lion-headed fountain spat water into an urn.

'When I lost your older brother, I was heart-broken. I threw myself into the shop, working to near exhaustion to try to dull my grief. No matter how much I tried to bury myself, your father never gave up on me.' She gazed serenely down on the garden, but sorrow laced her words, as palpable as Philip's grief had been when he'd first mentioned his late wife. 'Then one day, the darkness lifted and your father was still there, as loving as ever. Soon you were there, too, and I was happy again.'

Mother slid her hand beneath Laura's and gave it a squeeze. 'Mr Rathbone needs you. I know it's difficult to see right now, but if you're stubborn and refuse to give up on him, you'll capture as deep an affection as he shows to all he loves. I know it.'

Laura studied her mother's long fingers, thinking of Philip's hand in hers last night and the faint connection it'd created between them. She'd experienced it again when he'd apologised this morning, only that time it was him, not her, asking for something deeper. Both moments had been as fragile as fine silk thread. How could she possibly grab hold of something so delicate and make it strong enough to hold them both together?

'I don't even know where to begin.' She waved her hands over her dress, herself. 'I'm hardly going to arouse a grand passion in him.'

'I don't think Mr Rathbone is the sort of man easily ensnared by superficial things like dresses.' Mother's lips drew up in one corner with a mischievous smile. 'Though a finely turned-out figure doesn't hurt where men are concerned.'

'It will be easier to dress myself than it will be to figure out how to catch his fancy.' She knew almost nothing about gaining a gentleman's attention, especially such a stern gentleman.

'Follow your instincts, Laura. They'll guide you well.'

Philip looked up at the window, suddenly meeting Laura's eyes. He didn't turn away or nod, or do anything except study her as he had from the copper tub. She stroked her chin with her thumb and forefinger, almost able to feel Philip's hand on it. If there was one thing she knew to be true of Philip, it was his adherence to the contracts he made. When they stood before the vicar and uttered the vows, he'd be bound by what he said to her, what he stated before all his friends. It would be up to her to see he did more than simply uphold his promise.

'It won't be easy.' He'd fight like a dog to guard the wounded part of himself, but Laura had faced worse battles over the past year and in her own way won them, keeping a roof over her and her mother's heads, even staring down her uncle Robert on more than one occasion.

'Nothing worth having is ever easy.'

Laura nodded in silent agreement. No matter what she might wish for or think she wanted, the truth was, her future lay with Philip. If she hoped to have even a small portion of the life she'd once imagined for herself, a life of love with a true partner in the business and her bed, then she must find a way into Philip's heart.

## Chapter Five

Mrs Fairley fastened the last button and Laura turned to face the full-length mirror in the modiste's fitting room, moving slowly so as not to tumble off the small fitting stool. She sucked in a surprised breath at the reflection which greeted her. After a year in tatty black, the light-green muslin dress Mrs Fairley had chosen to alter first was a stunning change. Laura pulled out the skirt, then shifted from side to side to watch the material move. With the swish of the fabric, she caught a little of the excitement of that Christmas morning when her parents had given her a yellow silk dress, her first adult one. For a week afterwards, she'd crept down to the shop mirror at night to admire it.

The excitement of the memory faded and she let the skirt go. The silk dress had been one of the first things she'd sold to pay for the meagre rooms in Seven Dials. More than once while walking through Petticoat Lane with the rest of her dwindling wardrobe, she'd wondered which lady's maid or shop girl wore it now.

'It suits you as if it were made for you.' Mrs Fairley came to stand beside her, a box of pins in one hand. She nodded with approval at Laura's reflection. 'Brings out the green in your eyes.'

Her eyes weren't the only part of her the dress emphasised. The bodice was cut deeper than any she'd ever worn before, exposing the tops of her breasts which rested higher on her chest thanks to the temporary new stays Mrs Fairley had secured for her. It was by no means immodest, but Laura wasn't accustomed to it.

On the *chaise* next to the mirror lay the other dresses Mrs Fairley was to alter. They would keep Laura respectably clothed while Mrs Fairley prepared the rest of the new wardrobe in accordance with Philip's list. The sheer number of garments he'd requested was staggering. It didn't even include the gloves, fans, stockings and various other small items he'd sent instructions to other merchants to secure.

'Do I really need so many dresses?' Laura questioned as Mrs Fairley leaned down to begin pinning the hem.

'If Mr Rathbone says you need them, then I suppose you must.'

Laura tugged up the low bodice again. Even when the draper shop had been a success, her father hadn't spent like this on clothing, not even for his wife. Her father had insisted his family dress well, but simply, and with as few items as they could make do with. He'd believed in selling material, not spending their profits on it. 'I'm not usually so extravagant with my wardrobe.'

'Neither is Mr Rathbone. He never lets Miss Jane indulge in this manner, though she tries.' She slid a sly look up at Laura. 'He must have quite a fancy for you to be so generous.'

'I suppose he must.' Laura fingered the side of the gown, wishing she were a better liar.

'You don't sound so sure.'

'I am, I mean he does. I'm sorry, there's a great deal on my mind right now.'

'I don't doubt it,' Mrs Fairley agreed as she slid a pin in the hem. 'What happened to your things for you to need so many new ones?'

It was an innocent enough question, but Laura's embarrassment flared at the need to answer it. She'd kept her dignity in Seven Dials. Out of it, she didn't want anyone to know the degradations she and her mother had suffered. She was terrified they would judge her, just as Mr Williams had. 'They were lost in an accident.'

'You mean to debt.' Mrs Fairley rose to face her. She was young, maybe only a year or two older than Laura, but with an amiable nature, making her a good friend to anyone in an instant. 'You needn't be embarrassed with me, Miss Townsend. I came close to losing everything once, too. It's nothing to be ashamed of.'

'You won't tell anyone, will you?' She didn't want her shame to reflect on Philip.

'Miss Townsend, a modiste's first task is to help her clients choose flattering dresses to best emphasise their assets.' She tugged Laura's bodice back down into place, revealing more of the tops of Laura's breasts. 'A modiste's second task is to listen to her client's problems and offer advice. I assure you, I'm very skilled in both.'

Laura examined Mrs Fairley, sure that Philip wouldn't hire any woman to dress his sister or his future wife who wasn't both an excellent seamstress and discreet. Given the things Jane had already told Laura and her mother in the short time they'd been here, she could only imagine what the girl must reveal during her private fittings with Mrs Fairley.

What was Laura prepared to reveal? She

fingered the small ribbon pinned beneath her bust line while Mrs Fairley waited, as patient as she was buxom. She wore a demure light-blue cotton gown of superior weave with a high chemisette rimmed with delicate French lace. Beneath her generous breasts she'd wrapped a yellow cord, tying the knot just under the small separation almost visible through the sheer netting covering them. It was tasteful yet alluring, the pale blue of the dress matching her soft blue eyes, the yellow of the cord mimicking the rich gold tones of her hair. If there was anyone who might know how to turn a man's head with subtlety, it was this woman.

'What do you know of Mr Rathbone?' Laura began cautiously, still unsure how much she should reveal, if anything. Surely Mrs Fairley would think it odd for Laura to seek advice on capturing the attention of a man she was already betrothed to.

'He's a very fine gentleman.' Mrs Fairly selected a piece of wide netting from a nearby table. It was embroidered with the same flowers as Laura's dress and she draped it over Laura's shoulders to make a fichu. 'A little stiff in the breeches, but his heart is in the right place.'

'How do you know he has a good heart?' She hoped it wasn't for the reason flitting through her mind, but with the slender gold band encircling Mrs Fairley's finger, she suspected the attractive modiste had discovered Philip's better qualities in a less sensual way.

Mrs Fairley stepped back and the glowing smile which had graced her face since she'd first greeted Laura faltered around the corners. 'My husband, John, was a soldier. He was injured at the Battle of Waterloo. He recovered, but it took a great deal of time and I was forced to put aside my business to nurse him. Once he was well, the war with France was over and, with all the soldiers coming home, he couldn't find work. We fell into debt and were on the verge of losing everything. Mr Rathbone loaned me the money I needed to rebuild my business, sent me new clients and, as you can see, has been most generous with his patronage.'

All Laura's objections to the number of items on Philip's list vanished. Mrs Fairley needed the money as much as Laura once had.

Mrs Fairley chose a ribbon from the selection laid out next to the completed gowns and held it up to Laura's face, judging the colour against her skin. 'My husband has found a new life helping me manage my business, keeping accounts and dealing with inventory while I continue to see to clients. Without Mr Rathbone's help, I don't know what would have happened to us.'

Mrs Fairley's voice wavered and Laura recognised her fear of what might have happened whispering through the soft-spoken words. Laura had felt it, too, many times herself in Seven Dials, when each passing day had made their situation worse and lessened Laura's options for changing it.

Mrs Fairley wiped away the tears glistening in the corners of her eyes and fixed a bright smile back on her face. 'What of you? Are you excited for your wedding?'

Now it was Laura's turn to be honest. 'I'm unsure.'

'Unsure?'

Laura was unable to believe what she was about to reveal, but speaking to a married woman closer to her age proved too tempting to resist. 'What do you know of my betrothal to Mr Rathbone?'

Mrs Fairley flipped out the skirt to make it lie better, then examined the line of the hem. 'I know it was sudden and unexpected.'

'It was far more than that.'

While Mrs Fairley knelt down to adjust the pins, Laura told her the story of threatening Philip and the strange proposal. At first Mrs

Fairley continued to work but the more Laura revealed, the more the modiste sat back on her heels to listen, her work forgotten.

At last Laura finished, barely able to hear her voice over the noise of her heart beating in her ears. If Mrs Fairley wasn't as discreet as she claimed, if she told every client she possessed about Laura and Philip's betrothal and if he heard of it, she wasn't sure how he would react. She couldn't imagine him being pleased, nor doing anything but hardening him against her and their impending marriage. The task of capturing his heart was daunting enough without her creating more obstacles.

Mrs Fairley clapped her hands together, her eyes round with amazement. 'If I hadn't heard it from his intended myself, I never would have guessed Mr Rathbone harboured such romantic tendencies.'

Laura nearly fell off the stool. 'It isn't romantic. It's a deal, a bargain.'

'He might have dressed it up in such terms to fool himself and you, but it isn't the real reason for this hasty wedding.'

No. A man who knew his mind so well, who controlled himself with the precision of a tightrope walker like the one she'd once seen in Vauxhall Gardens did not need to invent such excuses to fool himself. Yet hadn't her father created a hundred of them to maintain faith in Laura's uncle? He'd been too honest and giving to realise how wicked his brother really was. Until the end, he'd held on to the idea Robert was still the young boy he'd once protected from street bullies, the one he'd felt guilty leaving when he'd left to apprentice with the draper. 'Perhaps you're right?'

'Oh, I know I am.' Mrs Fairley jumped to her feet, her excitement genuine. Her curls bounced as she snatched the fichu off Laura's neck. 'And I will do all I can to help prove it.'

The cold air sweeping over the tops of Laura's breasts startled her and she moved to tug up the gown again before Mrs Fairley caught her hands.

'You'll catch his attention with it lower, I promise you. And when you approach him, don't scowl with worry. Soften your face.' She pressed her thumb to the crease between Laura's eyebrows, smoothing out the skin. 'He's a confident man and obviously drawn to your confidence.'

'My confidence?'

'Any woman brave enough to threaten him with a pistol is most certainly confident.'

Laura would have called it desperation, but

if Mrs Fairley and Philip wanted to believe otherwise, then she'd let them.

Mrs Fairley looked over the selection of
dresses, tapping one finger against her chin.
'When will you see him next?'

'Dinner. He's quite busy today.'

Mrs Fairley selected a pale, rose-coloured
silk dress and held it up to Laura. 'Then we'll
make it a meal he won't soon forget.'

The rich scent of sage and cooked chicken
drew Laura to the dining room. Her stomach
growled, reminding her how late she was for
dinner. She'd sent Mary down earlier to ask
Philip and the others to start without her. Given
how hungry Laura was, she didn't want to keep
others from their meal. However, neither tardi-
ness nor hunger pangs were strong enough to
stop her from pausing at the mirror hanging in
the hallway to admire again the changes Mrs
Fairley had wrought.

She and the young modiste had gone well
over their appointed time together. A few
stitches through the shoulders of the pale rose-
hued dress had tightened the bust, bringing the
silk up snug against Laura's breasts. Then Mrs
Fairley had arranged Laura's hair, sweeping it
up off the back of her neck and using heated

tongs to create small curls which danced about her nape.

For such little effort, it'd made quite a difference. Laura appeared elegant, like one of the rich merchant's wives who would occasionally visit her parents' shop whenever her father had acquired a bolt of rare material. Perhaps with a simple necklace and a little more confidence, she would become more like those assured women, and learn to take pride in her position as the wife of a well-to-do moneylender.

Laura turned her face from side to side, pleased with the way the two long curls at the back bounced around her exposed neck. Pausing in her turns, she threw herself a sideways look, trying to mimic the coquettish smile Mrs Fairley had flashed when Laura had asked if Philip would be pleased with the new dress. She'd begged the woman to show her how to flirt, but Mrs Fairley had only laughed and told her she'd know what to do when the time came.

She hoped she was right. Laura's experience with gentlemen was greatly lacking. The stationer's son down the street had once shown an interest in her, but the dalliance hadn't lasted more than a few days. Her father had sent the boy off with a stern warning, reminding him he was in no position to set up house with a wife. She'd railed at her father for driving the boy away until the scandal of the weaver's daughter broke. Afterwards, she'd completely understood her father's concern. A solicitor's apprentice had got the weaver's daughter with child, then abandoned her, leaving her to face the scrutiny of the neighbourhood alone.

No doubt the old neighbourhood would look down on Laura if news of her nuptials to a moneylender became known. Pinching her cheeks to bring some colour into them, she dismissed her concern. Despite the years they'd lived and worked beside the other merchants, not one of their neighbours had helped her and her mother when the business had begun to fail and they'd been forced to hire a smaller, less expensive shop in a sad little neighbourhood many streets away. Instead they'd all stood around whispering while the removers had loaded the cart with what was left of their belongings, blaming Laura and her mother for Robert Townsend's mistakes.

Let them judge her for marrying Philip. Her opinion of them and their behaviour was no better.

Her stomach growled again and Laura reluctantly left the mirror, unable to avoid supper and Philip any longer. For all her thoughts of how to impress her betrothed, she had just as many of eating, especially with the scent of cooked chicken growing stronger with each step she took towards the dining rom.

'The dress is cut too immodestly for a young woman.' Philip's voice carried from the dining room, exasperation thick in his words.

'It's cut exactly like Princess Charlotte's,' Jane protested, sounding much the way Laura had done years ago when she'd wanted an expensive fan and her father had refused to purchase it. 'I altered it myself based on the pattern in the lady's magazine.'

Laura stopped at the dining-room door, unnoticed by the quarrelling siblings or her mother. Philip sat at the head of the table, his frustration with his sister evident in his tight grip on his knife and fork. Laura tried not to laugh at how easily his sister could rattle him when men like Mr Williams didn't seem to trouble him at all. Then again, she knew more than anyone how frustrating family could be. She'd been ready to scream more than once when her father had refused to listen to her arguments against her uncle. He'd always wanted to believe the best of his brother, especially at the end.

'You are not Princess Charlotte, nor are you

her age.' Philip cut his food, the knife scraping lightly across the plate. 'You will return the dress to Mrs Fairley to alter at once.'

'I won't.' Jane's foot stamped beneath the table, making the glasses on top rattle. 'I like the dress this way. Tell him, Mrs Townsend, tell him this is the style.'

'It is the style, Jane, but Mr Rathbone is right, it is too revealing for a young lady your age,' Laura's mother responded with measured patience.

'But—' Jane began to protest before Laura's mother laid a tempering hand on hers.

'I think I might have a suggestion which will suit you both. A width of gorgeous French lace along the top edge, like Miss Lamb wears, will encourage more modesty without ruining the line of the dress. It will be quite elegant and modest.'

'May I alter it as she says, Philip?' Jane bit her lip in anticipation, looking back and forth between her brother and the older lady. 'Mrs Townsend is right, it would be modest just as you like and, oh, so in fashion.'

Philip took a deep breath and Laura caught something of relief rather than frustration in the gesture. She wasn't sure if it was the desire to end the debate or his glimpse of the wisdom in the matron's suggestion which led him to nod his head tersely.

'You may keep the dress if you add the lace.' He levelled his knife at her. 'But if you alter one more dress on your own, I won't buy you another until you're sixteen.'

'I promise I won't change any of the others,' Jane stressed, before exchanging a conspiratorial glance with Mrs Townsend.

Philip didn't notice, reaching for his wine glass. Then his hand paused, his attention snapping to Laura.

She tried to steady the rapid rise and fall of her chest, but it was a fruitless struggle. She couldn't stop breathing, not unless she wanted to faint from the same shock she saw in Philip's eyes. They dipped down the length of her. The motion was fast, efficient yet potent, making her feel as if it had been her and not him who had crossed his room the other night naked.

Under the force of his gaze, Laura nearly tugged the ribbon from her hair and escaped upstairs to don a less revealing dress. She didn't flee, but strode into the room, her chin confidently in the air, her mother's words about working to win Philip following her like the swish of her slippers over the wood floor. She'd certainly succeeded in catching his attention tonight.

'My goodness, look at you,' Jane exclaimed.

'Miss Rathbone, that is not an appropriate response.' The older woman nudged the girl with her elbow before raising an approving eyebrow at Laura. 'Laura, you look very lovely this evening.'

'Indeed, you do,' Jane chimed in, fixing her brother with a devilish smile. 'Doesn't she, Philip?'

Philip didn't answer, but rose, his expression as stiff as his posture, except where his eyes widened. Yet it wasn't surprise illuminating their blue. It was something hotter and more potent, like the subtle flash of anger she'd caught just before he'd struck her uncle. This wasn't anger, or anything like what she'd experienced with the stationer's son. The stationer's son had possessed the ridiculous passion of a schoolboy. Philip's reaction was of a man, albeit a man trying not to react.

Heat swept up from the pit of Laura's stomach and burned over the tops of her exposed breasts. She nearly reached out and pulled the napkin from the footman's arm to cover herself before Mrs Fairley's assurance came rushing back.

'Good evening, Miss Townsend,' Philip greeted as she paused beside her chair to let the footman slide it out.

As she took her seat, she threw Philip the sideways look she'd practised in the mirror in the hallway. 'Good evening, Mr Rathbone.'

A muscle in his jaw twitched and his chest paused before he resumed his steady breathing.

Once she was seated, he took his seat again and she withheld a smile of delight, enjoying this new power over him.

Across the table, her mother's and Jane's astonishment was palpable, but Laura didn't dare look at them. It was difficult enough to maintain her composure in front of Philip. She didn't need an interested audience distracting her.

She unfolded her napkin and laid it across her lap, then sat back to allow the footman to present the cooked chicken, small potatoes and asparagus draped in a white sauce. Laura accepted a serving of each dish, trying not to overfill her plate. When at last she had sufficient, she took up her knife and fork and sliced through the potatoes, moving slowly so as not to fall on the food like some ravenous dog. Her concentration was disturbed when Philip spoke.

'Did you enjoy your time with Mrs Fairley?'

'I did. I hope you don't mind it taking longer than expected. I'm not usually one to spend so many hours fussing over my appearance.' Though she'd certainly take more care with her *toilette* from now on.

'Take whatever time you need with Mrs Fairley. I heartily approve of her work.'

'Do you?'

'I do.' He picked up the wine decanter and moved to fill her glass. 'She's exceeded my expectations.'

Laura didn't taste the wine, not wanting it to fuddle her senses any more than this conversation already had. 'No mean feat, I imagine.'

He leaned a touch closer and beneath the clove of the chicken, the faint hint of his bergamot cologne lingered, the scent heady and distracting. 'You've imagined correctly.'

'Then I'll have to discover how else I may exceed your expectations.'

He didn't smile, but she caught the glint of humour in his eyes. 'I anticipate your efforts.'

She focused on her plate, as unnerved as she was emboldened by this flirting. She didn't think it in him to be so charming. Thankfully, Mrs Fairley had promised to alter and deliver two of the other gowns by morning. It would keep Laura from turning back into a vagabond dressed in borrowed clothing and help her maintain something of the heat flickering in Philip's expression.

If the sharp and subtle blend of cloves and parsley sprinkled over the chicken's golden skin wasn't so distracting, she would have tried to be more intriguing. Instead, she set her knife to the bird, eliciting from the tender flesh a thick drop of juice as she pressed down. Spearing the piece with the fork, she raised it to her mouth. Her lips closed over the meat and she slowly drew it from the tongs. She closed her eyes and sighed as the savoury spices melted over her tongue.

After a year of ugly brown gruel, this was heaven.

Swallowing, she opened her eyes, eager for another taste, but Philip's expression made her pause.

He flushed as if his bite had stuck in his throat, except the strangled look suggested he'd been hit somewhere lower. His intense gaze warmed Laura's insides more than the chicken, burning through her like the chilli pepper she'd once tasted from an Indian silk merchant. She'd never thought of herself as a wily charmer of gentlemen, yet without even trying she'd done something, she wasn't sure what, to Philip.

'Is the food to your liking?' Philip coughed,

as if struggling through a dry throat. He took up his wine and sipped quickly before setting it at the corner of his plate.

'Yes, very much.' Closing her lips over another bite, she tried to recall the weaver's daughter and the way she'd flirted with her solicitor trainee. She could recall very little about their relationship except the aftermath. At least whatever came of this odd flirtation, it would do so with a ring on her finger.

'After dinner, I'd like to discuss the advertisement for Thomas's new governess,' he announced, seeming to recover his usual poise.

'I already saw to it this afternoon, before I left for Mrs Fairley's.' She sliced a potato, jumping a little when it rolled out from under her knife. 'Mrs Marston showed me the old advertisement, we discussed Thomas's present needs and I wrote the new one accordingly.'

She speared the potato with her fork to keep it in place as she cut it, watching Philip from the corner of her eyes, waiting for his reaction, unsure what it would be. She'd taken it upon herself to complete the task, eager for something to do and the chance to impress him. For all the advice Mrs Fairley had given her about her physical appearance, she suspected efficiency in handling domestic matters might be the second-best way to gain his admiration.

'You don't mind, do you?' she pressed. 'I thought it best to do it so you had one less item to see to.'

'I don't mind at all.' The stern businessman from this afternoon had vanished, replaced by a more relaxed gentleman, if one could call the straight line of Philip's shoulders relaxed. 'I appreciate your desire to help.'

She hoped it wasn't all he intended to appreciate. Sitting up a little straighter to best highlight the new gown and everything it exposed, she was about to tell him the contents of the advertisement when Jane called out from across the table.

'Miss Townsend, Philip asked Mrs Townsend to serve as my tutor and she's agreed.' The girl was more excited than any thirteen-year-old should be about lessons. 'Isn't it wonderful?'

No, it wasn't. All thoughts of impressing Philip vanished. 'Mother, you aren't well enough for such exertion.'

'I'm not an invalid, Laura,' her mother chided, closing her eyes in delight as she sipped her wine. 'Nor will I be one, not with food this grand and a warm bed.'

She raised her glass to Philip, then turned to

Jane. 'I think we should start with Beadman's *Principles of Accounting*, don't you?'

'I think it's a marvellous idea,' Jane concurred and the two fell to discussing the curriculum.

Laura gaped at them. She'd been dismissed, as if she were sitting here in her child's dress, not with her womanly figure filling out every inch of the silk. How could her mother do it? And how could Philip ask her mother to do such a thing without consulting his wife-to-be first? It was arrogant of him to be so presumptuous.

She sliced at her bird, then stuck a larger piece than intended in her mouth. It caught in her throat and she snatched up the wine everyone else seemed so eager to indulge in. The bouquet was as heavenly as the tender chicken, making the bird slide down her throat. If only the continued barrage of surprises would go down as easily.

Setting her wine glass on the table, she caught Philip watching her, his brow wrinkling in question at the change in her mood. Thankfully, Jane drew his attention away before he could say anything, then the girl dominated the conversation with her thoughts on women's education.

Laura focused on her food as the topic changed from bluestockings to the Prince Regent's latest scandal. Her mother and Jane exchanged details of it with the same animation which used to dominate her conversations with Laura while they'd tidied up the shop in the evenings.

Laura pushed a piece of asparagus through the sauce, hating to admit she wasn't just worried about her mother's health. She was jealous of her tutoring Jane. In a matter of hours it seemed as if Laura had been tossed aside while a new young lady had been whisked in to take her place. It wasn't a charitable thought, but she couldn't help herself. If she lost her mother's affection and failed to secure Philip's, what would be left for her?

Laura's discomfort soured her mood, but it didn't dampen her appetite and she enjoyed hearty helpings of the next two courses. It was only her fear of looking like a glutton which prevented her from asking for a second serving of trifle at the end of the meal.

At last, with her mind still troubled but her stomach full, Philip rose, as did Jane and Mrs Townsend. Laura was glad for the end of the meal, eager to be in her room and to let out her now very tight stays.

'Philip, you must show Miss Townsend Great-Great-Grandmama's knife,' Jane suggested, mischief in her eyes. 'You must see it, Miss Townsend, and have Philip tell you the story behind it. It's quite thrilling.'

Laura looked to Philip, expecting him to resist his sister's obvious attempt to see them alone together. She wasn't prepared for him to agree with the idea.

'Would you care to accompany me to the sitting room?'

No. Yes. She wasn't sure. She could almost hear her mother urging her to accept the invitation, but she'd been through so much already today. She wasn't sure she could endure being alone with him dressed so boldly.

'Please, lead the way,' she answered at last, not wanting to leave them all standing in the dining room waiting for her to make up her mind.

He didn't offer his arm as he escorted her out of the dining room. She wasn't surprised or offended. With the exception of last night and this morning, he'd avoided touching her since her arrival. She wondered how he intended to manage their marital relations if he could only be coerced into touching her by an apology. It seemed just another of the many things she'd be forced to overcome if she were to draw them together, yet it might prove the most difficult. She could hardly pounce on him and kiss him the way the stationer's son had done with her in the dark hallway between the shop and the store room. Or could she?

'Why did your great-great-grandmama need a knife?' Laura prompted once they reached the sitting room.

Inside, a warm fire burned in the grate, making the room more intimate and inviting than when she'd met him there that morning.

'She was a moneylender, the one who introduced our family to the business.'

'A woman? I don't believe you,' she teased, but his expression remained solemn.

'She and my great-great-grandfather lived in North Carolina and owned a tobacco plantation.' He removed the slender knife from its place of honour above the mantel and brought it to her. 'After she became a widow, she began lending money to planters and merchants and amassed a sizeable fortune.'

'If your family was so successful, then why did they leave the colonies?'

'My grandparents saw the threat the American Rebellion posed to their business. Well before war was declared, they sold the plantation at a profit and returned to London. The two of them re-established themselves here.'

'And the knife?' Laura's fingertips brushed his palms as she tilted it so the engraving could catch the light. Philip's heat was so distracting, she comprehended not one word of the inscription on the blade.

'Great-Great-Grandmama helped fund Lieutenant-Governor Spotswood's attack against Blackbeard.' They stood so close, she could hear the uneven rhythm of his breathing. 'When Governor Spotswood repaid the loan, he gave her this in thanks. It belonged to the pirate. It was one of many he was wearing when he was killed. It's been in the family ever since.'

'I should have known you were right.' She looked up at him through her lashes and a strange sort of panic flashed through his eyes. Beneath her fingertips, his hands stiffened on the blade. He'd been bold enough to stride in front of her naked when she'd threatened him. Tonight, when he held a weapon and there was no more flesh showing than the curved tops of her breasts, it was as if he wanted to flee. 'You don't lie.'

'I've never had a reason to.'

'Yes, I suppose it is one of the many things I admire you for.'

He arched one eyebrow at her. 'Then I assume you've forgiven me for this morning.'

'I have.'

Something like relief rippled through his eyes. She withdrew her hand from the knife, stunned. She thought nothing besides his sister's strong will could upset him, but it seemed their row this morning had troubled him too.

'I apologise for placing you in a situation you weren't ready for. It won't happen again.'

'Thank you, but what about my mother? Have you placed her in a role she's not ready for?'

'No.' He lowered the dagger, untroubled by her question. 'When I approached her with the suggestion, she readily agreed.'

'I'm sure she felt compelled to.'

'No, not at all.' A moment ago he'd been willing to admit he was wrong. Now he was so arrogantly sure of himself.

'You still should have discussed it with me first.'

'Why?' He returned the dagger to its place above the mantel. 'Mrs Townsend is a woman of mature years and doesn't need anyone's approval to do as she pleases.'

'She's ill. She needs rest.' Laura's voice rose before she brought herself back under control. 'Too much exertion might be bad for her.'

'I must disagree.' He wiped the fingerprints off the blade with the cuff of his sleeve. 'Mrs Townsend, like you, is not used to being idle. With your attention directed elsewhere, she needs an occupation. My sister will gain from the benefit of your mother's maternal care and business knowledge, and your mother from having another young person to guide and teach.'

Laura had no answer for him because he was right. She'd been wrong about him. Once again, he hadn't acted out of arrogance, but concern. If she didn't learn to think better of him, it would undermine everything she was trying to accomplish.

'I'm sorry and I don't mean to sound ungrateful.' She gripped the edge of the mantel. The cold marble corner dug into her palm. 'Only, I've been taking care of her for so long, it's difficult to think I won't have to any longer.'

He laid his hand on the mantel in front of hers. The heat of his skin radiated across the short distance between their fingertips. 'She does still need you. She always will.'

'Just like Jane still needs you.'

He heaved a weary sigh. 'She doesn't believe she does, but, yes.'

If only he needed Laura. Dread made her long to pace. If something happened to her mother, Philip and his family would be all she'd have left. It would be a lonely future if she failed to capture his affection. 'You make it look so effortless, managing your business and your family. If I'd had your talent for it, I might have saved the shop.'

'Then you wouldn't be here.'

She straightened, stunned by the faint hope woven into the words. Maybe it was possible. Maybe she could win his heart. 'Are you glad I'm here?'

After this morning, she wouldn't be surprised if he regretted his proposal.

'I am.' The honesty of his admission stunned her, as did his question. 'Are you?'

She wasn't sure. She'd wanted only the shop for so long. Now she wanted something else, something she wasn't sure she could achieve. If she couldn't win him, at least she was safe here. For that she was grateful. 'Yes.'

He looked down at the marble and traced a dark swirl in the stone. It brought his fingers achingly close to hers. She thought he might take her hand, but then he slid his away.

'It's taken me a long time to become comfortable raising Jane, and then Thomas and managing the business.' Loneliness and heartache tainted his words. Like her, he'd taken care of his loved ones while shouldering the burden of continuing on after a loved one's death. Philip might have been more successful with his business, but grief had left its mark on him just as it had on Laura. 'It wasn't easy. Some days it still isn't. It will help to have someone to assist me. I hope to offer you the same comfort.'

'In many ways, you already have.' She slid her hand over his, eager to chase away the darkness filling his eyes.

Beneath her fingers his muscles stiffened. The easy intimacy of a moment before vanished, the pain straining his expression dampening to something more solid, something she couldn't read.

She expected him to pull away and increase the wall forming between them. To her surprise, he turned his hand over in hers and slid his thumb along the line of her smallest finger. The slow caress ripped through her, as startling as if he'd stroked her nearly bare chest. If the same excitement raced through him she couldn't tell. His eyes remained fixed on hers, serious yet tempting, his true feelings as hidden from her as they were from his clients.

Despite his stoicism, she silently willed him to close the distance between them, to take her in his arms and kiss her until she could think of nothing except his touch, his warmth, his body. The urge frightened her as much as it made her heart race with anticipation, but the moment never happened. She pressed her fingertips against his wrist. His pulse beat a soothing rhythm against her skin. It didn't flutter wildly like hers. It seemed he was reaching out to her, but still holding something of himself back, retreating just when she wanted him to press forward.

The deep bells of St Bride's tolled nine times, marking the hour. Beneath their ringing, Laura caught Thomas's faint cries from upstairs. The sound didn't draw Philip's eyes from hers, but it interrupted the quiet moment and brought it to an end.

Philip slid his hand out from beneath hers, dropping it to his side. 'I must help Mrs Marston settle Thomas.'

'Of course.'

'Would you care to join me?'

'No, I'll stay.' She'd risked enough of herself

with him tonight. She didn't have the strength for more.

'Goodnight then.'

'Goodnight.'

He made for the door, stopping just outside it to face her. 'In the future, I'll do my best to consult you on matters pertaining to you and your mother before decisions are made.'

'Thank you.'

His assurance given, he strode away.

Beneath her palm, the marble still radiated with Philip's heat. Nothing had happened between them except the faintest of touches, yet it was as if he'd swept Laura in his arms and kissed the breath from her.

If only he had, then she wouldn't feel so unsettled. For all the passion his fingers had aroused in her, there'd been something rote about his touch, as if he'd known what was expected of him and performed his duties accordingly.

She traced the same marble swirl he had, coming close to the white base of a porcelain shepherdess before retreating. Despite the stiffness in his touch, when he'd spoken of his challenges and his true feelings about her being here, he'd been completely honest. It provided the faint hope that there could be something between them and that he might want it as much as her.

'Did he show you the knife?' Jane strolled into the room, attempting to not look too curious and failing.

Startled, Laura jerked her hand off the mantel, nearly sending the small figurine toppling to the floor. She caught it just in time.

'He did. It was quite fascinating.'

'So was the trick you played with the fork at dinner.' Jane smirked, strolling to join her at the fireplace.

'I didn't play any trick.' To her horror, Laura knew exactly what Jane was referring to.

'Yes, you did. I saw it.' Jane reached up and straightened the statue. 'Philip saw it, too. I've never seen my brother so stunned. You must do it again at breakfast.'

Laura laced her fingers in front of her, trying hard not to laugh at the absurdity of receiving flirting lessons from this sober thirteen-year-old girl. 'Should I die in ecstasy over the eggs just to get your brother's attention?'

Jane failed to see the humour in the remark, regarding it seriously, the way Philip regarded any proposal. The resemblance to her brother was striking. 'No, you're right. One time was good, too many will make it comical. You must continue to employ the subtle approach. Mrs Templeton was quite aggressive and put Philip right off her.'

'Who's Mrs Templeton?' It was the second time she'd heard the woman's name in connection to Philip.

'Mrs Templeton's a widow, all large breasts and red hair. Quite crass, though she doesn't think so. Her husband was another money-lender, an old man. Mrs Templeton set her cap at Philip after Mr Templeton died, but Philip wasn't interested. She wasn't right for him.'

'Am I right for Philip?' Laura felt quite brave with her enquiries tonight.

'You wouldn't be here if you weren't,' Jane stated, as if informing Laura of the day's wool prices.

If only Laura could be so sure. Jane was still a child. There were numerous things she might not know or understand about her brother.

'If Mrs Templeton was married to a money-lender, then she must know the business and still have her husband's clients. Wouldn't it have been prudent on his part to marry her?' Philip was nothing if not prudent.

'Her? Here?' Jane wrinkled her face in disgust. 'It never would have worked. She's too fond of her independence to marry again and she isn't like Philip; she lends to all sorts of questionable people. She's quite nasty when they don't repay. No, he's much better off with you.'

Laura wished she shared Jane's confidence in her suitability for Philip and his uninterest in the widow. He might not have married Mrs Templeton, but what Jane truly knew about Philip's relationship with her was sure to be limited. She couldn't imagine Philip parading his paramour through the house. It was quite possible his proposal to Laura had only come about because Mrs Templeton had rejected his.

The hope she'd experienced earlier dimmed. If his heart lay elsewhere, her chances of securing it were slim. She rubbed her thumb along the tips of her fingers, unwilling to give up so soon after she'd started. There had been something between them tonight, however faint. Whatever his relationship with the widow, Laura possessed the advantage of being here before him each day. She would use that to her advantage, even if she wasn't precisely sure how.

Philip sat behind his desk, the ledger open, the pen settled in the crease in the centre. He needed to finish the accounts tonight or it would be one more task to do tomorrow. Through the window, the moon grazed the top of the sill, looking down on the garden outside as Laura had looked down on him this morning.

Philip shifted in his chair, the tension low inside him as disconcerting as when Laura had entered the dining room. He'd sent her to Mrs Fairley out of necessity. He hadn't expected the results to be so striking. The pale rose-coloured silk had highlighted the slight blush of her skin and exposed the roundness of her breasts. The effect had hit him hard, as had the sigh of delight when she'd slid the morsel of chicken from the silver tines with her full lips.

Philip tugged at the knot of his cravat, working the tightness off his throat. Justin had told him stories of men with strange tastes, ladies' shoes and stockings driving them to the height of need. Philip had scoffed at the idea, until tonight. If Laura relished every meal in such an uninhibited fashion, he might develop a taste for watching her eat, naked, in the middle of his bed.

He pulled his list of things to do in front of him and wrote a reminder to instruct Mrs Palmer to remove chicken from the menu. He couldn't endure another meal like the one tonight. He might have walked naked in front of

Laura when she'd been a stranger, but he was not about to parade his more carnal needs in front of his future mother-in-law or his overly precocious sister.

The item added, he studied the list. Only a few things remained. Almost every one related to Laura. He stuck the pen in its stand, disturbed by how quickly she'd wound her way into his life. Though if any of the tasks on the list wrought the transformation the single visit to Mrs Fairley had achieved, he'd gladly put everything aside to see Laura off to the stay maker.

It was what lay beneath the stays which interested him the most.

His loins tightened again and he stood, trying to pace off the agitating desire. There'd been no one since Arabella. Many times Justin had urged Philip to follow him to his pleasure haunts, but he'd refused. Unlike Justin, Philip didn't allow his carnal cravings to guide his decisions, though he'd come perilously close to letting them influence him tonight. Only the greatest control, and the open door, had kept him from kissing Laura. She'd have allowed him the liberty, he was sure. He'd caught the invitation in the faint parting of her lips and the eagerness in her eyes.

His steps slowed as he reached the centre of the carpet. It wasn't just the unexpected surge of desire which had made him pull back tonight. It was the other, more subtle urge driving him—the craving for her presence as much as her curving body. Her willingness to express her fears and troubles had almost drawn him into revealing his own. It hadn't been false comfort when he'd said he needed someone to share his burdens with. He did. He wanted her here. He wanted her help. How much more he desired was difficult to discern above the cracking of the ice surrounding his heart.

He stopped and removed his watch from his waistcoat pocket and checked the time. It was early still. He and Justin could spar a few rounds at the club and he might shift some of the lingering discomfort distracting him tonight.

He closed the watch case and slid his thumb over the smooth gold, the memory of Laura's skin beneath his as troubling as his behaviour with her tonight. She'd caught the reluctance in his caress as easily as he'd noted the hesitation in her answer to his question about being here. At least her hesitation had been honest and affirmative. It was more than he'd expected after this morning's debacle. Sadly, he hadn't been as unguarded with her.

He dropped the watch back in his pocket and rang for Chesterton, eager to be at his boxing club. He didn't need to bare his soul like some poet to establish a solid relationship with Laura. What he needed was time and knowledge. In the coming days, as he taught her his business and she became further enveloped in his life, they would come to know each other and the awkwardness they'd experienced today would lessen. He would keep the hardness inside him hidden as well as the sense of failure fuelling it. They would build a relationship on mutual respect and affection, not worries and fears. They would enjoy a solid future together. The past need not trouble them.

## Chapter Six

Philip sat in the big chair by the window in the sitting room. Outside, the sunlight was dampened by the darkening clouds beginning to cover the city. They thickened the shadows in the room and made it seem as if sunset had arrived early today. A lively fire danced in the grate and candles burned in the holder beside Laura's chair, flickering in the faint light streaks in her amber hair. Thomas sat snug on her lap, his little head against her full chest as she read the horse story to him for the third time.

Gone was the ragged, desperate woman who'd slipped into his dressing room a short time ago. In front of him sat a poised lady and her confidence increased each day. Whether it was due to the gowns Mrs Fairley sent over every morning or Laura's growing confidence in her place here, he didn't know. He did know the modiste's bill at the end of the month would be substantial and he would gladly pay it.

'You're staring again,' Laura chided with a sideways smile when she reached the end of the book.

'I'm enjoying listening.' Philip laced his fingers beneath his chin. Over the past three days, he'd made a point of spending time with Laura, instructing her on the management of his business or, like tonight, joining her and Thomas in the evenings. 'You have a way with him.'

'He's a sweet boy.' She pressed her lips to Thomas's neck and kissed him, eliciting a peel of baby laughter from the child. Then she threw Philip a teasing look from beneath her long lashes. 'And not nearly as serious as his father.'

Philip lowered one hand to trace the curve of the chair's carved arm, fighting to douse the heat licking through him. 'Good.'

Thomas slapped his little hands against the book, demanding Laura start the horse story again.

'Yes, Master Thomas, I will read it once more.'

Thomas clapped with delight as Laura turned to the first page, ready to begin their fourth reading when Chesterton entered the room.

'Dr Hale,' the butler announced.

Philip's ease vanished as he rose to greet his father-in-law. 'Dr Hale, I didn't expect to see you today.'

'I was on my way to visit a patient. Thought I'd stop in and see my grandson.' Dr Hale reached for Thomas, who held out his chubby arms to his grandfather. 'How is my little man?'

Without hesitation, Laura rose and handed Thomas to the doctor. He bounced the boy on his hip, making Thomas squeal with delight. The two of them shared the same smile, top lips flat whilst the bottom lips spread wide to reveal the gentleman's full set of teeth and Thomas's small scattered ones.

Over Thomas's shoulder, Dr Hale examined Laura with an appreciative eye. 'You must be Thomas's new nurse?'

'No, I'm...' Laura's voice failed as she looked to Philip for assistance.

'Miss Townsend isn't the new nurse. Mrs Marston doesn't leave until the end of the month,' Philip corrected, reluctant to announce the end of his mourning, but he had no choice. 'Miss Townsend, allow me to introduce Dr Hale, Arabella's father. Dr Hale, Miss Townsend is my intended. We're to be married.'

Dr Hale looked back and forth between them

so fast, the fine wisps of grey hair at the sides of his head swung out. 'Married?'

Philip's eyes darted to Thomas, then the floor before fixing on Dr Hale. Until this moment, Philip had ignored the guilt lacing this marriage, the guilt which had pricked him when he'd engaged Mr Woodson, his solicitor, to secure the common licence. He didn't want to admit how much this new union felt like a betrayal of the old. 'Yes.'

Dr Hale moved Thomas to his other hip. 'I see.'

'I apologise for not informing you of the situation sooner.' He'd written the note summoning Dr Hale to discuss the matter. It still sat on his desk, unsent, just as the common licence now rested there unopened after Mr Woodson had delivered it this afternoon.

'I'm sorry if the news has come as a shock,' Laura soothed, dispelling some of the increasing awkwardness threatening to suffocate them all.

Dr Hale stroked Thomas's cheek, then offered her a grandfatherly smile. 'Miss Townsend, I've found there's very little news in this world, good or bad, that doesn't come as a shock to someone. Don't let me make you feel awkward. I wish you and Philip the greatest happiness.'

'Thank you, and please know you may continue to come here at any time. I want Thomas to know his grandfather, and his mother.' She brushed Thomas's hair off his forehead, then squeezed the doctor's arm.

It humbled Philip to see her so welcoming when all he could do was stand there.

Thankfully, Mrs Marston's arrival prevented yet another uncomfortable quiet from settling over them.

'It's time for Thomas to prepare for bed,' the nurse announced.

'Don't want to keep the lad from his sleep.' Dr Hale kissed the boy's chubby cheek, then handed him to the nurse. 'There you go. Sleep well.'

Mrs Marston presented Thomas to Philip. He pressed a kiss to his son's temple, lingering with his eyes closed, seeking comfort, not giving it. Philip was flailing this evening and he hated it.

'I must be going, too. I have a patient expecting me,' Dr Hale announced as Mrs Marston carried Thomas from the room. 'Mrs Linton. Healthy as a horse, but convinced she's dying. I suspect its unhappiness keeping her in bed. Husband ignores her. I do what I can to encourage her to pursue other interests, but instead she focuses on every twinge and cough.'

'Wish her good health from us,' Laura said.

'I will. Congratulations again to you, Miss Townsend.' He turned to Philip, his smile fading. 'Will you see me out?'

'Of course.' Philip might have avoided telling him of the marriage, but he would face like a gentleman whatever harsh words the doctor wished to level at him.

Laura remained behind as Philip accompanied Dr Hale to the entrance hall. The house seemed unusually dark, and when Chesterton opened the front door to let in the fading daylight it didn't dispel the gloom.

'You've chosen well with Miss Townsend,' Dr Hale offered as he accepted his hat from Chesterton and settled it over his hair. 'I can see she'll love the boy as if he were her own. It's the most I could've asked of you in choosing your next partner.'

Philip stiffened, wishing the man would curse at him for all his mistakes and failures the way he cursed himself. 'I do still grieve for Arabella.'

'And part of you always will, just as I grieve for my dear wife.' There wasn't blame in his long face, or hate, or any of the emotions torturing Philip, only a weary mask of resignation, like the one he'd worn the morning of Arabella's funeral. 'But time passes and eventually the pain fades. Let it and give yourself a chance to be happy with Miss Townsend.'

He clapped Philip on the arm, then made for the street, his trim figure silhouetted against the grey wall of St Bride's churchyard as Chesterton swung the door shut.

'Is there something you need, sir?' he asked when Philip didn't walk away.

'No.'

When Chesterton left, Philip didn't move or return to the sitting room. He stared at the carved panels of the door, struggling to push back the guilt threatening to crush him. Dr Hale was right, Philip needed to think of the future, but all he could see was that cold morning cloaked in misery and devastating grief.

'He's a very nice man.' Laura's voice filled the hall from behind him.

'I should have told him sooner. I wanted to, but I couldn't.' He regretted the words the instant they left his mouth. Laura's opinion of him mattered, especially while his own was so low. He'd been a coward and now both she and Dr Hale knew it.

She came to stand beside him and slid her hand into his, twining their fingers together. The gentle grip steadied his desire to stride out of the house and follow the pavement until the hole inside him engulfed all of London.

'My mother told me once that sometimes, after I was born, she would think of my dead brother and feel guilty for being happy with me,' Laura gently offered. 'She loved him very much, she still does, but at times it felt as if letting go of him was wrong.'

Something inside Philip cracked and he tightened his hand in hers. The words rose up inside him, despite every effort to stifle them. She understood and he wanted her to know.

'She wasn't like you, healthy and strong. When she wanted a child, I refused, but in the end I couldn't deny her and it killed her.'

Laura laid her hand on his cheek and turned his face to hers. 'It's not your fault, Philip. It's no one's fault when people get sick and die.'

'It was my fault. I should have known better. I should have kept her safe and I failed.' He let go of her hand and leaned away from her palm as the hardness rushed back in to surround his heart. He hadn't wanted her to know his gravest mistake. Now she did and he couldn't stand it. 'I have business to see to.'

He made for his office, ashamed of himself and his past.

\* \* \*

Laura didn't follow, recognising the grief pulling Philip inside himself. If she tried to draw him out now, he'd only push her away. All she could do was wait until he was ready to reveal more. Then she would listen and help him as best she could, assuming he ever placed as much faith in her as he had in Arabella.

She wandered back into the sitting room and lifted Thomas's discarded book from the chair. Until Dr Hale's arrival, she'd failed to realise how tight a hold the past still had on Philip. It was stronger than any power Laura possessed or could hope to forge in so short an amount of time.

Closing the book, she clutched it to her chest. In a few days, Philip's claim over her had tightened. It wasn't just the food, clothes and his house, it was him and his unwavering presence. She needed him as much as he needed her. Yet tonight he'd strode away from her help and she worried he always would. Then some day, she might take to her bed, focusing on every ailment as she grew old with a man who'd never regard her as more than part of a contract, a deal.

She quit the room, heading upstairs to see to the numerous packages which had arrived today from the glover and the stocking maker. Becoming an invalid like one of Dr Hale's patients wasn't her future. Philip might withdraw from her today, but she wouldn't give up on him, or their life together.

The clock on Philip's bedroom desk chimed nine times. The rain outside had been falling steadily for over an hour, striking the portico below. He barely heard it as he flipped through the papers again, searching the endless paragraphs of agreements and ship's inventory. Everything seemed in order, but experience told Philip something about this deal wasn't right.

'Is everything well with you?'

Philip looked up to see Laura lingering warily in the doorway, her white cotton day dress replaced by one of lemon-yellow silk. It sat snug against her breasts and shoulders, flowing out to cover her hips and sweep the tops of her white slippers.

He set down his papers, cautious of her presence. It'd taken hours of correspondence, accounts and a meeting with Justin to settle him. It might only take a moment with Laura to undo it all. He rose and splayed his fingers on the desk as if to balance himself against any lingering anxiety, but it never came. Instead, something in him softened with her appearance, as if it'd been too long since he'd last seen her and he'd missed her company.

'A potential client has me perplexed.' He waved her into the room.

A small sigh of relief escaped her as she approached his desk. He couldn't blame her for being wary. He'd fled from her in the entrance hall like a frightened debtor from the constable, then sent his excuses for missing dinner. It wasn't Philip's best moment. He'd enjoyed a number of poor moments since Laura's arrival, but she wasn't to blame. The fault was with him. 'The man intends to import a special silk from India. There's no reason why I shouldn't lend him the money.'

'But instinct is warning you off the matter.'

'I need more than instinct. I need proof.'

'Why? It's your money to lend or not. Simply tell him you can't give him what he wants, the way you told me.' She cocked her head at the bathtub visible through the open dressing-room door.

He rewarded her slight teasing with the smallest of grins. She noted it with a subtle rise of her eyebrows. 'It may be that simple, but I prefer to make decisions based on evidence, not suspicion.'

'Perhaps I can help you?'

'If you'd like.' He handed her the papers. 'Read these and see if anything strikes you as odd.'

She sat in one of the upholstered wingbacks flanking the window and set the documents on her lap to review. Beneath the parchment, the yellow silk flowed over her long legs, brushing the slender ankles crossed beneath the chair. Philip tried not to stare as he settled in the chair across from hers. He was glad his actions in the entrance hall this evening hadn't made her shy with him. It spoke to her courage and her concern, something he found endearing and as unsettling as his desire to watch her.

Laura's fingers moved to shift the papers, the whisper of their movement as quiet as her steady breathing. Then she turned to the last page and her brows scrunched a touch.

'You've found something?' he asked.

'I'm not sure.' She shuffled back to the previous page. 'Come and see.'

Philip rose and leaned over the back of her chair, forcing himself to focus on the pages in her hand and not the clean scent of roses and soap heightened by her warm skin.

'Here, in the list of French textile merchants.

I recognise only one of the three companies. I've never heard of these two.'

Philip straightened, all but forgetting the alluring little mole he'd noticed just above her collar-bone. He returned to his desk and removed a thick folio from the bottom drawer.

'Did I find something?' Laura twisted in the chair to view him, her hands gripping the rolled and tufted arm.

He looked up from his file and nearly forgot the silk merchant. The eagerness illuminating her face and the way her body turned to tighten the silk of the dress against the points of her breasts struck him hard. It took all his effort to jerk his attention back to the newspaper clippings in the folio in front of him. 'I collect stories about swindles and fake businesses. More than one potential client has tried to present shares in false companies as collateral.'

He held up a newspaper clipping. 'Two years ago, an actress and her husband were caught cheating shops out of goods by offering fake stock in fake companies. The husband served time in the Fleet for the debts the two of them accrued.'

'I remember the story. It seems your investor did, too, and thought it a good idea. What'll you do?'

'Deny his request.' Philip slid the clipping back into the folio. 'Then I'll warn my more reputable colleagues. One of them will start a rumour and within a short time, the man's ploy will be revealed to all.'

'And he'll never know it was you who uncovered his dishonesty.'

'There's a great deal to be said for being discreet.' He strolled to her chair and laid one hand on the back of it, trying to ignore the enticing curve of her creamy neck. 'Thank you for helping me.'

'It was my pleasure.' She looked up at him, the gap between her breasts teasing him as much as her sparkling eyes. If he leaned down, he could sweep her lips with his. Despite fleeing from her earlier, he very much wanted to kiss her now. It was an unsettling urge, made worse by the subtle tilt of her head, the way she seemed to be inviting him to taste her. 'I'm always here to help you when you need it.'

A chill licked up his back at the intimacy curling between them. He strode to the fire, took up the poker and tapped it against the coals as much to elicit a bright flame as to try to regain his usual reserve. 'Good, for there's another matter I'd like your assistance with tomorrow. Mr Connor and I must seize the goods of a bookseller who gambled away my loan and has now defaulted. I'd like you to accompany us so you'll understand the way of it. I don't expect it to be a difficult matter, or a dangerous one.'

Laura's excitement at having helped Philip resolve his troubles with the silk merchant vanished with this request. The manner in which her uncle's other creditors had handled their affairs still burned. The thought of creating such anxiety in another person, even if they deserved it, didn't sit well with her.

'I understand how it might be troubling for you,' he added in the face of her hesitation. 'You don't have to come if you don't wish.'

His recognition of her reluctance touched her. He was trying to be careful of her feelings. As much as she wanted to take up his offer to refuse, she couldn't. Her presence tomorrow wasn't about hurting someone or exacting revenge. It was about his genuine interest in her sharing his life, both the good and the unpleasant, and she couldn't ignore that. She'd accepted him as her betrothed and with it came so many things, all of which she must face.

'I'll come. You're right, it's part of the business and I must learn it.'

'Thank you.' His gratitude was clear. 'I'm sorry for what happened with Dr Hale today, and afterwards.'

He straightened the poker in the stand, staring at it as if it held all the comfort she knew he was searching for.

She came to stand in front of him and laid her hand on his shoulder. Beneath her palm his muscles stiffened. 'You don't need to apologise. It couldn't have been easy for either of you.'

His shoulder dropped a touch, the muscles easing their tightness. 'No, it wasn't, but thank you for trying to help and for your understanding.'

He raised his hand and slid it along the line of her jaw, his solid touch dispelling the uncertainty from the hall along with Laura's ability to breathe. The fire crackled in the grate and somewhere outside a horse whinnied. She didn't move and neither did he. The force of his gaze sent her heart racing until she thought she might have to dart from the room to release the tension.

Then he leaned down, his eyes closing at the same time as hers. His breath swept over the arch of her nose until at last his moist lips met hers.

The taste of him touched places only disturbed once before, when the stationer's son had stolen a kiss from her in the alley behind the draper shop. His lips had been nothing like Philip's. They'd been wet, sloppy, inexperienced. Philip's were controlled, powerful, leading, and Laura was more than willing to follow.

He didn't press his body to hers though her whole being craved it. She didn't dare move too close. She didn't want him to back away, or change his mind, as she knew he could at any moment. His fingers were light on her face, his pulse steady, dizzying, the most wonderful and the most frightening thing she'd ever experienced.

For all her desire to lose herself, she felt him struggling between pushing forward and holding back. It was in the shifting pressure of his mouth against hers, at one moment hard and demanding, the next light and withdrawing until at last it was gone.

She opened her eyes. His face remained so close to hers, she could throw her arms around his neck to pull him close again, but she didn't. His unsteady breath and the way his hand lingered on her face told her they wanted the same thing, but the fight for self-control raged in his eyes. It won, it always did. One day it wouldn't, she'd see to it, but not tonight.

'I'm sorry. You're here under my protection until we're married.' His eyes flicked to something on the desk before focusing on hers again. 'I shouldn't have been so forward.'

She tilted her head and viewed him through her lashes, tempting and forgiving him all at once. 'I think that was quite mild compared to how you acted with me the first time we met.'

'You were much less tempting when you were armed with a pistol.' He withdrew his hand, then made for the desk, the tender lover replaced by the reserved businessman. Laura regretted his absence at once but was also glad for it. The kiss had moved the ground beneath them like an earthquake and they were struggling to find new footing. 'Speaking of meetings, tomorrow evening an associate of mine is holding a dinner party for his wife's birthday.'

The abrupt change in the conversation was startling. 'A dinner?'

'Yes. I'd like to introduce you to some of my associates and friends.' He stepped behind his desk as if deliberately placing the solid wood between the two of them. It reminded Laura of an engraving she'd seen in a magazine once of a man chasing a woman around a table in amorous pursuit. Laura was tempted to try the same with Philip, if only to bring the light of laughter back into his eyes. She wanted to see more of the passionate man she'd experienced during his unexpected kiss, not the one turning to stone in front of her. 'I have no desire to startle anyone else with the sudden announcement of our wedding. Do you mind?'

'I'd be delighted.' *Delighted* wasn't the correct word, but it would do. Hopefully, his friends and associates would be more favourable to the idea of their match than Mr Williams had been. 'What should I say when the wives of your associates enquire as to how we met?'

'Tell them your uncle was one of my clients and introduced us. Our situation is not without precedent. Mrs Moseley was a governess before she married Mr Moseley and Mrs Charton was the daughter of one of Mr Charton's clients.'

'Then we'll be in good company.'

He tapped an envelope beside the blotter. 'Not all of it will be good. Not everyone in attendance manages their loans the way I do.'

'I see.' The discomfort of being associated with such a questionable business filled her

again. To think she would have to be on familiar terms with less reputable people and enjoy
it almost made her take back her acceptance
of his invitation. However, she could hardly
hold up her head in sanctimonious condemna-
tion. Though her parents had tried to deal only
with the most ethical of merchants, not all of
their fellow drapers and cloth merchants had
been so fair minded. Her parents had insisted,
however, on dealing with merchants who did
not buy from men who used slaves on their
plantations. More than once she and her parents had attended some party where a guest or
client of the host was well known for not only
supporting slave owners, but dabbling in the
trade themselves.

'I look forward to meeting your friends.'
And learning more about him and his life. 'For
now, though, I think it's time for me to go to
bed. Goodnight, Philip.'

Before he could respond, or perhaps tempt
her to stay, she hurried back to her room. It was
early, but with her body still vibrating from
his firm lips against hers, it might take hours
to fall asleep. The brief intimacy and what it
might mean for their future excited Laura as
much as accompanying him tomorrow troubled

her. He'd surrendered to the passion inside him and kissed her. It gave her hope that some day he might surrender more.

# *Chapter Seven*

The landau moved quickly through the twisting streets, the morning traffic having eased after the first rush of the day. Laura sat across from Philip and Mr Connor in the semi-darkness, the roof having been kept up despite the fine day. Mr Connor rested with his eyes closed, the dark circles underneath them betraying something of his night-time activities. Philip reviewed a list of goods, shuffling through the papers with all the seriousness of a cabinet member reviewing war plans. It was a harsh reminder of what they were about to do, to ruin a man the way her uncle had been ruined.

No, she reminded herself, it wasn't she and Philip who were ruining the man, but the man himself.

She pulled at the fingers of her new gloves, the fine leather hot against her skin. Philip had apprised her of the situation at breakfast. The man, a bookseller, had gambling debts. He'd sworn to give up the cards if Philip loaned him the money to clear his debt and purchase a very popular selection of novels much in demand. The man had done neither, leaving Philip's house and heading straight for the faro tables to lose all the money and his last chance to save his business. It seemed there were more dishonourable men like Laura's uncle than she'd once realised.

Philip folded the papers and slid them inside his redingote pocket. At the unspoken signal, Mr Connor opened his eyes.

'You're quite serious today, Mr Connor,' Laura teased, trying to lighten the oppressive mood in the coach.

'I'm always serious when we're about to seize collateral. Men in desperate situations can prove unpredictable.' He slid his friend a chiding glance.

'I wouldn't have brought Miss Townsend if I thought it was going to be dangerous,' Philip interjected, his words comforting despite their firm delivery.

In the past few days she'd learned to gauge his moods, to see something of the man behind the sturdy moneylender. He wouldn't hold her in his arms and coo reassuring words, but she could always trust that he meant what he said. Her comfort was short lived as the carriage slowed to turn into a small side street, passing a man standing on the corner preaching universal suffrage. The landau rocked to a halt where the street widened a touch in front of a small bookstore. The store was wedged between a tobacconist shop and a print maker displaying a scathing cartoon of a fat Prince Regent extolling the virtues of the hated Gag Acts. Laura peered through the window at the dark and dirty street. The windows of the shops with eaves were dulled by the grime of London air or streaked with a half-hearted attempt to clean them. The more exposed windows were pocked with brown spots from where last night's raindrops had struck them. The only things each shop had in common were the shabby goods filling their shallow display spaces or overflowing on the rickety carts outside.

Mr Connor hopped out, but stayed near the door, his back to the carriage. Philip stepped down next, waiting by the kerb for Laura to alight. She had to shift to one side as she did to avoid a dead rat. Behind the carriage, the cart driven by Philip's men halted. The burly gentlemen slid down off the sides, disturbing the small puddles dotting the pavement. The sky was clear now and the stench of the street, previously dampened by the rain, was beginning to rise with the heat of the spring sun.

Mr Connor made for the door, Philip following behind him, but Laura paused. A bow-front window with painted green trim marked the shop. The box affixed to the outside of the building spilled over with geraniums glittering with raindrops still clinging to their petals. Behind the flowers, the square panes of leaded glass sparkled with the faint sun reaching down this depressing lane.

'What's wrong?' Philip asked, pausing at the door as she joined him and Mr Connor.

'There's something too genteel about this place for a man in love with the faro tables.' She cupped one of the large geranium flowers drooping towards the door. 'There's a woman's touch here.'

Philip's scrutiny jumped from one point to another, noting the details. He pulled on the top of his glove, stretching the leather tighter over his hand before letting it snap back into place.

'I investigated the man myself. There was no evidence of a woman,' Mr Connor added. 'At least not three months ago.'

'The man's situation has changed.' Laura

could sense Philip's fury, yet no one watching them would have caught the subtle shift in him.

They exchanged a look, understanding whispering between them. Despite the change, they must continue, no matter what or who they met inside.

Her heart sank, but with his men waiting by the cart and the neighbours coming out of their shops or pulling back curtains to watch, there was no halting what was about to happen. Even the man preaching suffrage had stopped to watch.

Laura pulled her pelisse closer around her. The gathering shopkeepers' sneers and curious whispers reminded her too much of the morning they'd left the draper shop in Wood Street.

'Come along.' Philip lowered his walking stick, pressing the tip against the ground. 'Let's be done with this.'

Philip opened the shop door, disturbing the bell hanging over it, and Laura and Mr Connor followed behind.

The tinkling noise brought a young woman out from the back room. She didn't have the look of London. The sense of the country was too strong in the cut of her dress and the fullness of her hips. If she wasn't standing behind the counter, Laura might have mistaken her for one of the many milkmaids who walked the streets each morning with jugs of milk hanging off the yokes balanced across their shoulders. Whatever her origins, the freshness of the country had faded from her pale cheeks. The fullness of her body would soon fade, too, Laura predicted, as it had from her when the meals had become sparse.

'May I help you, sir?' The woman's voice was bright and inviting, but there was a strain to it Laura recognised. It was the same tense hope she'd once greeted each customer with when the business had begun to falter and every sale was desperately needed.

The breeze from outside ruffled the pages of an open book on a stand as Philip's men filed in behind them.

The woman's bottom lip began to tremble as Philip approached the counter.

'Madam, my name is Mr Rathbone. I'm here to see Mr Hammond.'

'No, you're not. I know why you're really here.' She twisted her hands in front of her. 'Please do me the courtesy of locking the door so none of the neighbours come barging in to see my shame.'

Philip nodded to Mr Connor, who slid the

bolt on the door. 'Where is Mr Hammond? My business is with him.'

'He isn't here. Up and took the King's shilling. Sent me a letter telling me he wasn't coming back. Didn't even say where he was.' Mrs Hammond went white beneath her freckles. The poor woman must have known as little about her husband's failed dealings as Laura had about her uncle's. 'That's what you've come for, isn't it, the money he owes?'

'It is.' Philip's voice softened, but it didn't ease the woman's worry or Laura's discomfort.

'Well, there isn't any to give you.' Mrs Hammond huffed. 'When he wed me, he said he had a good business, a fine shop. It was all lies. He had his fun with me, then left me to deal with his troubles. The coward. I thought I could keep it going, save myself from the streets, but I was sinking before he even left. I don't know anything about running a shop, or keeping accounts. I don't want to end up on the streets.' Mrs Hammond shoved her fist in her mouth to hold back a sob.

Laura rushed to her, recognising herself in the despairing woman and wanting to relieve even a small measure of her pain. 'I'm so sorry.'

The woman dropped her fist to her side, a hard look replacing her tears. 'Are ya?'

'I've been where you are. I know what it's like to lose everything.'

'You haven't lost nothing, not if you're with him.' She waved a finger at Philip, her tone blunt, not cutting. She didn't want Laura's pity any more than Laura had wanted anyone else's. 'I don't have a man like that to save me. Mine's run off, the coward. I hope he gets shot.'

'Mrs Hammond, are there children?' Philip asked.

She shook her head, her dingy blonde hair waving over her forehead. 'No, thank goodness.'

'Do you have family you can go to?'

Again she shook her head, large tears welling in her wide eyes.

'Philip, can't we extend the contract, give Mrs Hammond more time to pay, or loan her more money?' Laura pleaded, hating to see the woman suffer or to think what fate waited for her once she, Philip and his men left with her possessions. 'She's running the shop, she might make good of it yet.'

Philip came to stand in front of her, his body so close she could see the fine needlework around the buttonhole of his redingote. Laura tensed, expecting him to pull her from the room like her uncle used to do whenever she'd question him in front of customers or the more dubious creditors. Philip didn't pull her outside. Instead, he leaned in close to Laura's ear, the heat from his cheek singeing hers. Her heart began to race with more than just the panicked memories brought about by this situation. She stared straight ahead, focusing on the stacks of books just visible behind the counter and the narrow opening between the shop and the storeroom at the back. She was afraid to look at him, not because of what she might see, but because of the primal reaction setting low inside her, a feeling she couldn't explain.

'Making a scene will not make this any easier for Mrs Hammond,' he said in a low voice. It wasn't a warning or a reprimand, but as straight a statement as any he'd ever made. 'I understand your concern, but Mrs Hammond does not possess the skills or experience to make a success of a business which is already floundering. If I fail to seize her goods, one of her many other creditors will do it. They may not treat her as kindly when they do.'

Laura blinked slowly, trying not to let the heat of his firm body so close to hers add to the faint feeling already gripping her. At last she dared to meet his eyes, turning her head just enough to catch his gaze from beneath her lashes. The muscles along his cheekbones tightened, his breath caressing her face in a steady, even cadence to match the rise and fall of his chest. If there weren't all these people watching, she thought he might kiss the fight out of her.

Over Philip's shoulder, Laura caught Mrs Hammond's eye. The woman watched the exchange intensely, hope returning to her tired face. It crushed Laura to think it was about to be extinguished. She was no expert on books, but from here she could see the frayed edges of covers and the dust covering many of the tomes. Philip was correct. Mrs Hammond couldn't revive the business with such sad offerings. 'Yes, you're right. She can't carry on.'

Philip didn't gloat at her acquiescence, but studied her face. That unsettling spark jumped between them again, hidden from the others in the room by his wide back. As she held his stare, part of Laura willed him to step away, to lessen the intensity between them so she could breathe again. As if hearing her plea, he turned and strode to Mrs Hammond.

'Mrs Hammond, if you would please show me where you keep the rest of the inventory, then we may conclude this business and leave you in peace.' The deep tones of his voice were almost soothing.

With a resigned nod, Mrs Hammond led Philip behind the counter and through the small door at the back. Mr Connor went about instructing the men to pack up the books and they began loading them in the cart.

While the men worked, Laura stood in the middle of the store, watching through the sagging storeroom lintel as Philip quietly spoke to Mrs Hammond. The cadence and tone of Philip's voice was audible, but not the words. Mrs Hammond nodded as she listened, her despair seeming to lift, especially when Philip removed something from the pocket of his redingote and handed it to her. Laura thought it must be a pound or two. It seemed Laura's plea had prompted him to do more than enforce his rights. Mrs Hammond took the item and Philip's hand, showing what Laura thought a touch too much gratitude for such small charity. There was no kindness in extending a few pounds. If the woman didn't have the knowledge to manage accounts, she'd soon spend the money and be no better off tomorrow than she was today.

Laura tugged at her gloves again, wanting to

be free of the store and this dirty business, to sit in the dark of the coach and quiet her mind.

She made for the door. 'Mr Connor, I'll be in the carriage.'

'Allow me to escort you.'

'No, I can go alone.'

She slipped outside before he could object, stopping to take a breath.

'Excuse us, Miss Townsend,' one of Philip's men said as he carried a crate of books from the store.

She moved aside, noting the crowd watching, their eyes narrowed with hate and disgust, all of it directed at her. They despised her and Philip just as she'd once despised the creditors, too.

She hurried to the carriage, waving the rising driver back into his seat. She twisted the brass handle and climbed inside, pulling the door closed with a slam. The horse rocked back and forth, startled by the noise and the driver's voice rumbled as he calmed the animal.

The settling of the carriage didn't calm her, it couldn't, not with the steady clap of footsteps moving back and forth, the clunk of boxes falling into the cart and the loud whispers of all the watchers.

Laura leaned back as far as she could into the darkness of the landau, trying to brace herself against the fear of the strangers in the street and the memories awakened by Mrs Hammond's situation. Today wasn't supposed to be like this. It was Mr Hammond who was meant to suffer for his mistakes, not his wife. Helplessness filled her, just as it had when she'd overheard her uncle Robert downstairs bargaining away the business while her mother had struggled to sleep in the next room. Tears stung her eyes and fell in fat drops of frustration down her cheeks. She hadn't been at the new shop the morning Philip's men had come to claim the inventory, but she'd shaken with anger when Robert had callously told her it was all gone. Despite Laura's engagement to the man who had lent the money, she could no more prevent the end of Mrs Hammond's livelihood any more than she could have saved her own.

She stared out the opposite window, unable to watch Philip's men, eager for this awful morning and her part in it to end. Then, over the shoulder of an old woman whispering fiercely to the thin one beside her, Laura thought she saw a face she recognised. Her heart thumped hard in her chest as she jerked up and pressed her hands to the glass, trying to get a better look, but the man turned and hurried away. His shoulders were wide, his chest thick as a barrel. A shock of salt-and-pepper hair sat below his worn cap as he lumbered down the street.

Uncle Robert.

The day she'd left Seven Dials, he'd promised she'd see him again. The memory of his scowl glaring from the rookery window sent a chill racing through her. With shaking hands, Laura reached down and slid the bolt on the carriage door in front of her, then leaned over to lock the other one.

She returned to the window and caught sight of the man's cap in the distance. She willed him to look back, to confirm or ease her suspicions, but he turned the corner, the profile of his face obscured by the bright light reflecting off the building behind him.

The carriage door on the far side rattled and Laura whirled around to see Philip and Mr Connor outside. She fought to calm herself as she reached over and slid back the bolt.

'Why did you lock the door?' Philip demanded, as he stepped inside and settled himself across from her.

Philip had warned her to tell him if her uncle ever approached her. His intense stare almost demanded it. Out of spite, Laura refused to tell him, though part of her wanted him to know, wanted his protection.

'Mrs Hammond will not have the luxury of a bolt soon,' Laura shot at him, her anger fuelled by the fear threatening to escape from her control.

Mr Connor paused, halfway into the carriage. He looked back and forth between them, then stepped back out. 'I'll ride with the men.'

Once he was gone and the door closed, the vehicle rocked into motion.

'I'm sorry this morning didn't go as planned,' Philip offered, but she was in no mood for his apology.

'It went exactly as you planned. Mr Hammond failed to pay and you seized his goods. Now Mrs Hammond will starve, or worse.'

'Remember, Laura, Mr Hammond applied to me for help and I gave it. It was his choice to throw the opportunity aside and squander my money.' He settled his walking stick beside him. 'Why did you lock the bolt?'

His return to this subject startled her and she stammered as she answered. 'I was afraid of the crowd. Their hate was obvious.'

'If they understood the amount of good I've done, they wouldn't be so eager for our demise. Neither would you.'

'I have no desire to see us fail,' Laura insisted, wishing he could understand how watching the end of Mrs Hammond's hope had been like reliving the end of hers. 'I only question the good you seem to find in seizing a man's livelihood.'

'I assume your father was forced to collect debts.'

'He was.' Laura shifted in her seat, wishing to be left alone to deal with this tumble of emotions instead of enduring his questions and explanations.

'Then you understand the need to collect mine.'

'No, I don't understand. If my father had seen such a situation, he would have given Mrs Hammond more time, found a way to allow her to make payments, anything but snatch away her things. You see such a situation and it does nothing to alter your course. How can you be so callous?'

The atmosphere in the coach grew as tight as a thread about to break.

'You think me callous?' His question was sharp, slicing away her anger.

She'd pushed him too far.

The carriage rocked to a stop in front of the house. Philip flipped open the latch and stepped down. She expected him to storm inside. Instead he turned, facing her as he had

Mr Williams before he'd ordered the man out of his house.

'Join me in the study.' He strode into the house, not waiting for her.

She reached for the open carriage door to steady herself as she stepped down, waving away the footman's offer of assistance. The heels of her half-boots clicked with each step she took up the path. He was going to end their engagement. He was going to throw her and her mother out to join Mrs Hammond on the street. She was going to have to face her mother and tell her they were now going to starve, or worse, because she'd spat on everything Philip was, just because he'd made her face her fears at Mrs Hammond's and that had terrified her.

It was dim inside the hall and the shadows closed in around her as she walked slowly to the study. The prospect of returning to Seven Dials made her stomach roil. It wasn't the cold or hunger she feared so much as the loss of Philip's presence in her life. Over the past few days, he'd been there to support her. He was fast becoming the rock on which everything in her new life was being built. Without his confidence adding to hers, Laura wasn't sure she could face the challenges of poverty again.

She should have thought of these things before she'd let her anger get the better of her. Now it was too late.

Inside the study, Philip stood behind the desk, leaning on his palms pressed flat on either side of a large, open ledger. Even with his eyes fixed hard on hers, she knew she didn't want to lose him, or the closeness she'd fought to build between them. Maybe she was no better than a child, knocking contracts from his desk and hurling insults whenever she was frustrated or scared. Maybe she didn't deserve his trust, respect and affection, but she wanted it, especially now when it was close to being pulled away.

Laura crept into the room, penitent, ready to apologise, grovel, explain, whatever it took to make him forget her ugly words and not cast her out of his life. 'Philip, I—'

'Sit, please.' He pointed to one chair in front of the desk.

She obeyed, more afraid of him now than when he'd disarmed her the night she'd stolen into his house.

'What questions do I ask men who apply to me for money?' he demanded.

'Their collateral,' she squeaked, then cleared her throat, trying to rouse her nerve. 'Their business plan.'

'What else?'

Her memory failed her. She tugged at the lace around her neck, wanting to rip it out by the seams and clear it away from her hot skin.

'I ask them about their private affairs, whether they have a wife and children and their other household obligations,' he reminded her like a schoolmaster lecturing an unruly pupil. 'Mr Hammond succeeded in keeping the truth of his situation from me. Had I known he'd placed his wife in jeopardy with his poor business practices, I wouldn't have helped him dig the pit deeper. However, having discovered the deception, I'm glad of it.'

'Glad?' It didn't seem possible.

'Because it afforded me the chance to help her.' He turned the open ledger around and pushed it across the desk to her. 'I want you to see this.'

She perched on the edge of the cushion to peer down at the ledger and the long list of women's names. Next to each was fifty pounds and under the amount, a list of withdrawals with notes for the money's purpose. She could make little sense of the entries or who the women were. 'What is it?'

'The accounts for Halcyon House.'

She sat back, stunned. Tales of Halcyon

House and the safety it offered women who'd fallen on hard times were rife in Seven Dials. Entrance was by voucher only, but no one knew who provided them. Laura had once tried to discover it but, for all her enquiries, she'd never even obtained the address of the elusive sanctuary. 'Why do you have them?'

'Because I'm the primary patron.'

Laura's heart dropped to the floor and the guilt that had been steadily rising since her outburst in the carriage increased until she thought it might drown her. Everything she'd believed about him in the landau, all the wrong she'd convinced herself he'd done, ended with this simple admission. She deserved to be tossed into the street.

'I saw you hand Mrs Hammond something. I thought it was money. It was a voucher, wasn't it?'

He didn't answer. He didn't have to.

Laura slumped in her chair wishing she could take back everything she'd said in the carriage.

'My father was one of the primary founders of Halcyon House,' Philip explained. 'Since his passing, I've continued to manage its affairs, extending vouchers when I see fit and helping to raise the necessary funds to feed, house and clothe the women and their children who live there. We employ appropriate teachers in different endeavours, providing the women with the skills necessary to place them in situations to support themselves. When they are ready to leave, we furnish them with the means to establish a shop.'

Laura stared at the figures, unable to look at Philip. 'And their husbands?'

'If they can be helped, we find them a position. If they are dissolute, then we establish a trust for the women, money their husbands cannot squander.' He laid his finger on the ledger. 'This page is one list of those trusts. Two lady patrons, wealthy widows, hold the funds in the women's names for their use so their husbands cannot spend it.'

'I'm sorry, Philip.' She looked at him at last. There was no anger hardening his stunning blue eyes, only disappointment in her opinion of him. He'd believed in her when no one else would. She'd offered her assistance, listened to his troubles, but deep down, she'd failed to act from her heart. 'You're right. I should have given you the benefit of the doubt. After everything you've done for me and my mother, I should have thought better of you.'

'Yes, you should have.' He rounded the desk.

She stiffened, expecting him to escort her from the room, his house, his life. Instead he strode past her, his coldness as brutal as any words he could have thrown at her.

At the door, he paused and regarded her with the same detached reserve she'd come to recognise. 'I would have extended a voucher to you, if I hadn't asked you to marry me.'

He walked away, leaving Laura with the ledger and to reflect on the truth.

She rose on shaking legs and staggered from the room, too agitated to sit still, but not sure what to do or where to go. She wanted to talk to her mother and hear her reassurances, but it would mean admitting her mistake. She climbed the stairs, remorse following her. If Philip cast her aside, she didn't know how she and her mother would survive. Hopefully, Philip would send her to Halcyon House, though she wouldn't blame him if he decided to cast her off with no help at all.

Upstairs, the hallway was empty and she slipped thankfully into her room without being seen. She couldn't face her mother and burden her with worries about their future.

She paced across the thick carpet, her mind flitting from one awful possibility to the next. Making a quick turn, she upset the small stack of envelopes on the corner of her writing table. She dropped to her knees to snatch them up, pausing to look at the names on each one. They were answers to the advertisement for Thomas's nurse.

Laura pulled herself off the floor and settled herself in the chair by the window to read the letters. She might have failed to give Philip her full support, but she wouldn't fail him with her tasks. If she was efficient in this matter and continued to prove her worth, then he might see the value in upholding the engagement. It would give her time to rebuild the trust she'd so thoughtlessly shattered, the trust she hadn't realised was so precious to her until it had gone.

'Shouldn't Mr Woodson have obtained the common licence by now?' Justin's grip tightened on the dummy as Philip pummelled it. 'Your constant need to exercise is impinging on my more pleasurable pursuits.'

'Mr Woodson delivered it yesterday.' Philip punched the dummy hard, but it failed to drive back the anger gripping him.

'Then why haven't you summoned the vicar, set a date and instructed Mrs Palmer to prepare a wedding-breakfast menu? Not having second thoughts, are you?' Justin teased.

Philip jolted upright, dropping his hands to his sides, but not unclenching his aching fists.

Justin's smile wilted. 'You are.'

'Despite the past few days, my intended is determined to see me as nothing more than a grubbing moneylender intent on ruining everyone who wanders across my path.' He slammed his fist into the leather, the blow vibrating up his arm. The control he'd maintained all day, in the bookseller's, then after Laura had thrown her aspersions in his face, nearly failed him. He straightened, closed his eyes and listened to the sounds of the room, concentrating on the slap of fists against flesh, leather and canvas, the shuffle of feet over the dirt floor and the yelling of the trainers until his calm returned.

He opened his eyes and struck the dummy again, his punch controlled and well executed.

Justin clapped his hands on either side of the wobbling figure. 'You can't expect Miss Townsend to possess unshakeable faith in you because you bought her dresses and made her mother happy. It'll take time, which you won't gain by putting off the wedding.'

'Perhaps marriage isn't the best solution to my problems.' Philip shook out the burning in his arms, but couldn't shift the uncertainty which had plagued him since this morning.

He's been so certain in his decision when he'd proposed, now he doubted both himself and Laura.

'Breaking the engagement will only cause more problems. Imagine Jane's tantrum when you tell her Mrs and Miss Townsend are leaving.' He pointed a warning finger at Philip. 'That alone should encourage you to set a date.'

Philip turned and strode to the far end of the sparring ring, the potential scene with his sister threatening to bring on a headache. However, it wasn't Jane's disappointment which kept the common licence sealed on his desk instead of discarded in the grate. It was his own. He didn't want to see the light go out of Laura's beautiful face when he told her he'd changed his mind. He didn't want to experience even a small measure of the despair which stung his chest whenever he imagined the scene.

He paced back to where Justin waited with a towel. Taking it, Philip rubbed the coarse cotton between his thumb and forefinger. He was allowing emotions to guide his decision and it unnerved him. Such weakness had allowed him to ignore Arabella's frailty and it had killed her. If he continued on this path with Laura, he might be the one to suffer this time.

'What if marrying her is a mistake?' After

her actions in the entrance hall and their kiss the previous evening, he'd thought her concern for him extended further than the mere convenience of his money and name. Today, he wasn't so sure. He despised this confusion. He wanted to see the situation as plainly as he had the day he'd proposed.

'The only mistake you're making is putting off the wedding.' Justin threw one arm around Philip's shoulders, the rogue returning to replace the concerned friend. 'What you need is a wedding night. It'll clear your head.'

The memory of Laura's mouth eager and open beneath his nearly sent him back to pummelling the dummy. Twice yesterday he'd lost control, once after Dr Hale's visit and again in his bedroom. It'd taken the better part of the night and reviewing nearly every contract on his desk to forget the sweet taste of her kiss and how her soft sigh had nearly been his undoing. Not even his embarrassment over his confession in the entrance hall had been enough to drive the unsettling urges her tender cheek beneath his fingertips had raised. How easy it was to forget himself in her presence proved unsettling. 'I don't think the more intimate demands of marriage will make things clearer.'

'I know you don't, but trust me, intimacy

is exactly what you need to settle yourself. So take my advice and set the date.' Justin punched Philip's arm lightly. 'Now, come on, we have to get you cleaned up and home before Mr Charton's party tonight.'

'You're coming, then?'

'The lovely widow Gammon will be there. With her, I expect to be very settled by the end of the night.' He whistled as he strolled off to the bathing room.

Philip followed at a slower pace. He was done fighting for the day, fighting Laura, his feelings, himself. He wasn't ready to hurry to the church or to terminate his agreement with Laura, but something had to change before he entered into this most binding of contracts. He needed some assurance his future with Laura would be one of mutual companionship, not derision and disgust. Hopefully, tonight, he would find it.

## Chapter Eight

Laura held on to Philip's arm as they walked up to the Chartons' wide front door, careful not to squeeze too tight. Tonight there was none of the warmth she'd experienced in the previous times they'd touched, only an awkwardness she attributed to that morning's row.

Despite an afternoon of attending to household business, worry continued to cling to her like moist linen on a hot day. Not even Mary arriving to help her dress for tonight had eased her concerns. Mrs Fairley had sent over a cream-coloured silk gown with matching elbow-length gloves. A black ribbon edged the bodice, curling down to nip in beneath her breasts before falling in a straight line to her feet. Upon seeing the dress, Jane had insisted on instructing Mary in arranging Laura's hair into a pretty new style displayed in one of her fashion magazines. The tumble of curls gathered near the nape of Laura's neck and spilling over her shoulder to rest on the top of one breast was both demure and suggestive. Mother and Jane had been effusive in their praise of Laura's appearance tonight. Philip had not uttered one word, good or bad about it, nor had he stared at her in the carriage the way he had the night she'd surprised him with her dress at dinner. Instead, his focus had remained on London passing outside the landau window.

Now, as they stepped into the Chartons' columned hall, the fears his indifference raised settled a little. If he was still intent on introducing her to his associates and friends, then it must mean he intended to proceed with the wedding. Perhaps after a few glasses of port and convivial conversation with his associates had put him at his ease, she might gently press the subject of the wedding and put her mind at rest.

'Mr Rathbone, good to see you.' An older gentleman with a round stomach concealed by a fine red waistcoat and dark jacket swept down the curving marble staircase, to grip Philip's hand. 'And you've brought a guest?'

'Allow me to introduce Miss Laura Townsend. We're engaged to be married.'

'I never would have guessed it.' Mr Charton gaped back and forth between them. As reassuring as Philip's announcement might be, she was growing tired of seeing surprise on people's faces when she was introduced. 'But I should have known you'd simply spring her on us. With how close you keep things to the vest, it's a wonder you didn't marry her and then tell us.'

'I wouldn't have wanted to deny the ladies their share of the conversation and excitement.'

Laura tried not to stare at Philip. His near-joke had come out in his usual straightforward tone, but there was no mistaking the humour in it. Mr Charton certainly didn't miss it.

'No, they'd never forgive you.' Mr Charton laughed, then turned to Laura and made a small bow. 'It's a pleasure to meet you, Miss Townsend. You must be quite a lady to catch Rathbone's eye. Well, come up to the drawing room, both of you, Margaret and the others will be all in a flutter when they hear the news.'

Philip inclined his head, the only indication he agreed.

They started for upstairs, Laura struggling to watch her step and admire the fine plasterwork on the ceiling at the same time. She'd thought Philip's house grand until she'd entered this one. Philip's was more modest, his wealth was whispered rather than proclaimed.

Near the top, Mr Charton moved to Philip's other side, mumbling in a voice which wasn't quite low enough for Laura not to hear. 'Mrs Templeton won't be pleased about your engagement.'

'Her opinion doesn't concern me.' It was difficult to tell if Philip's declaration was the truth or merely made for Laura's and propriety's sake.

'No, I don't suppose it does,' Mr Charton conceded honestly.

It did little to calm the anxiety growing inside Laura or the very real fear she would have an enemy among his friends before she uttered so much as a good evening.

Mr Charton led them into the long drawing room just off the top of the stairs.

'Lily, stop playing,' he called out above the chatter to the young woman seated at the nearby piano forte. Then he looked over his shoulder at Laura. 'My middle daughter, no talent for drawing, but quite the musician.'

Mr Charton raised his hands, making the port in his glass slosh up along the sides. 'Attention, everyone.'

The conversation ceased as the guests turned

to face them, their scrutiny and curiosity fixed on Laura, the stranger. Among them she spied Mr Connor lounging near the widow with a buxom woman with deep-brown hair. At least there was one person Laura knew here. She settled her shoulders and stood proudly next to Philip. In time, there would be more, she was sure of it. She had to be sure. The alternative was too frightening to contemplate.

'Mr Rathbone has joined us with some surprising news,' Mr Charton announced. 'He's engaged to be married.'

The gasps of surprise nearly rattled the house to its rafters. Laura's fingers tightened on Philip's arm, digging in hard to the stiff muscle beneath. Neither of them was used to being the centre of so much attention and neither approved of it.

Mr Charton tossed Philip a ribbing smile. 'Now that's out of the way.'

'I would have preferred something more subtle,' Philip chided, both amusement and irritation dotting his words.

Beneath her palm she felt his arm relax, just as her hand tightened as one of the ladies hurried up to them.

'Mr Rathbone, how clever of you to spring such a thing on us,' exclaimed the tall woman in an expensive red silk gown and matching turban. 'Who knew you could be so surprising?'

'I did,' Laura answered, her cheeks burning with her boldness.

'I bet you do.' The woman waved her closed fan at Laura. 'I'm Mrs Charton. You don't know how excited I am to have you here.'

Laura flicked a glance at Philip, wondering if he was excited to be here with her, or if he was regretting it. His demeanour was as unyielding as always and she could discern nothing from it.

'Mr Rathbone, when you wrote to say you were bringing a guest you could have given me at least some hint as to her importance,' Mrs Charton scolded with a laugh.

Before he could answer, they were surrounded by nearly all the other female guests and some of their husbands. The women chattered and chirped, offering excited congratulations. The men were more sober as Philip made the introductions, acquainting Laura with the Moseleys, the Feltons, Mrs Gammon and Mr Jones.

'Enough of this ladies' business, Rathbone, come and give us your opinion on all those uprisings in Manchester. Jones doesn't think the weavers have the right to riot, but I say they do,' Mr Moseley, a lithe man with a long chin, insisted. 'If anyone can get to the meat of the matter, it's you.'

At last Philip turned to Laura, truly acknowledging her for the first time since she'd come downstairs to join him in the carriage. 'If you'll excuse me.'

She gripped his arm, preventing him from leaving.

'What shall I tell the ladies about our engagement?' she whispered, the women's excited voices keeping her from being overheard. She hadn't dared to broach the subject, or break the silence between them in the landau.

'Whatever you wish. The men aren't likely to ask for details so you needn't worry about me contradicting your version of events.'

This slim reassurance given, he strode off with Mr Moseley, the damage from this morning evident in his swift dismissal of Laura in favour of his friends.

Fear rippled through her, but a comforting hand on her arm steadied her. She turned to find Mrs Charton drawing her deeper into the room.

'I know we must be very intimidating with all our fussing,' Mrs Charton offered. 'But your announcement is the most exciting news we've had at a gathering in some time.'

'It is,' Mrs Moseley chimed in, joining Laura on her other side. Mrs Moseley was near Laura's age with round cheeks and her round stomach indicated she was expecting a baby. 'And for it to come from Mr Rathbone is most unexpected. I don't know what to make of it.'

Neither did Laura, but she resolved to appear happy and excited. It wouldn't do any good to worry and raise pestering and pointed questions among the wives of his associates.

Mrs Charton stopped them before the fireplace. Inside, a cosy fire consumed a thick pile of coal. Despite the warm spring day, the night had taken on a chill. 'Allow me to introduce you to everyone.'

The women formed a tight circle around Laura as Mrs Charton made the introductions. Mrs Felton was closer to Mrs Charton's matronly age, but plump and short where Mrs Charton was slender and tall. Even Mrs Gammon with her wide bosom and round hips had stolen away from Mr Connor to join the conversation.

Only one woman showed no interest in the discussion and Laura guessed she must be Mrs Templeton.

She remained across the room near the escritoire, her willowy form akin to the table's fine legs, her bust as full as the round clock behind her. Her long fingers with long nails sharpened almost to claws tightened on the wine glass she held as she observed Laura.

Laura swallowed hard, wondering at the true depth of Philip's interest in the woman. It was impossible to gauge it when he remained with his back to all the women as he talked with the men.

Whatever disappointment his indifference created, there was little time to entertain it as the women began to question Laura about the proposal. She stammered as she answered, doing the best she could to describe it without revealing the pistol, Seven Dials or her uncle's true financial situation. Then, with a few well-placed answers, she shifted their interest from the proposal to the wedding itself, focusing on the finer points of her dress, the only details of the ceremony she possessed. Nothing else had been settled or, if it had, Philip had not seen fit to inform her. She could well imagine him appearing in her room one morning with the news the vicar of St Bride's was standing at the altar and ready to perform the ceremony. After this morning, she didn't care how it happened as long as it actually happened. Only that would end the bleak uncertainty hovering around her.

The conversation with the ladies continued until the butler appeared to summon everyone to dinner. Philip and Mr Jones, a well-turned-out bachelor, stood deep in debate. Laura watched as one by one the other ladies' husbands came to lead them down to the dining room, leaving her to stand alone by the fireplace. She feared she might have to go by herself, but at last the gentlemen ended their discussion and Philip came to fetch her.

'How are you fairing?' He held out his arm to her.

She took it with the same hesitation as she had outside the carriage, unsure if his question was driven by manners or genuine concern. She glanced to Mrs Templeton and saw her full lips press thin before she recovered herself and fixed them into a wide, if not cunning, smile.

'I'm doing well. Mrs Charton is very nice, as are all the ladies.' She inclined her head to where Mr Connor and Mrs Gammon sat together on a sofa situated so far at one end of the room it was nearly in the hallway. 'Mr Connor is certainly enjoying himself. He's barely left Mrs Gammon's side since we arrived.'

'Nor is he likely to do so at any time this

entire night.' He cocked an eyebrow at her to drive home the meaning of his words.

Laura's eyes widened, but not in surprise at Mr Connor's nocturnal activities. No, she was more surprised at the way Philip spoke to her with the ease and comfort of a long friendship. It gave her hope they could move past what had happened and reclaim some of the intimacy which had developed between them over the past few days.

Mrs Gammon wasn't the only widow looking to snare a bedfellow this evening. Mrs Templeton strode across the room towards them. With each step, her large breasts jiggled above the edge of the blue silk dress, which clung to her round hips. The silk was of inferior weave and not as well cut as Laura's. She guessed Mrs Templeton had paid more attention to the way the colour emphasised the whiteness of her skin and the red curls piled thick against the back of her head than the quality of the material. Her dress reminded Laura of the buxom young women who used to stand across the street from the rookery in their garish second-hand frocks, trying to entice men. Hopefully, Mrs Templeton wasn't as experienced a temptress as those women, or Philip as willing as their clients.

The widow met them near the door to the hallway, all but blocking their way.

'Mr Rathbone, it's a pleasure to see you to-night,' Mrs Templeton purred, standing so close in front of Philip that, if she took a deep breath, her breasts would brush his chest. 'I've missed you at all the dinners of late.'

Laura slid her hand up Philip's arm, making her claim on him clear. If Mrs Templeton noticed, she didn't seem to care, remaining far closer to Philip than propriety dictated.

'I've been greatly occupied.' Philip's even voice and posture offered no clue to his thoughts about the widow's appearance or her proximity.

Mrs Templeton laid one finger on his chest, the large garnet adorning it sparkling over his dove-coloured waistcoat. 'You're always occupied with the wrong business.'

She slid a wicked glance at Laura before focusing back on Philip.

Laura wanted to pull Philip away from the cat's claws and chide the widow for behaving so inappropriately. Instead she stood firmly beside him, biting her tongue to keep silent. Laura hadn't seen Mrs Templeton in intimate conversation with any of the women, but it didn't mean they wouldn't rally to her defence if Laura insulted her. If Philip still intended to honour their engagement, Laura couldn't afford to make herself an outcast among the wives of his associates and friends.

To her relief, Laura didn't have to pull Philip away. He moved back without any prompting, placing a more appropriate amount of room between himself and the widow's breasts. Whatever dance Mrs Templeton hoped to engage him in, he wasn't rising to the invitation.

'Allow me to introduce my betrothed, Miss Laura Townsend.' He levelled his hand at Laura.

'Miss Townsend. A pleasure.' The slight sneer along the curve of Mrs Templeton's lips told Laura it was anything but pleasurable.

Laura didn't allow her smile to falter and matched Mrs Templeton's shallow curtsy with a deep, polite one. 'It's a pleasure to meet an *old* friend of Philip's.'

'I'm not so old as some are young and inexperienced.' She fixed her eyes on Philip, but he ignored her, turning instead to Laura.

Laura couldn't discern if he was proud or embarrassed by her exchange with the widow. Hopefully he admired her ability to face the subtle sneer of this woman as much as he'd admired her ability to stand up to Mr Williams.

Before any of them could say more, Mr Jones appeared at Mrs Templeton's elbow. A head taller than her, Mr Jones wasn't afraid to inspect the assets the widow so blatantly displayed. 'May I escort you in to dinner?'

'You may.' She took his arm, flashing Philip an enticing smile before following the more accommodating Mr Jones from the room. Mr Connor and Mrs Gammon followed close behind them.

If Philip regretted the widow's departure, it was difficult to tell as he led Laura downstairs to the dining room.

Dinner itself was a far more relaxing affair than the introductions in the drawing room. Laura was seated between the friendly Mrs Charton and Mr Connor, who remained deep in conversation with Mrs Gammon, who sat on his other side. Yet for all the welcome Laura received from the other ladies, she felt Mrs Templeton's attention on her frequently. Philip was unlucky enough to be seated next to the widow, who leaned too close to him as she listened to Philip's conversation with Mr Moseley, offering her opinion on many occasions. Philip kept his gaze on his plate whenever she spoke. Once, he raised his eyes to meet Laura's before shifting them back to the fish. Laura wondered if this reluctant show of attention was for her benefit.

'I'm so happy to see Mr Rathbone entering back into life again,' Mrs Charton observed, drawing Laura's attention from Mrs Templeton.

'Have you known Philip a long time?'

'Oh, yes, since he was a very young man and his father began doing business with Henry.' She nodded to her husband, who raised his glass to her, the open affection between them touching. 'Mr Rathbone's father used to bring him here when he was teaching him the business.'

'What happened to Philip's parents?' There was so much about his life and past he hadn't told her.

'Fever—seven years ago. Took his father first and then two days later his mother died. It was all so sudden and unexpected.' She shook her head in sorrow. 'After Mr Rathbone's parents passed away, he'd come to Henry for advice. There was one particular occasion when a silversmith he'd loaned quite a sum defaulted. It nearly ruined his entire business.'

'Philip almost lost his business?' It didn't seem possible.

'Oh, yes. It was such a hard time for him

after his father died, you understand. And then to lose his mother so soon after. I tried to help where I could with Jane, but I was newly delivered of my twins and could do so much less than I wanted to. Then, after so many years, when all was well, to have another tragedy befall him. The poor soul.' She touched her hand to her chest and threw a motherly look at Philip. 'But to see him tonight, looking so much happier and more like the old Mr Rathbone, it warms the heart.'

'You think him happier?'

'Oh, most definitely and I must say there's no doubt you're the cause. Isn't she, Mrs Gammon?'

The widow leaned forward to peer past Mr Connor. 'Isn't who?'

'Isn't Miss Townsend to thank for the change in Mr Rathbone?'

Mrs Gammon looked from Laura to Philip, then nodded, her pearl earrings brushing her smooth cheeks. 'Oh, yes, I noticed it at once, the moment they entered. I'm so happy for you both.'

She offered a bright smile before returning to Mr Connor.

Laura threw a glance at Philip, struggling to see what the other ladies did. She only noticed how the light from the wide chandelier hanging over the long table softened the set of his nose but deepened the shadow along the edge of his jaw. 'No, I don't think it's me.'

'Oh, indeed it is.' She laid her hand on Laura's, giving it a small, reassuring squeeze.

'What is?' Mrs Moseley called from across the table.

'Almond blancmange,' Mrs Charton answered without hesitation. 'It is one of the best dishes to serve at a wedding breakfast.'

'Oh, yes, you must have almond blancmange.' Mrs Moseley slipped a forkful of fish into her mouth, filling out her already round cheeks. 'It's heavenly.'

Mrs Charton winked at Laura as the conversation turned to the wedding breakfast, leaving Laura to wonder at the woman's comments about Philip. With Mrs Templeton practically pushing her breasts in Philip's face as he passed her the salt, Laura was hesitant to place much hope in Mrs Charton's observation. Maybe seeing his paramour again tonight was the reason for the change in his behaviour. If there was anything between him and Mrs Templeton, perhaps he felt it a welcome relief to be in her presence, rather than facing Laura's doubts about his character.

\* \* \*

Throughout the rest of dinner, Laura did her best to enjoy herself despite Mrs Templeton's shameless flirtation across the table. Mrs Charton was the centre of attention at dessert, with a large cake placed in front of her as everyone offered their congratulations. Then Mr Charton presented her with a stunning gold necklace, sweetly fastening it around her neck before leaning in to brush her lips with a kiss. Laura clapped with the others at the presentation, smiling despite the twinge of jealousy at witnessing such love between a man and wife. Before this morning, she thought she and Philip might obtain such happiness. She was no longer so sure.

At last, with the cake eaten and the present given, Mrs Charton rose and led the ladies back to the drawing room. If Laura expected the women to talk of domestic affairs once alone, she was surprised. They settled on the suite of furniture near the fireplace and set to discussing their husbands' business. Laura listened, learning as much about moneylending and dealing with clients as she had from her time with Philip. The conversation only turned to more feminine matters when Mrs Moseley complained to Mrs Charton of trying to manage small children when her husband required so much of her help. Their hostess and Mrs Gammon offered encouraging advice which Laura raptly took in. It was a comfort to know she would be able to draw on these women's experiences to help her manage her and Philip's affairs when the time came. Assuming it came.

Too agitated to sit still, Laura excused herself and made for the refreshment table near the window. If Philip decided not to go through with the wedding, it would only take a few words in private to the Chartons to undo everything done tonight. Then Laura would vanish from all of these people's lives as quickly as she'd come into them. The bitter taste of fear and regret filled her mouth. She wanted to know these people and enjoy the friendship they offered as much as she wanted Philip.

She poured herself a glass of punch, but the tart drink didn't ease the worries determined to needle her. Neither did the subtle rustle of cheap silk joined by a purring voice behind her.

'Tell me, Miss Townsend, when is the happy day?' Mrs Templeton asked, coming around to face Laura.

Laura set down her unfinished punch, viewing the woman with the same detached interest she'd directed at so many of Philip's clients over the past few days. 'The date has not been set yet.'

Mrs Templeton laid her talons over her large chest, her mouth forming a wide O in surprise. 'A sudden engagement, but not sudden enough to secure a date?'

'A date cannot be set until we have the common licence.'

'Strange he hasn't already obtained it.' Mrs Templeton's lips curled into a devious smile. 'Surely if he was so eager to get married, he would hurry things along.'

Assuming an air of carefree indifference, Laura shrugged, not about to let this woman cow her. If she did, it would give Mrs Templeton permission to treat her shabbily every time they found themselves together at such gatherings. 'I'm not concerned. If he had doubts, he would hurry the matter.'

Behind her, Laura heard the deep rumbling of the men's voices as they entered the room to join the ladies.

Mrs Templeton ran her finger over the rim of Laura's half-filled glass sitting on the table, eliciting a low sound from the crystal. 'Nothing is settled until the ring is upon your finger, Miss Townsend, and even then a man may find more tempting entertainment elsewhere.'

She fixed her gaze over Laura's shoulder and the sheer heat in it seemed enough to evaporate the punch from the bowl. No doubt she was eyeing Philip, making her disgusting invitation clear.

Laura didn't turn to see if the invitation was acknowledged. It didn't matter. Whatever happened, Laura wasn't going to allow this woman in the poorly cut silk to knock her down.

'You mustn't know Philip very well if you believe he'll dishonour a vow once it's given, or renege on a contract once it's been made. He has too much integrity to act in the way you've implied, or for me to doubt for even a moment that he will not honour his word. So suggest what you like about the two of you, I refuse to believe it for a moment.'

Mrs Townsend's painted lips twisted together in irritation. Laura had fought her with the truth and she had no answer for it. It *was* the truth. Laura felt it deep in her heart and not even all the fears swirling there since this morning could chase that away. Philip was a man of great integrity, as he'd proven to her time and again. He'd made Laura a promise and he would keep it. Whatever happened between them from this evening on, she would never doubt the man again.

The scent of bergamot swept over Laura and she sensed more than saw Philip beside her. 'Miss Townsend, are you ready to depart? I must rise early tomorrow.'

'Yes, let us go at once.' She held out her hand, ready for him to offer her his arm.

Instead, he slid his hand beneath hers and raised it to his lips. Even through the silk of her gloves the heat of his feather-light kiss seared her skin. He might as well have enveloped her in an embrace and kissed her with the passion of a Gothic hero, his claim on her was so clear.

It nearly knocked the breath out of Laura, especially when his eyes held hers as he rose. With not one glance at Mrs Templeton, he straightened, tucked Laura's hand into the crook of his elbow and led her away.

Philip settled against the squabs, the stiffness in his back he'd experienced on the drive over replaced by a more unsettling stiffness lower down. Laura sat across from him, the dim light from the carriage lantern dancing over her high cheeks and sparkling in the gold ear-rings Jane had lent her. Ever since Laura had come downstairs to join him in the carriage, the cream dress spilling over her curves, the tender curls of her *coiffure* lying sugges-

tively over one round breast, he'd fought his
desire to stare at her. Not even conversation
with his friends had set him at ease. He'd spent
half the night across the room from her just to
avoid the pull of her body over his. There was
no avoiding it now.

'Did you enjoy the evening?' he asked, curious about her thoughts on his associates and
friends.

'I did. The ladies were very gracious and
friendly.' She adjusted one sleeve of her dress.
'Most of them.'

'My apologies for Mrs Templeton. She has a
greatly inflated sense of her desirability.'

'Were you ever intimate with her?'

The question startled Philip. He wasn't used
to her being so direct. 'No. Mrs Templeton is a
handsome woman, but she offers little beyond
physical gratification.'

Laura nodded, seeking no further explanation.

Mrs Templeton had tried to snare him early
last year, when the darkness of losing Arabella
had gripped him the hardest and he'd been at
his weakest. It hadn't taken long for him to
see through her feigned concern to realise she
was more enamoured of his money than him.
That he was, even for a moment, tempted by

her charms rattled him as much as the mistakes he'd made with Arabella. He'd thought he might be making the same mistakes with Laura until he'd overheard her praising him to Mrs Templeton.

She'd defended him when she hadn't known he was listening. She might have said anything, but instead she'd defended his integrity, his commitment to his word, the one aspect of his character that Mrs Templeton continued to underestimate, judging by her behaviour tonight. It was something Laura might have dismissed after the incident today. She must have believed her words to defend him with such enthusiasm, instead of allowing Mrs Templeton's threat to make her doubt his commitment to her.

Relief filled Philip, strong enough to drive away the doubt the rational part of him had stubbornly clung to. Laura was the right choice. It was time to stop dallying. 'The common licence arrived today.'

The air in the coach thickened and Philip's back straightened along with Laura's. He fingered his watch fob, but the awkwardness he'd expected in the moment didn't come. He'd avoided the subject for days and now it was done the world had not tilted to throw them both off. He was also relieved to find the aching guilt he'd experienced when he'd faced Dr Hale did not return.

'When do you plan to hold the wedding?' More trepidation than enthusiasm laced her question..

Her measured reaction was his fault. He should have told her about the licence sooner, not left her to dangle in a limbo where he held the power to fulfil his promise or to cast her aside. Such a situation would not occur again. 'I thought we might plan it together. It's your wedding as much as mine.'

'Not the most romantic answer, but I suppose it will suffice.' The teasing he'd come to enjoy over the last few days warmed him as much as Mr Charton's port. 'When shall we stand before the vicar?'

'We must wait seven days.'

'Then in seven days we'll wed. It will give Mrs Fairley time to finish my wedding dress.'

He flexed his hand over his knee, as eager to see the dress as what would lie beneath it. 'In seven days it is.'

'You're sure the vicar will be available?'

'Reverend Clare is a former client of mine.'

'Gambling debts?'

'His son needed to purchase a living from a less-scrupulous man of the cloth who consistently ignored his flock.' He rested his ankle on one knee. He caught her surprise at his relaxed attitude in the slight tilt of her head.

'You never cease to surprise me, Philip.'

'It's not my intention.'

'No, I don't suppose it is, but you do it all the same, which I suppose will make for an interesting life with you.'

'I should hate for you to be bored.'

'I don't think it's possible.' She laughed and the sound almost brought a smile to his lips. No, they would not be bored together. She was too intriguing to him, her happiness suddenly too important.

'I'll leave you and your mother to see to the details of the wedding breakfast with cook and Mrs Palmer.'

'If my mother has time. She and Jane are as thick as thieves. I hardly see either of them any more.' Her happiness faded along with these last words.

'It troubles you to see them together so much?'

'A little.' She tugged at the fingertips of her gloves before resting her hands in her lap. 'But you were right, having something to do has made such a difference to my mother.'

'She's affected quite a change in Jane. Not

once this week have I been hounded for an inappropriate dress. Also, there is now the tempering influence of Mrs Townsend to counteract the questionable influence of the novels she reads.'

'You know about her books?' Laura rocked forward, looking surprised and, as a deepening blush spread across her chest, a touch guilty.

'There's very little in my house I don't know about.'

'No, I don't suppose there is.' She sat back, pulling one sagging glove tighter over her curving elbow. 'I'm surprised you've allowed her to continue reading them.'

'She's prone to be rebellious. Better she rebel with a salacious book than a more salacious tradesman.'

'A very wise position. Though she'll forget her books once I tell her the wedding date is set. Jane had already told me I must have beef and tonight Mrs Moseley insisted on almond blancmange. I haven't the faintest notion what almond blancmange is.'

'Then be sure to have cook prepare it so you'll know.'

'I would like Mrs Moseley, Mrs Charton and their husbands to be invited, and of course Mrs

Gammon. I wouldn't want Mr Connor to feel lonely at such an event.'

'It might inform him how best to proceeded with Mrs Gammon.'

'I think he has ideas of his own.' A tempting smile spread across her lips, bringing a few intriguing images to Philip's mind before he forced them aside.

'What other thoughts do you have for our wedding day?'

Philip listened, enjoying the sweet cadence of Laura's voice. Her hands waved through the air when she was excited or folded quietly in her lap when she became thoughtful. He enjoyed the happiness this control over this aspect of her life gave her, though her confidence took time to cultivate. At first, she searched his face after each proposed wedding detail to see if he approved. When he raised no objections, her subtle apprehension faded. It took many suggestions before she no longer looked to him, but gave full vent to her ideas, her hands moving in time to the rapid cadence of her speech.

As her confidence increased, he realised how unfair he'd been to make so many decisions without consulting her. He remembered the helplessness of not having a say in life. When he'd turned sixteen his father had decided it was time for him to learn the family business in depth. After years of watching his parents, he thought he'd known so much. In truth, he'd known next to nothing. For the first year, when his father had insisted he only listen and learn, it'd frustrated him. Remembering the pride he'd felt at being given his first client still made his chest swell.

Laura wasn't a youth. She was a mature woman with as much experience with hardship, business and struggling as him. It'd been unfair of him to deny her the control she craved, needed and deserved.

Suddenly, without warning, she lowered her hands, facing him with as much seriousness as Jane whenever she was about to ask for something. 'Mrs Charton said you almost lost your business once. What happened?'

Philip dropped his foot off his leg, allowing both feet to rest flat on the floor. He wasn't prepared for this. He felt his reserve returning, a dismissive answer to the question forming before he bit it back. Laura wanted honesty, the kind he should have shown her by sharing the details of Halcyon House sooner. He shouldn't have kept it hidden until revealing it was a necessity rather than a joy. Admitting his past mistakes would not be pleasurable, but she'd asked and he must answer. 'As you know from experience, it's difficult to continue a business when the person you relied on to guide you is gone.'

She twined her fingers together in her lap. 'Yes, it is.'

Philip shifted against the squabs, resting his elbow on the narrow ledge below the window. 'The year after my parents died, I loaned a large sum of money to a silversmith. He'd received a commission from a marquis for an expensive dinner service, but said his young daughter's illness over the last year had left him without the necessary funds to purchase the silver he needed to craft the order...'

'Or so he'd told you,' Laura finished when he paused.

Philip nodded. 'At the time he approached me, Jane was ill, so I sympathised with him. I was also distracted by numerous other difficult clients and didn't properly vet the man's claims. The loan was made and squandered at the faro tables. Had I not taken Mr Charton's advice, and the loan from his solicitor, I may not have proceeded quickly enough to seize the silversmith's shop or the merchandise he'd kept hidden there. The silversmith enjoyed gambling with other people's money instead of his own.

The amount I seized was almost enough to pay back what he'd borrowed. If he hadn't hidden his merchandise from more prosperous days, the loss of his loan would have ruined me.'

'I wish you'd told me sooner.'

'Mistakes aren't always easy to admit.'

'No, they're not. I made one this morning.' She stared out of the window at the passing buildings. 'When I saw Mrs Hammond, it was as if I were seeing myself again, losing everything because of something someone else had done. I thought I was over it, I thought it behind me, but it's not.'

The raw pain in her words touched him and he slipped across the carriage to sit beside her. The heat of her body next to his penetrated the wool of his jacket and the linen of his shirt. Without thinking, he wrapped his arm around her shoulders and drew her into the hollow of his arm. She nestled against him, her rose water perfume wrapping around him like a twining vine. He closed his eyes, revelling in the comfort of her body next to his, the weight of her cheek on his chest, the sweet sound of her steady breathing.

'You aren't the only one to blame. I shouldn't have expected you to follow me blindly into a situation I should have known would trouble you. I was as insensitive to you as—'

'I was to you today.' She curled her finger around the lapel of his jacket, the movement tender and trusting. 'I'm ashamed it troubled me so deeply.'

'It will for some time.' Philip rested his chin on her head, curling his arm tighter around her. She didn't fight it, but settled in closer, her breath sneaking in to caress his chest through a small opening at the top of his shirt. 'I can't deny this isn't always a straightforward business. At times it won't be easy for you. If you're ever uncomfortable again, please tell me at once. I will always have your best interests at heart.'

'I want to be able to extend vouchers,' she whispered.

'You will be. I trust your judgement.'

'And I trust yours.'

He wrapped his fingers around hers and squeezed them tight. All would be well between them.

# Chapter Nine

As the late morning sun stretched out over the carpet, the savoury scent of beef filled the bedroom. Laura inhaled with a sigh, making Mrs Fairley laugh as she fastened the buttons on the back of Laura's wedding dress.

'I knew I was right to make this dress and all the others a little larger through here.' Mrs Fairley tapped the ribbon beneath Laura's bust. 'I suspected the good food would fill you out in no time.'

'I hope it doesn't fill me out too much. I'd hate to split a seam.' Although a split seam was quickly becoming the least of her worries. It was nearly eleven o'clock and, across the street in St Bride's Church, Philip, the Chartons, the Feltons, the Moseleys and Mrs Gammon eagerly waited for Laura to become Philip's wife.

'I think other things might fill you out faster.'

Mrs Fairley hummed as she fastened the last button. 'Mr Rathbone is sure to have quite a surprise in store for you tonight.'

Laura gaped over her shoulder at the modiste, who shot her a knowing smile in return. Laura wasn't used to discussing such matters so openly. Nor was she completely prepared for the very real future the modiste hinted at. She knew the details; her mother had explained them to her years ago. There'd also been too many conversations between the women of ill repute in the rookery to keep Laura ignorant of what passed between two people in the dark. It was the intimacy it would require with Philip which made her stomach flutter.

'I hope he doesn't surprise me too much.' She shifted the slim gold necklace, an engagement present from Philip, over her chest. Even the delicate metal felt too heavy on her heated skin. As nervous as she was about what was to come tonight, she also craved him.

'Oh, I think he might. You must surprise him as well.' Mrs Fairley withdrew a thin, flat box from her case. 'I have something which will help you do just that.'

Unless it was a book of suggestions on how to please a husband, she couldn't imagine what the modiste might give her to accomplish such a goal.

Mrs Fairley removed the lid and held it out to Laura. 'I brought you these.'

Laura lifted the fine clocked stockings from the tissue paper. As the silk unfolded, the beautifully embroidered roses twining up the back were revealed one after another. They clung to a fine silk so sheer it took on the tone of her hand beneath it. Rubbing her thumb over the wispy weave, she inhaled as much in surprise at the delicate gift as at the thrill of holding such finely wrought fabric.

'It's gorgeous.' A bright red ribbon ran through the embroidery at the top, the satin as smooth as the silk. 'I hate to think of something so beautiful being hidden.'

'They won't be hidden from everyone.' Mrs Fairley winked.

Laura felt her cheeks turn the same colour as the ribbon. She wanted Philip to see these.

'Now, let's get them on you.' Mrs Fairley led Laura to a chair and helped her raise the long hem of her skirt. Laura slid her feet into the stockings, slowly pulling them up over her calves before tying the ribbon just above her knee. The material rubbed her skin like the finest goose down, making it tighten with a shiver.

As she stood, the silk of the dress whooshed out around her legs, fluttering the ends of the ribbons underneath against Laura's calves.

'You make sure he is the only one who sees these tonight,' Mrs Fairley instructed, as she picked up the satin slippers and placed them on the floor in front of Laura. 'Don't allow your maid to undress you, let him.'

Laura struggled to breathe, nervous yet excited about what was to come. In the week since the dinner at the Chartons' house, there'd been a new bond between her and Philip. They'd worked together on planning the wedding and other business matters as if they'd been together for years. Even their dinner with Dr Hale last night had been a relaxed affair, the sadness and awkwardness from their last meeting gone. Mr Connor had remarked on the change, thanking Laura for ending Philip's frequent need to exercise.

She slipped her feet in her soft slippers, the silk stocking pressing down against her toes and up against the arch of her foot. A wicked little smile graced her lips as she wiggled her toes. At least she possessed one advantage over Philip tonight. She already knew what he looked like naked.

She adjusted the necklace again, twining it

around one finger before allowing it drop down against her chest. The confidence she'd witnessed in every ripple of his muscles as he'd moved across the room naked in front of her gave her a sense of how it might be with him. It would take great restraint to retain a hold on her senses long enough to display her stockings, especially if he pounced on her with any of the pent-up energy she'd tasted in his kiss the other night. Then, he'd held back for propriety's sake. Tonight, there would be no reason for him to do so.

The doorknob turned and Laura's mother slipped into the room. At the sight of her daughter tears sprung to her eyes.

'Oh, my dear.' Her mother hurried to her, crushing Laura in a deep embrace. 'I used to dream of this day when you were a little girl. When we were in Seven Dials, I thought it would never come, yet here it is.'

Laura hugged her mother close. 'Though not as either of us could have imagined.'

Her mother gently pushed her back, holding her at arm's length and admiring her before fluffing out the flattened lace lining the bodice. 'It's exactly as I imagined. You're young, beautiful and marrying a man of integrity who cares for you.'

She knew he cared as much for her as Laura did for him. The strength of her feelings for him surprised her. It didn't seem possible to come to care so much for someone in so short an amount of time.

'Look at me carrying on when it is time to go.' Her mother dabbed her eyes with the handkerchief Mrs Fairley handed her. 'Reverend Clare is waiting and the guests are ready.'

Laura's palms went moist and she was glad Mrs Fairley had decided against gloves for this solemn occasion. She said it would be too much trouble with the ring, but Laura sensed it was to keep her nervousness from soaking the fine satin.

'Are you ready, Laura?' her mother pressed.

'Yes.' Excitement swept over her as Mrs Fairley knelt to fluff out the skirt of the dress.

Taking her mother's arm, the two of them made their way downstairs, Mrs Fairley following behind them. Laura walked proudly through the house, not skulking along the shadows of the walls as she'd done the night she'd broken in. What a strange change in circumstances it all seemed, a welcome reprieve after the nightmare of life with Uncle Robert.

Downstairs, they were greeted by the chatter and laughter of the servants gathered in two lines flanking the front door. Quiet settled over the house as they all turned to watch her with bright eyes and wide smiles. Mr Connor strode from where he waited by the front door, appearing in a fine mood. Laura suspected his joviality had more to do with Mrs Gammon's attendance than Laura's wedding ensemble.

'You're beautiful, Miss Townsend, as a bride should be.' He bowed before her then straightened. 'It's an honour to escort you and to stand beside Philip. Shall we proceed to the church?'

'We shall.' She took his arm, walking with him out of the front door. Two footmen flanked the walk, asking the people rushing by to pause and make way for Laura. Two more halted a cart in the street and Laura and Justin hurried across, Mrs Fairley and Mrs Townsend following closely behind. They moved quickly across the pavement and up the few stone steps to the churchyard.

Laura stepped on to the path leading to the church door, impatient to be inside and beside Philip, but Justin held back, forcing Laura to slow down in order to stay by his side.

'All in good time.' He chuckled at her eagerness. 'I don't want to hurry your happy day.'

'One would think you'd be eager to hand me off and see to Mrs Gammon,' she teased, his good nature only increasing her anticipation. 'When can we expect your nuptials?'

'This will be my second time before the altar and neither time will I have been the groom. However, for now, that will suffice.'

They moved on, passing beneath the tall trees spreading out over the walk and the churchyard. The breeze rustled through the green leaves and the towering branches obscured Christopher Wren's magnificent bell tower. Then at last it came into full view as they made the turn to enter the church. Just as they reached the door, Justin halted.

'Mrs Fairley, would you be so kind as to inform the bridegroom we are here?'

'It would be an honour.' Mrs Fairley hurried around them, her blonde curls bouncing as she slipped into the church.

'And, Mrs Townsend, if you would care to proceed inside,' Justin encouraged, with a wide smile.

Laura's mother turned to face her. She tried to say something to Laura, but the tears threatening to spill from the older woman's eyes left her silent. She placed a swift but tender kiss on Laura's cheek, then followed the modiste into the church.

Laura watched her go, her own eyes blurring, glad of Justin's voice helping to steady her.

'Are you ready, Miss Townsend?'

She took a deep breath which managed to settle the flutter in her stomach, but not the excitement coursing through her. After all the apprehension and excitement of the past two weeks it was at last time to tie her life to Philip's. There was no hesitation this morning. She wanted him for her husband and to share his life. 'Yes, I'm ready.'

Laura followed Justin's steady lead into the church, the excited whisper of the guests calming her nerves as she came down the aisle.

Laura saw almost nothing of the people, the highly polished wood choir stalls, or the white-and-gilded arched ceiling. Not even Jane silently clapping her approval at the dress from where she stood beside Laura's mother was enough to draw Laura's attention away from Philip.

He stood before the altar next to the silver-haired vicar, a dark-grey jacket covering the sharp cut of his shoulders. His hands were down at his sides as always, but the faintest hint of a smile raised the edges of his lips and made his blue eyes dance. As Mr Connor escorted her down the aisle, Laura's smile widened with Philip's approval and the unspoken eagerness hovering between them. Euphoria flooded Laura. In mere moments she would be beside Philip, speaking the vows that would bind them together for the rest of their lives.

Mr Connor escorted her to Philip's side, then stepped away to let the ceremony begin.

The words of the service filled the air as the scent of her rosewater perfume mingled with Philip's bergamot cologne. With his sturdy form next to hers, it was all Laura could to do to focus on Reverend Clare and not shift in her slippers. When they were instructed to face one another, she turned and the ribbons of her stockings grazed the back of her knees beneath the dress. Determined to say her vows with a seriousness to match Philip's, she held his eyes, carefully repeating every word, taking each promise and all their meaning to heart. When he spoke his vows, there was no mistaking his earnestness. He'd been her saviour less than two weeks ago, now he would be her partner.

'The rings, please,' Reverend Clare instructed.

Mr Connor laid the gold bands on the open prayer book. The diamonds in Laura's ring winked in the candlelight from the mantel. She tossed Philip a questioning glance. In the slight incline of his head, she could almost hear him telling her the ring had come from a client, another merchant he'd helped who she would no doubt see when time and need called for it. Reverend Clare blessed the rings, then instructed Philip to take her hand.

Philip slid his palm under hers and raised it between them. Her fingers stretched out over the warm skin of his wrist before she lowered her hand on his. Beneath her fingertips, the quick beat of his pulse mimicked hers. He stood so close that his breath whispered across her forehead. Reverend Clare's august words were lost in the heady strength of Philip's touch as he slid the ring over her finger. She could feel almost nothing of the smooth metal encircling it, only the softness of his skin grazing hers. Nothing in Philip's touch changed and yet, at the same time, everything felt different.

When instructed, Laura took up Philip's ring and held it just beyond his strong fingers. She repeated Reverend Clare's words, ready to abide by everything she was promising today, including the vow made in her own heart to honour the man facing her, the man she loved.

Shock at her emotions forced her to pinch the ring tight so as not to risk fumbling it. Yes, she loved him. It'd crept up on her during their quiet conversations in the sitting room, his study, the garden. It didn't scare her as it might have done a week, or even a few days, ago. There was something between them now. It was slender yet strong, growing sturdier as the days passed, like gentle threads of silk bound together in a twist strong enough to edge even an admiral's uniform.

'With this ring, I thee wed.' She slid the band over Philip's finger. It caught a bit on his knuckle before she eased it down to fit snugly around his finger, to claim him as he'd claimed her.

Reverend Claire finished the ceremony with his last instruction. 'You may now kiss the bride.'

The kiss in Philip's room the other night seared through Laura's memory as she tilted her face up to meet her new husband's. He bowed forward and she closed her eyes in anticipation, her body tingling as they drew together. When their lips merged, heat leapt between them like sparks flashing between pieces of wool on a hot, dry day. The kiss was tender, light, but in the press of flesh to flesh, she felt him struggling between pushing forward and holding back. Behind her the muffled applause of the guests faded away. There was only Philip, his lips warm against hers, his hand firm and fast in hers, a beautiful, wonderful assurance of their future together.

All too soon, she opened her eyes to watch Philip pull away and she was left wanting more of him and his lips against hers. Without his kiss to muddle her, the sweeping architecture of the church and the presence of the vicar and the guests rushed back. Her cheeks burned with the embarrassment of having enjoyed the kiss so much as she turned with Philip to accept the congratulations of their friends and family.

'Oh, it was so romantic,' Jane gushed as she hurried forward to throw her arms around Laura, hugging her with girlish delight before stepping back to allow Dr Hale to approach.

'Congratulations, Philip.' Dr Hale vigorously shook Philip's hand.

Philip returned the gesture, at ease with the gentleman. 'Thank you.'

'And the very best to you, Mrs Rathbone.' He bowed to Laura. The sound of her new name was startling, but she loved it, just as she'd come to love so many other aspects of Philip's life over the past few days. 'One day I hope to see a little brother or sister joining Thomas in the nursery,' he said, stepping away to speak with Mrs Townsend, as a faint flush of embarrassment rose to Laura's cheeks.

'Shall we return home for the wedding breakfast?' Laura asked Philip.

Philip raised her hand to his mouth, pressing his lips to her skin. He gazed up at her, the promise of the night to come heavy in his gaze. 'Yes, please.'

Laura shifted on her feet and felt the stocking ribbons ruffle again. She didn't know how she would make it through the next few hours with such anticipation pooling deep inside her.

After the register was signed, Laura and Philip led a chatting and laughing parade of guests out of the church and back across the street to their house. The lively wedding breakfast extended well into the late afternoon, the conversation flowing as steadily as the port.

The cook had prepared a scrumptious meal and Mrs Moseley raved no end about the almond blancmange while Mrs Charton and Laura's mother discussed the challenges of raising a daughter. Mrs Charton had seen her eldest daughter married last year and talked at great length about her new grandbaby. As they spoke, the older women tossed Laura more than one suggestive look.

If Philip was anxious about the wedding

night, it didn't show in his spirited discussions with Mr Charton and Mr Felton. Even if he never quite smiled, in the midst of such warm-hearted and festive people, he was cheerful and his dry humour flourished to Laura's and everyone's delight.

At last, when the best of the French wine was gone and the candles needed to be lit, Mrs Charton rose, sending a secret signal to the other ladies. Mrs Felton, Laura's mother and Jane stood as well, the women forcing the men to their feet.

'We do not wish to intrude on the rest of your celebration tonight,' Mrs Charton explained, barely containing a mischievous smile. 'Mr and Mrs Rathbone, we wish you all the best.'

'Hear, hear,' Mr Charton chimed in, raising his wine glass before finishing the last of the deep-red liquid and staggering after his wife into the entrance hall.

All too soon the guests were gone. Mr Connor and Mrs Gammon melted away along with Laura's mother, Jane and the servants, leaving Laura and Philip alone at last.

In Philip's room, they stood across from one another. The fire crackled in the grate and a candle sputtered. Mary worked near the dressing table, laying out a chemise and robe.

'Shall I leave you to prepare for bed?' Philip trilled his fingers against his thigh, one foot turned as if he intended to go.

Laura's bravery nearly fled. It would be easier to meet him beneath the sheets with the room dark than to face him in the soft glow of the candles. She curled her toes in her shoes and the silk stockings slid along her skin. She wouldn't deny herself, or him, the pleasure of seeing the fine needlework.

She reached out and stilled his fingers. 'No, your assistance is all I require tonight.'

Without being asked, Mary removed herself from the room, closing the door behind her.

Philip drew Laura to him, step by slow step until they were nearly touching. As he looked down at her, a strand of dark hair fell over his forehead. She reached up to brush it aside, then stopped, still hesitant to be so intimate with him. His hand squeezed hers, as if nudging her on, and she stroked the faint lines of his forehead. With the backs of her fingers she traced the angle of his cheek, dropping to the smooth jaw below. He remained steady beneath her touch, not alarmed or uncomfortable at her caress. Heat began to build in his eyes and he ran his thumb tenderly across her palm. At last she slid her hand along the skin above his collar, bringing it to rest in the short hair at his nape.

Accepting her subtle invitation, he leaned forward and Laura closed her eyes, waiting, expecting. She wasn't prepared for the intensity of this kiss.

He didn't hold back this time, but covered her lips hard with his. His arms encircled her waist, pressing her stomach to his need rising beneath the fine material of his breeches. The ribbons from one of the garters brushed the back of her leg as her form curved to fit into the arch of his. The strength of his embrace kept her from falling on to the carpet he'd been so worried about ruining the night they'd first met.

Twining her arms around his neck, she held on tight, not frightened but excited by the passion building between them. His tongue traced the line of her lips, nudging them open. She took in the firmness as it teased and tasted her, urging her to do the same. She surrendered to the thrilling caress, heeding nothing but his body against hers, his breath on her cheeks, his fingers sliding over her shoulders. His desire reverberated through her and she didn't hold back, eager to ride the crest of it into the unknown.

It wasn't until the first prick of cool air on her back awakened her from this delicious fugue that she noticed he'd undone the buttons of her dress. Whatever fears she'd had of coming together with him dropped like the silk pooling around her feet. Breaking away from his kiss, she stepped out of the circle of the garment, noting how his eyes widened at the sight of her near undress.

'Your stay-maker does excellent work,' he choked, sliding his hand along the curve of her waist to rest on her hip. His shock emboldened her and she clutched the edges of his lapels in her hand.

'Your tailor is very talented, too.' She touched her tongue to her top teeth, feeling quite bold as she peeled the fine wool away from his chest.

He didn't help, but watched her, his chest rising and falling fast as she set to work on the buttons of his waistcoat. She slipped each one through the holes until the garment hung open over his trim waist. Her palms grazed his hard muscles as she pressed both the jacket and waistcoat off his shoulders and down over his arms.

He made the task easier by lowering his hands and allowing them to rest on either side of him as he always did, but tonight his stance was different. His fingers loosened from their fists to let the jacket and waistcoat slide free. They didn't curl back under when the clothing fell away, but reached for her urgently, as if she'd been away too long, drawing her to him so he could kiss her. Yet even in his grasp she felt Philip's steady self-control while her urges ran wild beneath the taste of his tongue against hers.

His lips never broke from hers as he pulled each tie of the new stays through the eyelets, loosening the fine garment. With the last few strings still fastened, he turned her around.

'Don't I get to see you?' She glanced over one shoulder, trying to tease him though she could barely speak through her nervousness. His warm cheek came up against hers, his body achingly close though just far enough away for his fingers to continue their work.

'You've already seen me naked. Now it's my turn.' His playfulness surprised her and increased the warmth spreading inside her.

Her stays opened and her heavy breasts bounced lightly as he moved the restraints away and let them fall forward on to the floor. The chemise billowed out around her naked skin, teasing the tight tips of her breasts. There was nothing separating her from him except the thin layer of cotton and a delicious heat radiated between them. His hands didn't retreat entirely as he moved up close behind her. He swept the curve of her hips through the cotton before his fingers tangled in the material and he began to draw it over her head. Her arms stiffened, the unfamiliar making her resist a moment before she raised her arms to let the chemise come free of her body. Philip was her husband now, there was no reason to hide herself from him.

*Husband.* The word curled around her heart. Now she was his, she would give her entire self to him tonight.

Cold swept over her, tickling her hot skin like his breath whispering across the back of her bare shoulders. She turned to press her body against his, something deep and primal she didn't understand urging her on, but he stepped back. The same passion burning low inside of her flared in his eyes as his gaze dropped lower and lower to the garters, red ribbons bold against her legs.

The sheer fabric and fragile silk were the only things still covering her and the vulnerability in her nakedness nearly struck down her bravery. He could pounce on her, satiate his lust and be done, leaving her confused and wanting. Instead, the control which dominated Philip's life kept him planted to the floor. It increased her courage and she turned on the balls of her feet, rising on her toes to give him a better view of the embroidery and her round derrière.

'Do you like them?' Her voice wavered as she lowered herself to rest the heels of the clocked stockings against the plush carpet. The ribbons fluttered a touch as she moved, sweeping her skin with the same feathery heat she'd witnessed in his gaze.

'I must remember to pay Mrs Fairley more the next time her bill is due.' His voice sounded strained, making Laura bold, her confidence in this new power growing ever stronger as she met Philip's burning gaze.

She turned again, faster this time so the ribbons danced against her knees before settling back to grace her calves. 'Add a little extra to thank her from me.'

It wasn't the ribbons Philip watched now, but her breasts as he moved forward, cupping the weight of each in his palms. 'I shall jump to comply.'

The heat of his touch stole her playfulness and a heady need rose up inside her as his palms kneaded the full flesh. She reached out and undid his cravat, revealing the firm Adam apple's punctuating the fine length of his neck. Loosening the laces of his shirt, Laura spied the sweep of dark hair on his chest. She ran her fingers through the coarseness of it, feeling his heart beat a quick pace beneath her touch. Then she grasped the sides of his shirt and tried to raise it over his head. He was too tall for her to manage and he slipped his thumbs beneath the linen, helping her to free him from it.

She'd been too stunned to truly appreciate his body the night they'd met. Now she could fully admire it. The hours at the boxing club had tightened the muscles of his stomach and chest and they rippled as he raised his arms to crush her softness against his solid body.

The thickness in his breeches pressed against her bare stomach as his lips claimed hers again, his kiss more hungry than before, but with the marked restraint she'd come to know so well. The maiden in her was glad for his contained reaction. The curious woman who'd already seen his body slick with water wanted his careful control to crack and for him to ravish her passionately as she'd read about in novels. She had no real knowledge of the act, but the yearning deep inside her offered a heady hint to the pleasure waiting for her under Philip's guidance. If his touch elsewhere proved to be anything like the delicate circles his thumbs made across the tender tips of her breasts, she didn't know how she would survive the night.

'Raise your leg,' he growled in her ear.

She did as she was told and his hand slid over the curve of her breast and down the length of her thigh to the satin ribbon. In one fluid move he pulled it free of the bow. With his wide hand, he pushed it over her calf, drawing it from her foot before dropping it to the floor. Without prompting, she raised the other foot, clutching his shoulders as he guided the second stocking over her pointed toes, his movements controlled and agonisingly slow.

As she lowered her leg, his fingers graced the length of her inner thigh. Her body tightened as he neared her need, anticipation making it all but impossible to stand as his feathery touch graced the top of her womanhood before sliding down to settle inside her.

She gasped at the fire ignited by his touch, which welled up inside her until she could barely breathe from the sensations racing through her.

'Philip,' she gasped, leaning hard against the hand at her back holding her steady and keeping her from falling into the tide of pleasure rushing in to consume her.

Then he withdrew his fingers and she settled against his chest, panting, her need heightened but not quenched.

She lowered her hands to his waist, tracing the skin above his breeches as she trailed her fingers to his front. The pressure of his hips against hers eased as he shifted slightly to give her access to the wool. She fumbled with the buttons, trying to undo them, but with him so close, his masculine scent as sharp as his breath that raced across her nakedness, she could barely grasp the round ivory. He brought his hands over hers, assisting her and sliding the buttons through the holes. Then he let go, inviting her to do the rest.

She didn't quite possess his grace when it came to lowering his breeches, but they soon lay around his feet and he stepped out from the fabric. As she rose to face him, she paused, taking in the sight of his hardness.

Nervousness filled her, but there was little time to entertain it as he stepped forward to press against her once more. She nearly jumped back at the slight twitch of him against her stomach, before settling herself into the circle of his arms, his hands firm and steady against her back.

He led her to the bed and pressed her down on to it, his weight against her bare skin even more heavenly than the clean sheets and chemise had felt on her first night here. In the past week, a happiness she'd thought had died with the shop had consumed her and Philip was the cause of it. The thought moved her just as deeply as his unexpected kiss against the tender tip of her breast. His fingers began to play over her skin as they trailed down her stomach and over the curve of her thigh. Then at last, when she thought she might expire from the steady teasing of his tongue and fingers, he settled himself between her legs. He didn't press forward, but paused, and she felt him hot against her skin as he silently waited for her invitation. She opened to him, drawing in a sharp breath as he slid slowly into her depths. He moaned as she accepted his body into hers, bringing them closer together than she'd ever believed possible.

He moved slowly at first, each stroke filling her, until she thought she might shatter from the intense pleasure. She moved her hips to match his thrusts, wanting more, to give to him as much as he'd given her in their brief time together. Wrapping her arms around him, she held on to the hard muscles of his back, pressing her chest against his. With his heart so close, there seemed nothing to stop it from becoming hers.

Philip groaned, his restraint faltering under her silent demands as he plunged into her. Pinned in the circle of her arms, he felt free, the guilt of leaving the past behind lost in her softness. He surrendered to his passion and hers, grasping her around the waist to hold her steady as she tightened around him, her pleasure evident in her soft whimpers. As his desire began to crest, he mustered his control to wait, to hold back until at last her body exploded around him in spasms. Then he surrendered to his release, crying out as it pulsed to meet hers.

Philip clutched Laura to him as the ripples of pleasure uniting them began to fade. Rising up on his elbows, he brushed the hair from her forehead and pressed his own against it. Breath after breath laced with the sweet tang of her perfume caressed his face.

At last he dropped down beside her and slid his arm under her to draw her close. He caressed the length of her arm, following the arch of it to where her hand rested on his stomach.

Their wedding bands clinked together and his hand stiffened at the noise before he settled it firmly over hers. He resisted flexing his fingers or raising them to examine the band. The weight of the gold against his skin was familiar and yet unfamiliar, comforting and awkward.

He pulled Laura closer to drop a kiss on her forehead, pushing away all other thoughts.

'What's wrong?' Laura asked, her ability to sense his unease disturbing.

'Nothing.' Guilt stabbed at Philip for holding back. Each day it was growing more difficult to withhold his whole heart from Laura. He cared deeply for her, but there still existed a part of him he couldn't relinquish, not even to her sweet charm. He ignored the shame just as he'd banished the melancholy thoughts threatening to taint this moment. She was happy and it was all that mattered.

'Liar,' she challenged, stroking his chest.

'I was thinking about today and how beautiful you looked,' he said, not wanting the past to intrude and deny either of them their happy wedding night. 'Justin was escorting you so slowly up the aisle, I didn't think you'd ever reach me.'

'Perhaps he was afraid Mrs Gammon would step in to spring the parson's mousetrap.' She giggled against him and he felt the joy of her humour welling up inside of him, pushing away the dark memories and nagging shame.

'I'm glad he took his time. It gave me the chance to admire you.'

She raised her head to him, her lips drawn into a seductive smile matched by her inviting eyes. 'Careful, Philip, I might become used to such flattery.'

'Good, for I intend to flatter you often.' He smothered her smile with his lips. In the whispered breath of their kiss, a calm settled over him. There was no logical reason for this feeling, nothing about it he could explain or rationalise beyond Laura's presence. He lost himself in it and the pleasure of her embrace.

## Chapter Ten

Laura sat at the desk in Phillip's bedroom, combing through the columns of numbers on the ledger in front of her. She'd spent the past quarter of an hour trying to tease out why the expenses for beef did not match those of the bills stacked in the pile next to her. Picking up the butcher's last bill, she was careful not to disturb the neat stack of contracts next to the blotter. The writing table in her room was elegant, but too narrow, and while Philip was downstairs with Mr Connor, she'd decided to come in here to work. Though she doubted he would mind her little intrusion, this was his space and she didn't want to completely upend it.

Below, in the garden, Thomas's happy giggles were punctuated by one of his high-pitched squeals as Mrs Marston, Jane and Laura's mother played with him. Laura longed to be outside with them enjoying the fine day, but the ledger needed to be balanced, not because Philip demanded it, but because she did. He was a fine manager, but in the past year he'd been pulled in so many directions, one or two things had gone errant, like cook overspending at the butcher. Laura was determined to address these small issues, no matter how much she wanted to crawl into the large bed, pull the covers up to her chin and fall asleep.

She stifled a yawn, struggling to continue on, but the figures blurred before her, the totals making no more sense than before.

'This is impossible.' She tossed down the pencil and fell back against the chair in a huff, then laughed at herself. Two weeks ago she'd have given her teeth for such a simple problem. Now all she could do was complain.

The breeze fluttered through the open window, making the fine curtains billow out. The small crystals dangling from the candlesticks over the fireplace shivered with the wind, creating little rainbows in their depths. They spilled over the tendrils of the vines woven into the carpet. She slipped out of her shoes and rubbed the bottoms of her feet over the thick pile. Then, folding her hands over her lap, she closed her eyes. It wasn't the figures which vexed her as much as the lack of sleep. Since the wedding, more pleasurable pursuits than rest had occupied her and Philip's nights. She curled her toes at the memory of last night and the delicious things he'd done to her. In the dark together, they were open and vulnerable with one another. It was only afterwards when the intimacy seemed to fade.

She relaxed her feet, trying not to worry. The hint of the reserve she'd detected during their wedding night had come over Philip again last night, intruding on the quiet conversation between them. One night, she hoped, that reserve would be gone for good.

The breeze filled the curtains again. The ruffling fabric soothed her along with the sounds of the birds and her mother and Jane's steady conversation outside. There was only one more thing she needed to ease the concern dancing along the back of her mind.

'Have you become a woman of leisure?' Philip's teasing question drew her from her silent reverie. His lips lilted in a near-smile and Laura's toes pressed deeper into the carpet, anticipation making her lick her lips before she recovered herself and straightened.

'If only I could be, but the accounts won't

allow it.' She waved her hand over the open book. 'It seems I've dropped a figure and can't find it.'

'Let me see.' He closed the door and came to stand beside her and examine the ledger.

All thoughts of the accounts flittered out of her mind. There was only him, strong and masculine, his scent permeating the smell of warm earth drifting in from the garden outside.

He bent over the book, hands flat on the desk as he studied her work. While he was occupied, she leaned back a touch to admire his solid buttocks hugged by his buckskin breeches. Her fingers trilled on the arm of the chair, the activity keeping her from stroking the firm roundness, but she wanted to, badly.

'Having trouble concentrating?' He looked back at her, his eyes inviting. He pressed one finger to the ledger, but she longed to employ it in another, more sensual activity. 'You didn't carry the four on line twelve.'

She slid her fingers over the open neck of her gown, drawing his eyes to her breasts, as daring this afternoon as she'd been the night she'd first slipped into his room. Only today she was his wife, not a client. 'Does it matter?'

'Not at all.' In one easy move he turned and drew her from the chair into his arms, his body hard against hers. She leaned languidly into him, twining her hands around his neck and arching back as he bent forward.

'And here I'd come to ask you to join me on a walk through the park.' His voice rumbled between them. 'I have something to discuss with you.'

She traced the line of his jaw with one finger as his hand found its way to her behind, gripping it tight and pulling her closer against him. 'What?'

'I can't remember.' He leaned forward to claim her mouth, but Laura didn't surrender, not yet, wanting to tease him a little longer.

'But I have things to do.' Her fingers twined in the knot of his cravat, drawing the ends out from beneath the waistcoat.

'They can wait.' He leaned forward again. A growl of frustration escaped him as she denied him yet another kiss.

'It must be a special day if you're asking me to put aside work.' She enjoyed this teasing and the unexpected reaction it elicited from him.

'One cannot work all the time.' There was mischief in the remark as his frustration turned to determination.

Rising up on her stocking-clad toes, she finally surrendered her lips to his.

* * *

Whatever matter Philip had sought her out to discuss vanished. There was urgency in her wanting, a demanding need to match the one welling inside him. This would be no leisurely afternoon lovemaking, but a fast coming together. He surrendered to the moment, channelling his restlessness into the hunger drawing them together.

He tugged up the sides of her dress and slid his hands beneath the fine cotton chemise. Tracing the line of her silky thigh, he found her centre. She tilted her head back, as he slid one finger inside her. She was ready for him and he almost lost what little control remained. Holding back, he ran his tongue over the sweet skin of her neck while his finger worked her pleasure until she was near panting, her hands tight on his shoulders. He drew her earlobe between his teeth, his fingers steady and firm in their work, withdrawing just before she reached her release.

Opening her fevered eyes to meet his, she caressed his chest, then undid the buttons on his breeches. She slipped her hands beneath the buckskin to stroke his hips, her touch as teasing as the kisses she pressed against the skin above his cravat. The feather-light brush of her fingertips over his hardness sent a tremor racing through him. He splayed his fingers on his thighs, allowing the woman who'd been little more than a stranger to him two weeks ago to explore his body, relishing her growing confidence and her gentle touch. When at last she took him in her hand, he groaned, clenching his teeth as she slowly began to stroke. Remaining still, he gave himself over to her until the quickening pace of her palm proved his undoing. He shoved the ledger aside and the contracts fluttered to the floor with it as he lifted her up to rest on the edge of the desk. She pulled up the hem of her gown, as eager as he was for their joining.

Her fingers wound through his hair and she stifled her cry of pleasure in the curve of his neck as he entered her. The window was open, the breeze teasing them both as he plunged into her, all other thoughts lost in the storm of his desire. His thrusts were hard and greedy but she matched each one with a subtle shift of her hips, drawing him in deeper. The swelling pleasure pushed them higher until with one last thrust his body shuddered into hers and they fell together in a slow descent of light and darkness. Only her curves against his kept them from toppling over the top of the desk in exhaustion.

Moments passed, until the room, the breeze, the sound of people outside came back to Philip. He slid his hand up the curve of her back. Twirling one dark curl around his finger, he treasured the soft sweep of her hair over his skin. On the floor around them lay the scattered contracts and the upended ledger. He ignored the urge to break from Laura to clean up the mess.

'I should tease you over figures more often,' Laura murmured into his neck, her hand making lazy circles over his exposed body. 'Though I fear I may not be able to join you on a walk today, or even perhaps tomorrow.'

She laughed, the bright sound as lovely as the whimpers which had met her release. He let go of her curl and it bounced back against her neck.

'It was not my intention to exhaust you.' He kissed her damp forehead, pushing the strands of hair which clung to her radiant skin, ready to dress and proceed with the day.

'Oh, please do.' She wrapped her legs around his waist and all thoughts of business were gone.

It was a full two hours before they finally left the room and arrived in Hyde Park. Laura

held Philip's arm as they made their way leisurely over the paths crossing the wide swathes
of grass. A few fashionable folk were out riding
or enjoying the fine day in their open-topped
landaus. The rest of the park occupants were
retired soldiers and their grandsons or young
governesses running after children.

Laura tugged her hat down a touch to shield
her eyes from the low sun. She strode beside
Philip in a new walking dress of deep puce, the
glow from their lovemaking still fresh on her
skin. After their adventure on the desk, they'd
closed the window and drawn the curtains to
take advantage of the comfort of the bed. Deep
inside, Laura's body quivered at the memory
and she was tempted to drag Philip back to the
landau and away from whatever he'd brought
her here to discuss. She smiled wickedly at her
wantonness and the shock Philip was sure to
greet such a suggestion with. However, after
their afternoon intimacy, he might just surprise
her and agree to a romp in the carriage.

'I have a proposal for you,' Philip announced,
jarring her out of her pleasant daydream.

Her hand froze at her neck and she wondered if he'd entertained the same scandalous
thought as her.

'Yes?' she braved, knowing she couldn't resist him if he ask her to do such a thing.

He brought them to a halt, turning her to face him. It clearly wasn't lovemaking he wanted to discuss, but something more serious.

He didn't speak right away, but studied her, increasing her curiosity. At last he moved them back into a walk. A week ago she wouldn't have understood his hesitation and would have fretted over it. Today she recognised his careful ordering of his thoughts and waited patiently until he was ready to say them.

'You've told me a great deal about your parents' business and how they built it. It reminds me of my father. After his death, had I lost my business, it would have been like losing him again.'

'Yes, at times, after everything was gone, it felt as if I'd somehow failed him and my mother.' She adjusted her hands on his arm, touched by how well he'd come to understand her.

'I want to offer you the chance to revive your father's business.'

This time it was Laura who brought them to a halt, surprised out of her steady step. It was what she'd wanted the most when she'd first stolen through his house, the one thing she'd been forced to give up the moment she'd accepted his proposal. Now the chance was before her again.

'I spoke to the gentleman who bought the contents of the shop after I seized them from your uncle,' Philip continued, squinting against the low sun behind Laura. 'He doesn't possess everything, but he's willing to sell back a generous portion of what is left. I can instruct Mr Woodson to find a suitable location for the shop and you and Mrs Townsend can manage it.'

'What about being your partner, understanding your business? How can I do that if I'm running my own?'

'I want you to be happy.' He guided her into the shade of a tall tree, its branches spreading out over the grass and the gravel path. 'After the incident with Mrs Hammond, I'm concerned you may not be.'

She laid her hand over his. 'You'd really do such a thing for me?'

'Yes.' He didn't waver in his declaration and she knew this wasn't a hollow offer. He was determined and ready to act if she accepted it, but she couldn't.

'Thank you, Philip. You don't know how much it means to me to hear such an offer, but I don't need the draper shop any more.'

'But it's your father's legacy. It's as important to you as my father's business is to me.'

'It was at one time, when I had nothing else to hold on to during all the cold nights in Seven Dials. Since then, you've given me so much more to cherish and to strive for. Going back to the draper business would be like sliding into the past when all I want is to move forward, with you.'

He raised her hand to his lips, the kiss tender and heartfelt. He'd offered her a gift and in refusing it, she'd given him something even more meaningful in return. It seemed strange to leave the past so firmly behind, but she wouldn't go back. Philip was her future now and though parts of him still remained hidden from her, with each passing day they drew closer together.

In the distance, a church bell chimed. Philip plucked his watch from his waistcoat and clicked open the gold case, the businessman Laura knew so well overtaking the caring husband once again. For all his sudden change, there was a new softness around his eyes and at the corners of his mouth.

'I'm afraid we must return home.' Philip clicked the watch closed and dropped it back in his pocket.

'I knew you wouldn't linger too long,' she chided with a laugh, running her hand over his back. 'Though at home, might I tempt you to dally for a time with me, upstairs?'

He met her daring question with a tempting look. 'I can always make time in my schedule for you.'

He dropped a searing kiss across her lips, heedless of them standing in the open where anyone who happened by might see them.

When at last they broke from their embrace and returned to the gravel path, they could not walk back to the carriage quickly enough. There was a great deal they could accomplish inside with the curtains drawn, even more when they arrived home.

Hand in hand, they neared the tall gates of the park entrance. Across the street, the landau waited by the kerb. A wide-shouldered gentleman in a rough coat peered inside it through the open window. Laura jerked to a halt at the sight of him, trying to catch a glimpse of his face, but a large town coach lumbered between her and the landau. Her desire shrivelled into cold fear as she realised the strange man ogling the carriage reminded her of her uncle Robert.

'What's wrong?' Philip slid his arm around her waist and drew her close.

'I thought I saw my uncle near the carriage.'

He peered across the street as the town coach wobbled away on its springs, but the man who'd ignited her fear was gone.

'Mr Rathbone, I must speak with you.'

Laura jumped at the deep male voice calling out to Philip from across the grass. They turned to see Mr Jones hurrying towards them, dressed in a finely tailored coat of expensive light-blue wool.

'Mr Jones, of course. Walk with us if you will,' Philip urged, but Mr Jones hesitated.

'What I wish to convey would best be spoken out of your wife's hearing.' He tipped his hat to her. 'My apologies, Mrs Rathbone.'

'She may hear anything you wish to discuss,' Philip insisted.

Mr Jones's troubled eyes darted back and forth between her and Philip. 'I don't wish to alarm your wife unnecessarily.'

Philip stood stiffly as ever, making it clear he intended for her to stay.

'Philip, I can wait inside the carriage,' Laura offered, recognising Mr Jones's unease. He would speak quickly and more freely if she was away and Philip could relay the matter to her once they were done.

'All right.' They left the park and crossed

the street in silence. Philip helped her into the
landau. 'I'll only be a moment.'

He closed the door and she settled herself
against the squabs, her nerves tightened by Mr
Jones's strange warning. Whatever he'd drawn
Philip to the back of the carriage to discuss, she
couldn't hear it over the steady clop of horses
and the creaking wheels of the numerous car-
riages beginning to arrive with the *haut monde*
for the fashionable hour.

She shifted to the back squab to try to catch
something of the conversation when the sound
of crunching paper drew her attention to the
floor. Against the dark treads lay what looked
like a ragged bit of old broadsheet tracked in on
her half-boot. She plucked it up, ready to fling
it aside when the dark, sprawling letters on the
unprinted side made her freeze.

*You owe me.*

The carriage door opened and Philip stepped
inside, his face set hard. 'The man you saw was
Mr Townsend.'

'I know. I found this on the floor.' She
handed him the note.

He offered it only a glance, his lips drawn
tight across his teeth.

'It isn't the first time he's approached us,'
she confessed cautiously. 'The morning at Mrs

Hammond's, I thought I saw him in the crowd. It was the reason I'd locked the carriage door.'

He settled his hands on his knees, his displeasure obvious. 'Why didn't you tell me before?'

'Because I wasn't sure. I didn't get a proper look at him. With everything happening in the bookshop and how upset I was, I thought it was only my mind playing a trick on me.'

'If you'd told me, then I could have done something to prevent the present situation.'

'The present situation?' Her stomach clenched with worry.

'Last night, your uncle approached Mr Jones about trading a gold necklace for money. During the transaction, he asked Mr Jones if he wanted to see me ruined and hinted at helping him achieve it. His suspicions raised, Mr Jones pretended to entertain the idea and tried to garner more details, but his questions made Mr Townsend suspicious and he left.'

Laura felt her misstep as sharply today as she had in his study that day he'd shown her the Halycon House ledger. It was an awful reminder of the lack of faith she'd displayed in Philip. 'What'll we do?'

'Mr Jones believes the necklace is stolen.

I'll contact a thief taker I know who'll see to it Townsend is arrested and we'll be rid of him.'

For once, Philip's confidence didn't put her at ease.

'I don't think the necklace was stolen, I think it was something he had hidden away, in the trunk he brought back with him from India. I tried to pick the lock once, convinced he was keeping valuables from us, but I couldn't open it.' Her wrist tingled at the memory of her uncle's rough grasp as he'd pulled her from the floor when he'd found her kneeling in front of the chest, hairpin in hand.

'Now you know what he was hiding.'

'I wonder what else he kept squirreled away while my mother and I sold what we had to pay the rent and buy food. The selfish pig.' She plucked the note from Philip's hand and crushed it between her palms. 'I never let him bully me before. I won't let him bully me now.'

She flung the wretched paper out of the window.

'Laura, not all moneylenders are as honest, or on as good terms with us, as Mr Jones,' Philip warned, dampening her resolve.

'What are you saying?'

'I don't know how serious Mr Townsend is,

or how determined, but he may find someone to assist him with whatever he has in mind.'

'He can't be serious, or sober enough, to do anything. He couldn't even keep himself fed without my help.'

'I agree, but we must still be cautious.'

'And do what? Hide in your house in fear?'

Philip flexed his fingers over his knees. 'There is a press-gang boss I've dealt with before, a Mr Walker.'

'You'd have him sent to sea?' Her uncle had hated the discipline of the army and returning him to service would be like Philip sending her back to Seven Dials with all the deprivations and uncertainty it entailed. She shifted against the squabs, unsure if she could wish such an awful fate on anyone, even her uncle.

'Only if Mr Townsend continues to pursue whatever plot he's concocted. I'll have Mr Walker locate him tonight and threaten him with being pressed. It should be enough to scare him away from implementing whatever foolish plan he has in mind.'

'And if it isn't?' Robert Townsend wasn't known for being rational, especially when drunk.

'Then he has no one to blame but himself if he wakes up aboard a ship.' Philip tightened his hands into fists, his determination and unease subtle, but none the less evident. 'Most likely, the encounter with Mr Walker will encourage Townsend to leave London and it will settle the matter.'

She hoped Philip was right.

'My uncle isn't the first person to threaten you, is he?' She knew about Philip's weapons and his boxing, but in all the time she'd been with him, she'd never felt in danger, until now, and that was due to her, not some indignant client.

'No.' He moved across the squabs to sit beside her, wrapping his arm around her waist and pulling her close. 'Not everyone who has threatened me is as lovely or talented as you.'

Laura smiled, his confidence raising hers. She might have doubted him at Mrs Hammond's, but she didn't doubt him now, nor his determination to protect her and keep her safe.

His brief spark of humour faded as he stared down at her. Philip slid his hand beneath hers, his grip tight with his concern. 'Until the matter is resolved, promise me you'll only leave the house escorted by me, Mr Connor or one of my men, and you are not to see clients by yourself.'

'I promise.' She didn't know if her uncle would resort to violence. Judging by his fury the day Philip had removed her and her mother from Seven Dials, she knew it was within him to lash out. Only it wasn't just herself she was worried about. It was Philip. 'What about you?'

'I'll be careful. I promise.'

She rested her head on the soft wool covering his chest and closed her eyes, breathing him in as if they were alone together in his bed and all the troubles of the day were put away in the darkness. Whatever juvenile ideas about revenge her uncle possessed, she knew Philip would deal with them.

The landau rolled up to their front door and Philip stepped out first, stopping to look up and down the street before beckoning her out. She took his hand, holding her head high as they strode up the front path, pulling Philip back when he wanted to hurry forward.

He paused and threw her a questioning glance.

'I won't let him intimidate me,' she answered defiantly and Philip's lips drew proudly to one side.

'Nor should you.'

Together they strolled into the house. Once inside, Philip handed his stick and hat to the butler and asked him to summon Mr Connor.

\* \* \*

While Philip and Mr Connor sequestered themselves in Philip's study, Laura went about the activities of her day. She tried to focus on each task, but she was so distracted Mrs Palmer, and even Laura's mother, asked more than once if something was wrong. Mrs Palmer didn't pry out of deference to Laura's new position as head of the household. Laura's mother wasn't so shy.

'Come, dear, what is it? You look worried,' her mother pressed. They sat together with Thomas in the shade of the house, watching Jane direct the gardener as he tended the roses.

'I'm tired, that's all,' Laura lied. She didn't want to frighten her with the truth.

'As a newly married woman, I don't doubt you are,' she observed knowingly. 'But your distraction is more than marital bliss.'

Thomas struggled to slide off Laura's lap, but she wouldn't let go of him. With its high walls, the garden seemed safe enough, but her nerves were on edge. She felt as if her uncle might appear at the iron gate at any moment, the pistol she'd left behind gripped in one hand and this time packed correctly. She didn't want this beautiful life torn apart or to see Jane, Mother or Thomas suffer yet another tragedy.

Guilt hit her hard. If only she'd trusted Philip sooner, this threat might not be hanging over them.

'It's only the household accounts.' She glanced at the study windows and the back of the drawn curtains. She wished Philip had left them open. She needed to see him, wanted to see him. His presence would calm the flutter of worry making her stomach turn over. 'They're in worse shape than I first thought.'

'I see. You're married now, so it isn't my place to pry, but if you wish to speak to me, I will listen.'

Her mother rose, taking Thomas and carrying him across the grass to join Jane.

Another wave of guilt hit Laura. Her mother had a right to know if they were in danger and she'd never kept anything from her before. However, as it might all come to nothing, there seemed no reason to disturb her peace. If only she could settle herself.

## Chapter Eleven

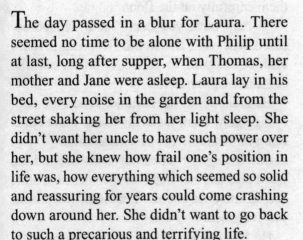

The day passed in a blur for Laura. There seemed no time to be alone with Philip until at last, long after supper, when Thomas, her mother and Jane were asleep. Laura lay in his bed, every noise in the garden and from the street shaking her from her light sleep. She didn't want her uncle to have such power over her, but she knew how frail one's position in life was, how everything which seemed so solid and reassuring for years could come crashing down around her. She didn't want to go back to such a precarious and terrifying life.

Rolling over, she pounded her fist into the warm pillow before flipping it over in search of the cooler side. Uncle Robert had ruined so much already. How much more did he plan to lay to waste now that he was done wrecking his own life?

At last the door opened and Philip slipped into the room. The tension in Laura eased as he made for the bed, shedding his coat and cravat as he walked. He draped the garments over the coverlet at the foot of the bed before unfastening his cufflinks and dropping them into the crystal bowl on the dressing table. He sat gently on the edge of the sheets, thinking her asleep, as he pulled off his boots and set them carefully on the floor.

'Where have you been?' she whispered. She'd sent word she would sleep in his room tonight, wanting to be close to him and the comfort he provided.

He looked over his shoulder at her, the faint orange glow from the coals in the grate flickering in his hair. 'You're awake, then?'

She sat up, wrapped her arms around his waist and laid her head on his back, his shirt soft against her cheek. 'I couldn't sleep until you were here.'

He twisted around in her embrace, stroking her back through the chemise. 'Justin and I have just returned from Mr Walker's. He's going to visit your uncle tonight. By morning, if he's smart, Townsend will be far from London and out of our lives.'

'I'm sure he will.' She shifted up on to her

knees, her arms draped loosely around him, her hair falling forward to brush her cheek. 'I'm sorry again I didn't trust you.'

'I understand why you didn't.' He pushed a lock of hair behind her ear, his hand lingering against her jaw. 'Besides, it's in the past now. There's no reason to dwell on it.'

If only she could forgive herself so easily. 'But I put us in danger by being foolish.'

'We all make mistakes.' He pulled out of her embrace, propping one arm against the mattress to lean hard against it. Guilt and anger shadowed his face, just as it had in the entrance hall the night he'd told her about his late wife's death. 'I don't want to fail you like I failed Arabella.'

'And you won't.' Taking his face in her hands, Laura forced his eyes to meet hers, refusing to let him retreat into his pain. 'You've done so many things right, Philip: maintaining your business, managing Halycon House, taking care of Thomas, Jane and me. Look to those and let the rest go, for your happiness and all of ours.'

She held her breath, waiting for him to trust her as she trusted him. If here, in the middle of the night in his bed, he couldn't be completely open with her, he might never be.

Then, at last, the pain faded from his expression. He slid his hand along her cheek and nestled it against the back of her neck. 'Perhaps some day, with your help, I will be able to.'

He drew her to him, covering her lips with his. Relief flooded through her and all thoughts of danger faded with the sweep of his tongue across hers. Tonight, he was hers and his past wouldn't pull him away.

Philip covered her body with his, protecting as much as seducing her. Anger had burned inside him from the moment Mr Jones had told him of Townsend, to the moment he'd entered the stinking air of Mr Walker's grimy lodgings. It wasn't danger to himself which fuelled his rage. He'd faced worse and survived. It was Townsend's threat against Laura and the happiness they'd found together which made Philip seethe.

His thumb grazed the hard point of one breast through Laura's chemise and her fingers dug into the muscle of his back. Cupping the full mound in his palm, he slid his other arm around her and pressed her hard against him, lowering them both into the soft sheets. The fears awakened by Townsend's threat shadowed Philip even as he caressed the tantalising roundness of Laura's hip and slid the soft cotton from her body. The worry demanded that he pull away and guard his heart. Intoxicated by his need for her, he couldn't.

He pressed himself into her, eager for the calming comfort of her soft curves. As they moved together as one, their intimacy and her fierce possession of him swept through Philip. He twined his fingers with hers, raising their hands above her head, both resisting and craving this closeness. She was here now beneath him, but nothing was certain, nothing guaranteed. He kissed her hard, the exquisite taste and heat of her driving back his worries. The word *love* lingered on the tip of Philip's tongue as he inhaled her delicate rose scent, but his breath came too hard, his body was too demanding to allow him to free the word. So instead he showed her, grasping her around the waist as her body tightened. She met his frenzied thrusts, drawing him deeper and deeper into her until they both cried out with their release.

It was a long time before Philip withdrew and settled in beside her. He said nothing as he held her, listening to her short breaths grow longer until it was evident she was asleep. Sleep eluded him and he stared at the folds of the canopy above the bed, refusing to disturb her though he wanted to rise, pace, exercise, do anything to shift the agitation burning a hole in his gut.

It wasn't until Laura had shown him the threatening note from Robert Townsend that Philip had realised the depths of his feelings for her. In the past week she'd become more than his wife, but a part of him, a part he could not survive without. With her, he'd been free to put aside the control he'd exerted over himself for so long and enjoy the passion of her body and being. It had lifted him above his past troubles and all the sorrows which had turned him to stone. The feeling hadn't come at once, but crept over him bit by bit. He'd failed to see it because it had simply become part of his life, like breathing or eating, and just as necessary.

'I love you,' he whispered, disturbing the fine wisps of brown hair arching over Laura's face.

'Hmm,' she murmured against his chest, snuggling closer to him before settling back to sleep.

He closed his eyes, struggling to join her in rest. He'd been this happy with a woman once before and she'd been ripped from him. He didn't want to face such torment again. A noise in the garden jerked him from his light sleep and panic loomed before he beat it back. Philip listened, but heard nothing except the faint whinny of a horse in the mews.

He stroked Laura's back, drawing from her peace to regain his own. He couldn't allow his worries to taint his time with her, or make him scurry back to the hardness inside him. He didn't want to live for ever in that cold, lonely place, but here with Laura and her love. He settled down closer to her and closed his eyes. Laura believed in him and his ability to keep her safe. He would prove himself worthy of her faith.

Loud thuds echoed through the room. Laura raised her head groggily from Philip's chest, thinking someone must be racing up the stairs and wondered who could be about at this hour. Then the bedroom door rattled on its hinges and Mr Connor's voice called through the wood.

'Philip, wake up. There's trouble at the warehouse.'

Philip flipped back the covers, snatched his banyan from the foot of the bed and flung it on before he cracked open the door.

Laura clutched the sheets to her, straining to hear. She couldn't make out the words of their muffled conversation. At last, Philip closed the door, then marched to the grate, lighting a reed and setting it to the candles on the mantel. Orange light filled the room, settling over the smooth skin of Philip's chest as he slipped off the banyan and made for the clothes laid at the foot of the bed.

'What's wrong?' She tugged the sheets up higher over herself, to ward off the chill of fear licking at her.

'There's a fire at the warehouse where I store collateral.' He pulled his shirt on over his head, then reached for the breeches. 'I must see what can be salvaged and ensure the two guards I pay to watch it aren't hurt.'

She snatched up her dressing gown from the chair beside the bed, wrapped it around her and pulled the ties tight across her waist. 'You shouldn't go. Send your men.'

'They'll come with me.' He tugged up his breeches.

Laura hurried to his side, trying not to panic. 'What if it's my uncle who set the fire? What if he's trying to get you there so he can hurt you?'

Philip sat in the chair and pulled on his boots. 'Most likely it was some sailor who was trying to keep warm. It's happened before, to Mr Charton and Mr Felton.'

'And if it isn't a sailor?'

He rose and cupped her face with his large hands. 'Even if your uncle did it, he was probably drunk at the time. He could barely strike me when he was sober. If he's inebriated, it should make it easier for Mr Walker to find him.'

He pressed a sweet kiss to her lips. She laid her hands at his waist, wanting to clutch him to her and not let go. Instead, she believed in his confidence and used it to bolster her own.

'I'll have my men with me. I'll be fine.' He stroked her cheek, revealing only a hint of worry in the gesture. 'I'll leave two men with you. While I'm gone, don't open the door to anyone except me, Mr Connor or my men, do you understand?'

'I do.'

'Then I must go.' He pulled on his redingote and hurried to the door.

Laura followed him out into the hallway. They weren't the only ones awakened by Mr Connor.

Jane rubbed her eyes as she staggered out of her room. 'Philip, what's wrong?'

Across the hallway, Laura's mother watched from her bedroom, her long braid falling out from under her nightcap and over one shoulder.

Philip took Jane by the shoulders and guided

her back to her room, giving her a little push inside. 'Only some trouble at the warehouse. I won't be gone long. Go back to bed. All will be well.'

His fatherly tone settled Jane and she returned to bed with far less resistance than Laura had expected.

Laura's mother remained. She wrung the end of the braid with her hands, throwing Laura a silent question with her eyes.

Philip closed the door to Jane's room, then made for the stairs. Laura followed, pausing to whisper to her mother, 'I'll tell you more once he leaves.'

'I'll wait up to hear it.' Her mother faded back inside her room as Laura and Philip hurried downstairs.

At the foot of the stairs Mr Connor met Philip. 'The fire company has been summoned. I've sent Mr Phelps with most of the men and the cart to try to remove what they can and make sure the guards are all right.'

'There isn't much there except the bookseller's stock and the remaining wine from the vintner.'

'The crates will make it easier to remove them, unless the fire has already reached them.'

'Let's hope it hasn't.' Philip looked to the two

men flanking the door. 'Mr Reed, Mr Marsh, stay here and keep an eye on things. I'm not expecting trouble, but be alert.'

'Yes, Mr Rathbone,' the two men answered in unison.

With a last, terse look at Laura, Philip strode out to the waiting landau.

'Take care of him, Mr Connor,' Laura instructed.

'Don't worry. I'll see to it he's back in your bed by morning.' With a saucy bow, Justin swung around on one boot and followed Philip out the door.

Mr Reed swung the door closed and slipped the lock, then both men took up positions on either side.

Laura made her way back upstairs, eager to put some of her mother's concerns to rest, though she didn't know how she'd accomplish such a feat with her own mind a tangle of fretting. She knew she wouldn't sleep until Philip was safely back home.

Philip stood at the kerb, the heat of the fire warming his face as a roar of flames raced up the east side of his building. Around him were stacked crates of books and barrels of wine his men had managed to save before the flames had overpowered them. His men now stood about, hands on their clubs, keeping an eye on the crowd. They'd been warned about Townsend and were on alert for any additional trouble. Philip might have worked to convince Laura it wasn't her uncle who'd set the fire, but he had his doubts. So far, there'd been no sign of the drunk. Philip imagined Laura waiting anxiously at home for him to return, the image of her fretting for his safety feeding his anger.

Nearby, two burly firemen pulled and pushed on the pumps while the rest directed the water from the river into the flames. Dark smoke alternated with white as one plume was extinguished only for another to sprout up nearby. The stench from the foul river water mixed with the acrid smoke filled the air. Philip's grip tightened on the walking stick he held as he watched the flames lick at the roof. He almost wished Townsend would stagger from the shadows and confront him. The buffoon deserved a beating for the fears he'd raised in Laura.

Mr Cramner, the stocky fire captain, approached Philip, his face greasy with sweat and soot. 'The flames are putting up quite a fight, but I don't think they'll win, not with the moist air tonight. You're lucky you got the books and wine out. If those had caught, it might be worse.'

'Good work, Mr Cramner.'

'Fight isn't over yet, Mr Rathbone.' He pointed at one of the men manning the pumps and stomped off towards him. 'Adams, put your back into it. I want the whole damned Thames sucked through there before the other brigade gets here and starts interfering. We don't want the whole block catching.'

Justin came to stand beside him, serious for once as the light from the fire wavered over his face. 'Neither of the guards saw or heard anyone before the fire broke out. Hard to believe Townsend could sober up enough to stagger here and do something like this.'

'Even if he did, by now I'm sure Mr Walker must have found him. I paid him plenty and he's never failed to find a man before.'

'Mr Rathbone,' a gruff voice called out over the roar of the flames. 'Mr Rathbone.'

Philip and Justin turned to watch Mr Walker push his way through the crowd and hurry over to them.

'Did you find Mr Townsend?' Philip demanded, eager to know if his plan had worked.

The press-gang boss shook his head. 'He doesn't live in the rooms in Seven Dials any more. I searched all the other places a man like him is likely to turn up, but he was nowhere to be found, not even at Mrs Topp's. Then I heard about this.'

He waved his hand at the flames.

Justin looked to Philip. 'Where do you think he went?'

The faint noise Philip had heard earlier from the garden came rushing back to him along with a sickening realisation. 'Townsend didn't do this to get me here and strike at me. He did this to pull me away from Laura. I have to get back home.'

Philip ran for the carriage, Justin close on his heels.

'My house, at once,' Philip called to the driver as he and Justin jumped inside.

The carriage took off in fits and starts, men hurrying to shuffle out of the way as the horses danced with agitation at the flames. A cracking noise filled the air, and through the window Philip watched as a portion of the warehouse roof collapsed.

At last the carriage broke free of the confusion and tore down the dark streets, passing the whores and drunks littering the shadows.

'I should have known. I should have guessed

what Townsend was up to.' Phillip banged his fist against the carriage side.

'Mr Marsh and Mr Reed are there,' Justin tried to reassure him. 'They'll see to it he doesn't get in.'

'If he got past the warehouse guards, he can get past them.' The same wrenching fear he'd experienced the morning Arabella had told him she was pregnant choked him again now. He tried to force it away, to keep it from distracting him from whatever needed to be done, but he couldn't shake free of it.

He balled his fist over his knees. If Townsend dared to touch Laura or anyone else in his house, he'd kill the man himself.

Laura sat by the window in her mother's room, the lantern hanging over the doors to the mews just visible beyond the garden wall.

'Watching won't bring him back any faster,' her mother reminded her, though she, too, kept glancing out at the darkness beyond the garden gate.

'I know, but I can't sleep until he's home safe.'

'You can't sit up all night worrying either.'

'I won't. I'll do the accounts. Do you mind if I bring them in here?'

'Not at all. I'm not likely to sleep any more than you are. I'll read Jane's new book.' She slid the slender tome off the table beside her chair and flipped it open. 'I like to know what happens before she does so I'm not too shocked by the content.'

'I'll return in a moment.' Laura made for her room, eager for the work to take her mind off Philip and what might be happening at the warehouse. Even if the fire wasn't her uncle's fault, there were other dangers to threaten Philip: a spreading inferno to trap him and his men perhaps, or a carriage overturned by a spooked horse.

Laura paused outside her room and took a deep breath, banishing the images of doom threatening to overwhelm her. Everything would be fine and in the morning this would be just another business matter to deal with. Philip was well protected by his men and experience. There was little her drunk, bumbling uncle could do to hurt him.

Laura pushed open the door, the chill inside cutting through her thin banyan. She hugged the dressing gown tighter to her chest as she went to the window and shoved the sash down to meet the sill. Then she took up the poker next to the fireplace, kneeled down and jabbed at the coals, sparking them back into life.

The flames danced in the grate as she rose, ready to return the poker to the stand when something in the mirror over the fireplace made her heart stop.

Uncle Robert's cold, red-rimmed eyes met hers from across the room. 'Hello, me darling niece.'

She whirled around, her fingers tightening on the iron. 'What are you doing here?'

He pushed away from the dark wall beside the thick bed curtains where he'd been waiting for her. In the light of the fire, she caught the dull nose of a pistol in his hand by his side. 'I couldn't miss the chance to congratulate me own flesh and blood on her advantageous marriage.'

He swept into a mocking bow, staggering a little, in danger of tipping forward on to the carpet before he righted himself.

'Laura, why is it so cold in here?' Her mother entered the room, then jumped to a halt, the book falling with a thud to the floor at her feet. 'Robert.'

He levelled the gun at Laura. 'Come in and don't say a word or I'll shoot your precious daughter and find a less pleasant way to silence you.'

The older woman hurried to stand behind Laura and the poker which offered them both slim protection.

'Whatever you think you're doing, you won't get away with it.' Laura seethed. 'Philip's men are downstairs. They'll kill you for this.'

'But they ain't up here, and they ain't likely to get to me before I send a bullet through you and the poker through your ma's head.'

'What do you want?' Laura demanded, determined to remain calm and steady as she knew Philip would. Then, when the moment presented itself, she would be able to give them a fighting chance to escape.

'I want what I'm owed for keeping the two of ya for the last year.'

'We owe you nothing,' Laura countered, refusing to show an ounce of the fear tightening her hold on the poker. 'You stole enough from the shop.'

'Don't think you're going to cast me out so easily, girl.' Spittle escaped with the words, a large drop sliding down through the thick grey stubble on his chin. 'You think you're so high and mighty, living here with your filthy moneylender, a man who makes his living off the backs of men like me. Tell me, how many weeks did ya both spend planning to ruin me?'

'You ruined yourself.'

'Don't think I didn't guess what the three of you were up to with this proposal coming so fast after he stole everything from me.' Her uncle took a step forward, his red-rimmed eyes blazing, and Laura and her mother backed up. Laura nudged her mother to the side, away from where they would be trapped against the fireplace and towards the open bedroom door. Hopefully, one of them could slip through it and alert Philip's men. 'Do you know what I've had to suffer since you two rode away laughing at me in your hoity carriage? I've been sleeping in gutters, bitten by rats and fleas, while you're here lounging in your silk sheets.'

'You could have sold your necklace to help yourself, but instead you used it to try to ruin us, wasting it like you wasted the chance my father gave you to make something of yourself.'

'Your father gave me a chance?' He snorted. 'He and our parents never gave me a chance. They shipped me off to hell before I was even a man while my brother was taught a trade, given a business, a wife and family. They were so eager to be rid of me they never stopped to think what I might have wanted.'

'Killing us won't change the past, it'll only make things worse for you,' Laura countered, careful to keep her words low and steady so trembles of fear didn't warble them. 'You think Philip will just let you go if you hurt us? You think life in gaol or swinging from the end of a rope will be any better?'

'My life will be better and you're going to make sure of it.' He jabbed his thumb against his dirty shirt. 'I want my share of the money from the sale of the inventory and whatever else the rat paid to take your virtue.' He moved a step closer and Laura and her mother took another cautious step back. 'You thought you could cut me out of whatever deal you made with the moneylender—well, you're wrong. You'll pay me and you'll do it now.'

'We don't keep money in the house.'

'Liar. He gave me a lot when I visited before so there must be something here.' He waved the gun in a large circle at the room. 'So fetch it.'

'I can't.'

He stepped forward again and Laura and her mother backed achingly close to the door. 'Don't think I won't send a ball through you.'

'The safe isn't here. It's downstairs, in the sitting room.' She said nothing about not having the key. All she wanted was to escape and alert Philip's men.

He waved her towards the door with the pistol. 'Then get to it and don't tell anyone what you're about or I'll kill your ma, do you understand?'

She adjusted her grip on the poker. 'You would stoop so low, wouldn't you? You're disgusting.'

'Look at both of you, cornered and still looking down your noses at me.' Her uncle's lip curled, revealing one dark tooth before his mouth twisted into a sneer. 'Now get me my money.'

Laura nodded. Her heart pounded in her ears as she turned slowly, gripping the poker tight. He was so focused on his hate and bent on revenge, he hadn't thought to tell her to get rid of it. Or he just didn't see Laura as a threat, dismissing her as he always had. Tonight, it would be to his detriment.

Laura took one step forward, shifted her weight to her legs, then swung the poker in an arc to slam against her uncle's arm. The pistol clattered to the floor as he clasped his wrist and howled, his heavy eyes flaring with hate and anger.

'You bitch!'

'Mother, run!'

Her mother fled, screaming out for Philip's men.

Laura bolted for the door. Her uncle grabbed her by the arm and tugged her back, flinging her at the other side of the room. Her feet left the floor before she stumbled and slammed hard against the wall. An explosion of light and pain ripped through her head and she sank to the floor, catching her head on the edge of the table and sending another sharp pain tearing along the tops of her eyes. Weakness washed over her and she reached up to feel warm blood slipping down her forehead. It streaked against the side of the chair as she rested her head against it, exhaustion settling over her like a heavy blanket. She fought against the sensation and the room spun as she rose to her knees to face the man storming towards her.

'You never respected me like you should've.' He swept the gun from the floor, his form growing larger and more menacing as he came to tower over her. 'You thought yourself too smart and too good for your own uncle. Well, I'll show you who's smart.'

Laura sagged against the soft side of the chair, aware of the dark end of the pistol barrel dancing before her. The thud of footsteps and deep voices sounded from somewhere down the hall. She'd be dead by the time her mother and Philip's men made it up the stairs. Regret and pain pounded hard through her head and her stomach clenched, threatening to revolt.

The pistol swam in front of her, the barrel dark, menacing, ready to swallow up her whole life the way the throbbing along her temples and the light dancing around the corners of her vision had swallowed the room. Somewhere down the hall Thomas let out a wail. No, she thought, she would live for Philip, for Thomas, and the life they would build together. She grabbed the arm of the chair, trying to haul herself to her feet, refusing to give up and be shot like a dog in her own house.

Her uncle stepped closer, eyes burning with hate and satisfaction for what he was about to do. 'Now you're going to pay, you little bitch, for everything your father did to me, for everything he denied me.'

The trigger clicked and the hammer hit the pan. A deafening roar filled the room, followed by the sharp stench of smoke and burning wood, metal and flesh. The mangled pistol dropped to the floor in front of Laura, the cracked barrel and singed handle smoking.

Behind it, her uncle tipped back, his bulk dropping to the floor with a thud.

A commotion of voices clattered through the swaying room, increasing the throbbing in Laura's head. Her mother's high-pitched voice stood out among those of Philip's men, but she couldn't see her. All she saw was the worn-out bottoms of her uncle's shoes before everything went black.

Philip was out of the carriage before it stopped, racing across the front walk and through the open door. The emptiness of the hallway confirmed his worst fear.

He started for the stairs when Jane swung around the banister at the top, her braid flying to one side. 'Philip! Philip!'

She rushed down the steps as he flew up, the two of them meeting on the landing. 'He came. He tried to kill her.'

Philip's hand tightened on the banister as he faced his sister, trying to guess what had happened from her expression.

'He didn't,' Jane whispered. 'But she's hurt, badly. I summoned Dr Hale. He's with her in your room.'

Philip raced past his sister, barely aware of

her soft footsteps falling in quick succession behind him.

He flung open the door to the bedroom, coming up short when he reached the poorly lit scene before him. In the centre of the carpet lay Robert Townsend, his face a mess of black powder and blood. The mangled pistol lay at his feet. Philip's stomach clenched, but not from the gore. It wasn't the first time he'd seen a man in such a state.

It was the scene greeting him in the four-poster bed that rattled him. Laura sat up against the pillows, Mrs Townsend rubbing her back as she retched into an old porcelain basin. A white bandage with a dark spot of blood covered her forehead. Dr Hale stood on her other side of the bed, his grey hair wild at his temples, his face grim.

It wasn't the blood or the vomit which nearly sent the contents of Philip's dinner up to join the mess on the floor. It was the terrifying familiarity of it all.

Philip rushed forward, but Dr Hale rounded the bed to stop him.

'Move aside,' Philip commanded.

Dr Hale clenched his arm, refusing to let him pass, his grip just as firm as it had been that fateful morning a year ago. 'Come with me into the hallway and keep your voice down. The noise will only disturb her and increase her suffering.'

'You can tell me here,' Philip insisted.

'The cut on her forehead is more bloody than serious, but she's suffered concussion. She's confused. The best we can do is to keep her awake tonight, not let her sleep. I saw too many men during my two years in the army fall asleep after hitting their heads only to watch them slip into a coma and pass before the night was out.'

Laura retched again, crying despite Mrs Townsend's soothing words. Philip looked to her, eager to be by her side. Dr Hale's hand tightened on his arm, keeping him where he stood.

'Will she be all right?'

'Her eyes are responding well to light and she's behaving as I would expect after such an injury. By morning she should be better, assuming there isn't some deeper wound which prevails. Sadly, all we can do is wait.' Philip tore his gaze away from Laura to meet Dr Hale's eyes. In the grey depths was the same sickening seriousness he'd used to deliver the news which had changed all their lives. 'She must not be allowed to sleep tonight.'

'I'll make sure of it.' Philip wasn't going to relive that dreadful morning.

'Brace yourself, Philip, she's confused. She may behave strangely.'

Philip nodded, drawing in a steadying breath before Dr Hale let go of his arm. He strode to the bed, barely aware of Dr Hale taking up his former position on the far side.

Mrs Townsend rose as Philip approached, removing the bowl Laura had been hunched over. The older woman's worried eyes met his, the concern in them so deep it was nearly Philip's undoing. He saw no blame in her gaze, but none the less he felt deeply responsible. He should have guessed, he should have sensed what Townsend was up to and prevented it. He should have kept Laura safe, but he'd failed her as he'd failed Arabella.

Philip settled on the bed beside her. 'Laura, I'm here.'

'I'm so tired.' Her eyes began to close and Philip slid his hand in hers. It was cold, deathly so. The terror of it struck him deep in his soul.

'You can't sleep. Dr Hale says so.'

'Who?' Her half-mast eyes cast about the dark room in confusion, alighting on Dr Hale.

He cast a smile at the patient, but she didn't offer one in return.

'I don't know him.' She looked to Philip to ease her confusion. 'Should he be here?'

'Yes, he should.'

Out of the corner of his eye he caught sight of his men moving in with a blanket. Philip shifted on to the bed, sitting in front of Laura to block the view of his men cleaning up the mess that was Robert Townsend's body. He'd send Justin for the constable and have him see to the legal matters. Helping Laura heal was all Philip cared about tonight.

'What's this on my head?' Laura tugged at the bandage.

Philip gently pulled her hand away from it. 'You've hurt yourself.'

'How?'

He looked to Dr Hale, who shook his head, warning him off the truth. 'You slipped and fell.'

The explanation left her more confused than before. Soon her eyes began to slide closed again.

Philip patted her hand. 'Stay awake.' *Stay alive.*

'Philip?' Jane's shaky voice carried through the semi-darkness. He twisted around to see his sister standing at the doorway, just as she'd done that morning a year ago, sniffing back her falling tears. The sound of her young, frightened voice rattled him, her fears too much like his own.

'I'll see to her.' Mrs Townsend laid one hand on Philip's shoulder and offered a light squeeze before going to Jane. 'Come, come, my dear, everything will be all right.'

Her reassurance seemed as much for Philip's benefit as Jane's.

Jane's scared sobs were muffled by Mrs Townsend's embrace as she escorted her into the hall.

'Why is it so dark in here?' Laura looked around the room in confusion, her voice weak and tired.

'We can light some candles if you wish.'

'No.' Dr Hale's objection stopped Philip from rising to see to the matter. 'The darkness is better. It helps the mind to rest.'

'Then what should I do?'

'Talk to her. Keep her awake.'

Philip settled in across from Laura, telling her first of the fire, his success in retrieving the merchandise and how his guards were safe. She didn't seem to comprehend, asking him who set the fire and where it had been. Casting about for something, anything to say, he studied her small hands in his. The clock chimed sweetly and the crystals on the candlesticks clinked together in the soft breeze from the slightly opened window. Philip wasn't a man to chatter, to fill the air with words, but once he began speaking to Laura tonight, he couldn't stop.

He spoke to her constantly as the hours wore on, surprised to find there were so many things inside him to say. He described his father and mother and his many happy memories of them both alive and in love. He spoke of the awkwardness of hearing, at sixteen, that his mother, after so many barren years, was with child again. He described the worry he'd experienced the night she'd been delivered of Jane. It was the same worry nipping at him now. His father had sent him to the boxing club with Justin to keep him away. Justin had made many jokes about the horror of his parents being intimate at their age while Philip had pummelled a dummy so hard, his hands had hurt for days afterwards. Then Chesterton had arrived with the news his mother and new baby sister were safe. In the midst of his relief, he'd realised how pernicious fear could be.

Laura listened, sometimes asking questions in her struggle to follow the thread of Philip's stories. He told her of warm Christmases in the sitting room with his parents and cuddling a very young Jane, who'd cried because she couldn't reach the red berries on the mistletoe hanging in the doorway. He asked Laura about her Christmas memories, hope filling him as she began one story about receiving a yellow dress she'd wanted so badly. Then her voice drifted off, along with all memory of the happy day.

'What was I talking about?' she asked and Philip's hope faded as another minute of this long night fell away.

Philip ran his hands over his face, exhaustion pulling at him, but he fought it, determined to keep his vigil, to keep talking, to keep Laura awake.

The clock chimed four times. Mrs Townsend slipped quietly back into the room, taking the chair next to the bed.

'How's Jane?' Philip asked.

'Sleeping. She's very shaken. We all are.' She leaned forward. 'How are you, Laura?'

'My head hurts.' Laura tugged at the bandage again before Mrs Townsend took her hands and laid them in her lap.

Judging by the questions Laura peppered her mother with about why she was in bed and why her head was bandaged, Philip guessed she would have little memory of the evening. He was glad. Glancing at the dark, stained wood floor, he wished he could remove tonight from his memory as easily as his men had removed the ruined carpet.

'You should get some sleep, Mr Rathbone,' Mrs Townsend urged.

He raised Laura's hand to his lips, pressing a kiss to the soft skin. 'I won't leave her.'

He'd lost one wife. He couldn't lose another, or face Mrs Townsend the way he'd faced Dr Hale that ugly morning.

'Then I'll sit with you and read.'

Mrs Townsend read aloud from one of Jane's novels. It was a simple story, but Laura kept losing the thread of it. It shook Philip each time Laura stopped her mother to ask a question. Mrs Townsend answered them with patience, often rereading a sentence two or three times until at last Laura seemed to grasp it.

Philip couldn't help Laura with the plot. He couldn't focus on anything but Laura's eyes and keeping them open and fixed on him. She blinked hard against the exhaustion making her shoulders sag and darkening the skin beneath her lashes. From time to time she would offer him a weak smile, propping up his spirits, only to make them fall again when she looked at him with puzzlement, unsure for a moment who he was or why people were gathered around her in the room.

Dr Hale's soft snores from the stuffed chair by the window punctuated the noise of a nightingale perched in one of the bushes outside.

Then slowly the darkness began to turn to grey, and the nightingale's call was replaced by the trills of songbirds. Dr Hale awoke and leaned over to look into Laura's eyes, holding up a candle to examine first one and then the other. Laura watched the flame move across her line of vision, the confusion which had so disturbed Philip a few hours ago replaced by a more concentrated scrutiny of Dr Hale.

The doctor blew out the candle and set the brass holder on the bedside table. 'I think we can let her sleep now.'

'Thank heavens,' Laura breathed, as if at last aware of the long hours which had passed.

Philip was relieved to hear something of the usual Laura in the remark, but it didn't ease the worry stiffening his back.

With Philip and Mrs Townsend's help, Laura settled down into the bed. She was asleep before Mrs Townsend could even draw the coverlet up to her chin.

Down the hall, Thomas's loud wail broke the morning quiet.

'I'll help Mrs Marston see to the lad,' Dr Hale offered. With his grey hair in some disarray, his cravat wrinkled and his waistcoat undone, he staggered out of the door, a sigh escaping him as he turned the corner. Philip recognised the release of tension in the subtle sound, and envied it.

His worry only increased with the daylight filling the room.

Mrs Townsend kissed her daughter on the cheek, then moved around the bed to the window. She tugged the curtains shut. The rings rattling against the rod made Philip flinch.

'Rest, Mr Rathbone. You won't help her by wearing yourself thin.'

'I'll sleep in a little while.'

Mrs Townsend studied him from across the bed. 'Thank you for all you've done for her.'

'I couldn't have done anything else. I love her.' The admission hurt because he hadn't yet told Laura. Somehow, for Philip, the intimacy they shared together in the darkness at times seemed just as terrifying as the sickroom.

'I know.'

'She doesn't.'

Mrs Townsend came around the bed, grasping one post. 'She does know, Mr Rathbone. She has for some time.'

She patted his shoulder, then left. The sweep of her feet over the floor reminded him of the quiet leaving which had taken place after Arabella had passed away. Mrs Palmer had shut the curtains as everyone who'd worked so fervently to try to save Arabella had drifted out of the room.

Only Laura wasn't dead. She was alive.

She shifted beneath the covers, mumbled something, then settled back to sleep.

Philip came around the bed, unable to take his eyes off her for fear that if he looked away she might drift away. He sagged down in the chair still warm from where Dr Hale had rested most of last night. It was the same chair he'd occupied a year ago when he'd watched Arabella and willed her chest to rise once more. Down the hall he heard his father-in-law's deep voice soothing Thomas, just as he'd tried to soothe him after Arabella had died.

Philip grasped the sides of his head, his fingers digging into his temples. It was all too much like before.

Something inside him shifted, solidifying around his heart like hot metal when it cooled, creating a shield between him and the emotions threatening to undo him. He'd been determined from the start to maintain his distance with Laura, to enjoy friendship and companionship, but not this soul-wrenching closeness which had cost him so dearly before. He'd allowed himself to stray from his original intent, like one of his clients who, holding the money in his hands, wanders back to the gaming table instead of his shop, squandering his second chance and all hope of salvation. Last night had been a warning, like the first lost shipment cautioning an investor from buying more shares.

Philip wouldn't walk away from Laura. He wouldn't abandon her or the promises he'd made. Neither would he continue to surrender his heart. He'd given it away as casually as some of the less-reputable moneylenders gave away sovereigns. It was a mistake, a dangerous one. There were more tragedies which could befall a person than the loss of their assets. He knew. He'd suffered through that loss once before. He would not do so again. He'd pull back his heart, guard the investment of his emotions as stringently as he did his business. Loss would not shatter his world ever again.

# *Chapter Twelve*

Laura opened her eyes and the room spun. She squeezed them shut, but it didn't block out the strange wavering light around her vision or the pain radiating from the back of her head. Her stomach flopped. If it hadn't been empty, she would have lost the contents of it.

Against the dark canvas of her eyelids, she caught flashes of images: her uncle, a looming circle of black. None of it came into detail, but wavered like a busy pattern of silk viewed from across a room. Nothing made sense to her now, not the pain, the strange light or whatever must have happened to leave her so hurting and confused.

Beneath the confusion, the image of Philip sitting on the bed beside her, the candlelight stroking the sharpness of his jaw and straight nose came to her. As the wavering light crowding her vision began to fade, the sense of Philip's presence and love enveloped her.

Love.

She could almost hear him speak the word, but couldn't untangle the memory of it from all the confusion smothering her like a heavy down coverlet.

The floorboard squeaked. Someone was here.

'Philip?' She didn't open her eyes. She didn't want to disturb the faint respite from the pain.

'No, my dear.' Her mother's voice came as both a comfort and a disappointment.

Laura opened her eyes. The room was dark, her mother's form shadowy as she came to sit beside Laura, the bed sinking under her weight. 'Where is he?'

'Resting. It was a long, difficult night.'

'Is he all right?'

'He is. And how are you? You've slept away most of the day.'

'Not well.' It hurt to talk, to think, to lie here.

Her mother draped a damp cloth over her forehead. Laura felt a little sting above one eyebrow, but the coolness eased some of the tension along her temples. 'You took quite a nasty bump last night.'

'What happened? I keep seeing snatches of

things, Uncle Robert, a dark circle, but nothing makes sense.' She opened her eyes and took a deep breath to steady her rebelling stomach. In the air lingered the faint aroma of smoke and gunpowder beneath the tart scent of lemon scouring soap. Whatever images she'd seen, they weren't part of a dream, but something real.

'Uncle Robert broke in here last night and threatened us.'

Laura's eyes flew open and she turned. A fresh wave of pain crashed through her and she gripped her head. 'What happened?'

Her mother reached up to adjust the disturbed cloth. 'I'll tell you all about it when you're better.'

Laura reached under the cloth and her fingers brushed the cut on her forehead. 'Is Thomas fine? Is Jane and everyone safe?'

Her mother removed her hand from the cut and laid it at her side. 'Everyone is fine, but if it will put your mind at ease, Robert is in no position to trouble us again. The poorly packed pistol killed him.'

'Then he's dead?' She was ashamed of the relief sliding through her.

'Yes.'

Laura closed her eyes, trying to recall what

had happened, but nothing came to her except the image of a dark hole and smoke. 'I don't remember anything.'

'It's better that way,' her mother reassured her, offering no more details about the events of the previous night. Laura didn't press her. She was too drawn out and hurting to take in any more than the facts she already knew.

'Is she awake?'

Laura's heart skipped a little at the sound of Philip's voice. She forced her eyes open and reached out, inviting him to hold her, to press his sturdy cheek against hers and wrap his long arms around her. The craving made her heart ache, but it didn't sting as much as the reluctance which whispered through Philip's eyes.

He moved forward slowly, as if compelled by duty, not by desire.

Her fingers curled over her palm and she nearly pulled her hand back, stunned and wounded by his reticence. Her mother had said he was fine, but something else had happened, something she could faintly detect, but couldn't work loose. It was all too tangled in her mind, like a tightly knotted thread.

Philip stopped by the bed, taking a chair beside her, staring at her hand as if reluctant to take it. When he finally did, Laura felt like she was holding a dead fish. 'How do you feel?'

'As if I've been struck by a carriage.' She rubbed her aching neck, then ran her fingers through her hair to feel the tender bruise beneath.

'Dr Hale assures me you'll make a complete recovery.' His words were as they should be, low, comforting, but even through her haze of pain she felt something missing. It was as if he spoke because it was expected, not because he wanted to.

She willed back the light obscuring her vision to fix on his face. He didn't look at her, but focused on her hand in his.

'Philip, what's wrong?'

At last he met her eyes. Warmth curled through her at the tenderness in his face. He softened his hand in hers until she thought he would take her in his arms and kiss away the fear seeping through her.

Then it was like a metal gate banged shut between them. He sat up straighter, something of the man she'd first met in this room, the stranger, coming over him.

'Nothing's wrong.'

Laura exchanged a look with her mother, who turned away to fuss with a basin of water. It wasn't the wound or exhaustion making Laura see things which weren't there. Her mother had caught his reserve, too.

She let go of his fingers, hating the stiff coldness of his grip. She laid her hand on his chest, startled at the way his heart raced beneath her palm. 'I'm sorry you had to suffer, too.'

'Your mother and Dr Hale were with me. It was a long night, but you're better now.' His face remained rigid as he leaned away from her touch. She lowered her hand back to the bed. It reminded her of the first time she'd touched him, outside Thomas's room. He'd struggled so hard to keep his distance then and again over the next few days. He was doing it again.

'Will you sleep here with me tonight and keep me company?' If she could hold him in the darkness, she might drive away whatever was hardening him against her.

He shook his head, resisting her. 'Dr Hale says you need rest. I would only disturb you. I'll sleep in your room.'

'What if I need you?'

Agony flashed across his face, as though he were fighting with himself to refuse her. The stoic man in him won the battle. 'There's a bell here on the table. Ring it and you'll have what you need.'

'I need you.' Weakness coloured her words, but Laura wasn't ashamed. She wanted him to know what he meant to her.

'You need rest.' He rose and laid his hands on her shoulders, pressing her gently down against the pillows.

She yielded, not possessing the strength to fight him.

Outside the bedroom, Philip sagged against the wall in the hallway, the pain so intense he struggled to breathe. She'd reached out to him and he'd pulled away and she'd seen it. Guilt gripped him hard as he felt the anguish of turning away from her when she needed his comfort the most.

'Are you all right, Philip?' Jane's voice cut through his agony.

He straightened, facing his sister as she approached him. She appeared less like a woman today and more like a child. Fear still danced around the edges of her round face and he knew it would be some time before the events of last night faded from her consciousness, just as it had taken months for her to recover from the shock of losing Arabella. 'I'm fine.'

'You don't look fine. You look as though you were the one who was thumped on the head.'

He rubbed his hand against his coat, Laura's warmth clinging to his skin, reminding him of everything he'd done wrong. 'Why don't you sit with her for a while? I'm sure she'd enjoy the company.'

'Why aren't you sitting with her?'

Curse her directness. 'A man from London Insurance will be here soon. I must speak with him.'

'Let Mr Connor or Mr Woodson deal with him.'

'It's my warehouse; I'm the one who must meet with him.'

He tried to slide around her and make for the stairs, but Jane blocked his way.

'She needs you.'

He studied his sister standing so defiantly in front of him. She was as determined as their mother had been whenever their father stubbornly refused to yield. 'And I'm here.'

'No, you're not. You haven't been here all morning. It's just like after Arabella died, like this whole year had been until Laura arrived.'

'What do you mean?' There was no need to ask. He already knew.

'You're distant, like no one and nothing can touch you, not me or Laura or anyone.'

Philip tapped his thigh. He'd pushed every-

one out of his heart except Thomas and Jane.
Or so he'd thought. A fresh wave of remorse
struck him. 'It's been a difficult night.'

It was a poor excuse for what he'd done to
Jane this past year and what he was doing to
Laura now. He was hurting those who loved
him the most, but he couldn't stop it or the increasing hardness encasing him.

'Everything will be fine, Philip, you'll see.'
Jane threw her arms around his waist and
hugged him tight, comforting him the same
way he used to comfort her. 'Laura is going to
get better and then she'll teach me to recognise
fine silk, like she promised she would.'

He wrapped his arms around Jane and laid
his cheek on her soft hair, revelling in her in-
nocence. It shamed him to think she could take
in the horrors of last night, of this past year,
better than he.

He removed her arms from around his waist.
Her eager eyes met his, waiting for him to agree
with her that all would be well. He wanted
to share her belief, but he couldn't. She was
young. She'd been even younger when they'd
lost their parents. She possessed no real understanding of the depths of suffering that loss
could inflict on a person.

'Yes, everything will be fine.' But not the

way she and Laura wanted it to be. 'Now, go in and help Mrs Townsend. I must see to the insurance man.'

He descended the stairs, cursing the pain crushing his chest. He didn't want this agony. He wanted everything settled as it had been before Laura had arrived, before Townsend had burst in and shattered their tranquillity, before he'd been foolish enough to fall in love.

Dropping off the last step, he strode to his office, squaring his shoulders as he struggled to regain something of the man he'd been two weeks ago, the one he both hated and needed.

Laura could neither wake nor fully sleep as the images haunting her semi-consciousness pulled at her like thick mud. Last night, Dr Hale had given her laudanum to dull her headache. The tonic tainted her dreams, turning them dark. Her uncle returned to harass her, threatening her and Jane and Thomas again and again until she cried out. As she struggled to free herself from the tortuous nightmare, she thought she saw Philip's face above hers and felt his hand on her forehead. His tender voice had soothed her back into a dreamless sleep which ended with the birds chirping outside the drawn curtains and her alone in bed.

Through a crack in the curtains, a thick shaft of sunlight fell over the desk. She peered through to the dressing room beyond, thankful the strange, flickering light from yesterday no longer obscured her vision. Everything in the room was as it should be, the desk neat, the coverlet wrinkled over her, the chair beside the bed empty and the bottle of laudanum corked on the table beside it. There was no evidence Philip had been here last night except her hazy dreams and the lingering memory of his voice.

A knock at the door made her roll to one side. The room swam a little, but to her relief the aching along the back of her neck and above her eyes was nearly gone. 'Come in.'

The door cracked open and Jane peered around it.

'Oh, you look much better this morning. The circles around your eyes are not nearly as dark.' She threw open the door and strode in, followed by Laura's mother and Mary carrying a breakfast tray.

Laura's mother marched to the curtains and pulled them open. 'What you need is some fresh air and sunlight.'

Laura blinked against the bright light filling the room, but it didn't increase her pain.

'How do you feel?' her mother asked as she raised the sash.

The cool air flowing in from outside drove away some of the exhaustion pulling at Laura. 'My head doesn't hurt as much, but I still feel so tired and sometimes dizzy.'

'Dr Hale says you probably will feel like that for a while,' Jane explained. 'He suggested broth and bread for today. Tomorrow you may have eggs.'

'Then I look forward to tomorrow.'

With her mother and Jane's help, Laura sat up. Mary rested the tray across her lap, then set to tidying the room.

While Laura removed the silver lid from the bowl, Jane plunked down on the bed in front of her, making the coverlet puff up around her knees. 'The coroner and the constable were here yesterday.'

'Were they?' Laura stirred the thick broth with the spoon, the rich, meaty scent of it heavenly. She tried a small amount, pausing to see if it would stay down. When it did, she eagerly ate the rest, thankful once again for the comfort of good food. If only Philip were here, it would help settle the lingering disquiet of her nightmares.

'Philip wouldn't tell me anything about it,

but Mr Connor told me the constable wasn't surprised to see the end of your uncle.' In the quick clip of Jane's words, Laura sensed her unease over what had happened and her desire to be brave and cheerful for Laura's sake. It was the same way Laura used to speak to her mother when her father was ill. 'According to him, in the past two weeks Mr Townsend got into trouble with at least two other moneylenders and someone named Mrs Topp. Who's she?'

'The owner of a bawdy house,' Laura mumbled through the last bite of the soft bread.

Jane's eyes opened wide. 'Oh, how exciting.'

'Laura, Jane isn't old enough to hear such things,' Laura's mother chided, removing the tray and handing it to Mary to take away. 'What happened at Mrs Topp's?'

'Mr Townsend was tossed into the gutter for fighting with one of her best clients,' Jane eagerly relayed. 'I think it's exactly what he deserved. I told Philip so, but he only said Mr Connor shouldn't have told me about it.'

'Where's Philip?' Laura asked, trying not to sound concerned. A man wasn't expected to attend the sick room, but his absence this morning was glaring and troubling.

Jane shifted hesitantly on the bed, looking

unsure about speaking for the first time since entering the room. 'At his boxing club.'

Laura picked at the sheet. 'I see.'

'He thinks he's being brave by staying away,' Jane rushed, as though revealing a bigger secret than the things Mr Connor had told her. 'And that if he is, then no one will know how scared he was for you, but of course we all know. We were all scared.'

Laura was also scared, not for herself, but for her relationship with Philip.

Before she could think on the matter further, Dr Hale appeared at the door, interrupting their conversation.

'Good morning, ladies.' He looked more rested than he had last night, his usual good cheer evident in his wide smile. 'How are you doing today, Mrs Rathbone?'

'She's much better. Ate nearly everything cook sent up for her,' Jane answered for Laura, jumping to her feet to stand at attention by the bed.

Dr Hale approached, setting his leather bag on the floor before leaning in to examine Laura's eyes. 'And the pain?'

'Mostly gone.' Laura followed his finger as he moved it in front of her eyes.

He examined her forehead. 'The cut is heal-

ing nicely. I'd say in a few days you'll be back
to your old self with this whole ordeal behind
you.'

She wasn't as confident as the doctor. She
might be the same as before, but things with
Philip wouldn't be. She sensed it in his absence.
She leaned back against the pillows with a sigh.
It was all too much to think about right now,
yet it was nearly the only thing occupying her
thoughts.

'You're tired so I'll leave you.' He picked up
his bag. 'Jane, I was so eager to check on Mrs
Rathbone, I didn't have my breakfast. Would
you be kind enough to escort me to the dining room?'

'It would be my pleasure, then I can tell you
what Mr Connor told me the constable said.'

Laura's mother shook her head as Jane and
Dr Hale left the room, arm in arm. 'She enjoys
gossip far too much.'

'So do you,' Laura teased, the levity light-
ening a little of the weight in her heart. 'Philip
hasn't been in to see me since yesterday.'

'Yes, he has.' Her mother lifted a shawl from
the back of a chair and began to fold it. 'He
was in here with you last night while you were
sleeping. I heard you call out and came in to
sit with you, but he was already here. He didn't

notice me. I don't think he wanted anyone to see him, so I didn't disturb him. He stayed for a very long time.'

Tears welled in Laura's eyes at the image of him holding his silent vigil. He was still caring for her as he had since the moment she'd come under his protection, but hiding it. 'Why wouldn't he want anyone to see him? Why is he avoiding me?'

'He's had quite a shock, my dear.' Her mother perched on the bed next to Laura, crumpling the shawl against her stomach. 'We all have.'

'Tell me what happened.'

'Dr Hale doesn't think it a good idea for you to know just yet.'

'I don't care, I have to hear it.' It was the only thing which might explain Philip's sudden distance.

In short sentences, her mother relayed her uncle's threat, Laura's bravery with the poker and finally his death caused by the poorly packed pistol. Laura looked to the now bare floor near the fireplace, noticing the dark circle staining the wood, the lingering scent of vinegar and lemon soap explained. None of it moved her like her mother's description of the long night afterwards and how Philip had sat beside her, determined to keep her awake and alive.

The throbbing behind her forehead increased and Laura closed her eyes. She struggled to remember the events her mother described. Only the vague awareness which had come to her late into the night, the peace and comfort of Philip sitting next to her and old memories of Christmas in their rooms above the shop revealed themselves.

She couldn't believe the same man who'd sat with her making her feel so warm and safe could be so distant now. What had happened between the darkest part of night and just before dawn to change him so much?

'Is she worse?' Philip's voice pierced the cloud of confusion swirling around her.

Laura opened her eyes and lifted her head from the pillows, wincing at the stab of pain at the back of her neck.

'No, she's much better,' her mother replied.

The bright statement didn't ease the firm set of his mouth. He didn't move into the room, but lingered by the door, hands stiff at his sides, just like yesterday.

'Laura was only worrying over you. She hasn't seen you this morning,' her mother remarked. It wasn't a chastisement but a reminder, a pointed one.

If Philip experienced any awkwardness he

didn't reveal it, waiting near the door as her mother rose to give Laura a hug.

Her mother leaned in and whispered in her ear, 'See, he's here now. There's nothing to worry about.'

She made for the door, pausing in front of Philip. 'Go and sit by your wife.'

She drew the door closed behind her as she left.

Philip didn't move, but studied Laura as he had the night she'd first faced him in this room when he'd been wearing nothing but soapy water. She smiled a little at the memory.

'It's good to see you smile,' he offered, cautiously approaching.

'I wish the same might be said for you.'

'When you're completely recovered, I will smile.' The words were tender but his tone was a little cold, like some posy of flowers obliged to be delivered. He sat down on the edge of the bed, near her waist, close but somehow distant.

'My mother told me what happened.'

He turned his hand over, bringing his thumb in to touch his wedding band. Nothing else about him changed. 'She shouldn't have.'

'I insisted.' She watched him stroke the ring, her worry sharp, pain thudding along her temples. 'When Uncle Robert was at his worst in

Seven Dials, I used to wish for him to meet with some accident. I didn't think one would befall him here.'

'He never should have been allowed to creep in.' Philip's fingers curled until his nails dug into the lines of his palms and his knuckles turned white.

'There was no way either of us could have known what he was planning.'

'I should have known. I should have guessed it.'

'It's not your fault, Philip.' She laid her hand on his cheek, wanting to comfort him as he'd comforted her during her nightmares. 'Everything is well now.'

'No, everything is not well.' He jumped to his feet and paced back and forth beside the bed. 'I should have done more to prevent last night. I should have made sure Mr Walker found Townsend before I left, I should have insisted Townsend be pressed instead of being lenient and waiting for him to strike. If I had, you wouldn't have been hurt. I failed you, just as I failed Arabella.'

'You didn't fail me.'

'I did. Can't you see it?' he blurted out, the shame in his eyes more powerful than it had been the evening he'd stormed away from her in the entrance hall. He jerked back his shoulders, the fight to regain control evident in the tightness along his jaw. He paced to the mantel, then turned and strode back to the foot of the bed, stern reserve descending over him. 'Now isn't the time to discuss it. I'll leave you to rest.'

He made for the door.

'I love you,' Laura cried, desperate to make him stay and not knowing any other way to pierce the wall encasing him.

He halted, but didn't turn around. The sun brought out the deep hint of blue in the darkness of his coat and another darkness threatened to consume them both. 'You shouldn't. You don't know who I am, how incapable I am of—'

'Love? You're wrong, Philip. I know you love me as much as I love you. I heard you say it when you sat with me and kept me awake through the night. I thought it was a dream, but it wasn't.'

She twisted the sheet, waiting for him to answer, to acknowledge at last what she'd suspected since their wedding night. Instead he stood in silence, his hands tightening into fists at his sides. She willed him to face her, to reveal the scarred and battered Philip he was fighting so hard to hide, but he didn't.

'It was a mistake to make our relationship more than an business arrangement, a bargain.' He reached for the doorknob, his words as chilling as the morning breeze that flew in through the window. 'I can't be the husband you want. I'm sorry if I led you to believe otherwise.'

Then he was gone.

Laura stared at the empty hallway and the painting of a dog hanging on the opposite wall. Tears made the room waver and she squeezed her eyes shut against them. Everything she'd fought for, everything she'd done to win Philip's heart came crashing down around her. She lay back against the pillows, her head hurting, her body too weak to do more than sink into the soft down. She cursed her uncle again. He'd severed Philip from her and Philip was all too willing to allow it.

She rolled on her side and opened her eyes. The bottle with Dr Hale's laudanum mixture sat on the table beside the bed. She was exhausted, but she didn't want to sleep, to face again the cloying dreams which had left her so ragged this morning. However, if sleep was the only way to bring Philip back to her, then the elixir was just tempting enough to taste.

She clasped the bottle, tilting it back and forth to make the liquid dance inside. For the first time she understood why some of Dr Hale's patients took to bed and the easy peace of the drug. Sleep was more comforting than the cutting loneliness of watching a once-loving husband turn away.

She ran her thumb up to the cork, ready to remove it and enjoy the sweetness inside. Her nail dug into the soft bark, peeling back a thin layer before she stopped.

She didn't want to be like Dr Hale's patients, trapped in a lifetime of loneliness, abandoned by the one man who'd vowed to love her the most. She set the bottle back on the table and pushed herself up on one elbow. This was not how it would be between her and Philip.

She flung aside the covers and swung her feet to the floor. The room spun as she sat up. She gripped the thick wood of the bedpost until everything stopped swaying. Then she pushed herself up, wobbling as she took her first step, catching the back of the chair to steady herself.

With her fingernails digging into the chintz, she wasn't sure how she would make it downstairs, or muster the strength needed to face Philip, but she knew she must. Another day could not go by like this, not another hour could pass with him retreating from her.

Her mother appeared in the doorway, stopping so quickly, the water in the pitcher she carried sloshed over the top and dribbled on to the floor. 'What are you doing out of bed?'

'I must see Philip.'

'You can't.' She deposited the jar on a low bookshelf and rushed to Laura's side. 'You'll make yourself worse.'

Her mother tugged her back towards the bed, but Laura fought to stay standing. 'No, I have to. You told me once you tried to push Father away because of your grief. Philip is doing the same to me now. He's retreating inside himself and I can't let him do it. I have to fight for his love, like you told me to do. I can't let him pull away.'

Philip sat across the desk from Mr Charton. Word of the fire and Townsend's demise had circulated among his friends and the affable man had paid a visit to make sure everything was all right. Assured by Philip that it was, he lingered now, sharing one of his many humorous stories. Philip was eager to draw the visit to a close, but he didn't want to insult his friend.

'And that's when I said he should try it and he did.' Mr Charton slapped his knee and let out a loud guffaw.

Philip laced and unlaced his fingers together

in front of him, unable to share Mr Charton's humour. If he let even one harmless emotion through, then everything else he held back would come rushing out with it. Before Laura, it'd been so easy to shove everything, his pain, his fear, into the deepest corners of his mind. Then Laura had unleashed it. Now it took all his effort to keep the tentacled beast in its box.

'Don't you agree, Mr Rathbone?' Mr Charton prompted eagerly as he waited for an answer to something he'd said.

'I'm sorry, Mr Charton. I failed to follow you.'

'I'm not surprised, not with you worrying about Mrs Rathbone. I always worry about Mrs Charton when she's ill, never so much as when she was delivered of our children. Soon, you'll have the same reason to worry and then another strapping boy in the nursery.'

Philip forced himself not to bolt from the study, hurry to the boxing club and pound the first dummy he saw into a pulp of feathers and leather. After last night, he knew he wouldn't be able to sit with Laura in her confinement, pacing the room until she and the child were either safe and well, or dead.

He snatched up the pen lying across the top of his desk and clutched it hard, working to ignore the beast inside him rattling against its cage. He'd been careless with Laura since the wedding, risking getting her with child instead of holding himself back. He set the pen down, lining it up with the ledger as Mr Charton prattled on about his children. When Laura was well, Philip wouldn't return to her room. To be alone with her in the dark was to risk both her safety and himself with their intimacy. He couldn't do it again.

A slight commotion in the hallway made him look up and the wind was knocked from him.

'I say, are you ill?' Mr Charton looked alarmed, before following the line of Philip's stare to turn in his chair and face the door.

Laura stood there, exhaustion clear in the darkness beneath her eyes. Mrs Townsend was beside her, helping her to stand.

At the sight of Laura, Philip's chest clenched, not with fear, but excitement. The life flaring in her eyes took hold of him, bringing him to his feet. He wanted to jump over the mahogany desk to reach her, hold her, kiss her, but he didn't move. The angry gash on her forehead was a reminder of everything she'd been through, everything he couldn't face.

He pressed his fingertips into the polished desktop, as if they might take root there and keep him anchored against the storm of emotions roiling inside him.

Laura ignored the other men who rose to greet her, focused as hard on Philip as he was on her.

'Everyone leave, now,' she commanded.

Justin pushed off his perch by the window and made for the door. 'Shall we, Mr Charton?'

'We shall.' Mr Charton moved fast on Justin's heels, following him around Laura. 'I've been married long enough to know when there's trouble brewing.'

Laura let go of Mrs Townsend and moved into the room, stepping cautiously. With surprising strength, she swung the door closed, then winced at the loud thud it made. Her heavy breathing betrayed her determination as she gripped the back of the chair before his desk, struggling as much as Philip to steady herself.

'You shouldn't be up. You should be resting.' Philip hurried around to her side and took her by the arm. The beast inside him roared at the touch and her nearness. The intensity of the moment was everything he didn't allow himself to be: irrational, unexpected, uncontrollable.

She resisted the gentle pressure he placed on

her arm, her body trembling under his hand, not from weakness but conviction. 'No, Philip. You won't push me away so easily.'

'I'm not pushing you away.' He balled his free hand tight at his side. He'd tried for so long to hide the ugliness inside him. Now she was seeing it and the awful man it made him.

'I know exactly what you're doing, even if you won't admit it. I won't let you crawl back into your stoic castle or live with me as a partner, but not as a true wife or companion.'

Philip scraped in a ragged breath, struggling for the strength which had carried him through the last two nights, determined not to crumble under the force of her determination. 'If you don't rest, you won't get better and then you might—'

'Die?' She stuck her chin defiantly in the air. 'Is that what you're afraid of, Philip?'

He didn't answer. He couldn't speak through the rigid exertion of beating down the helplessness and pain welling up inside him. It was a battle he was slowly losing.

She slipped her hand behind his neck, leaning heavily on him as she drew his forehead down to touch hers. The fortitude blazing in her eyes singed him and he dropped his gaze to the floor. Beneath her feet, the scratch on the floor snaked under the desk, white against the deep brown of the surrounding boards, a glaring reminder of his failings. He screwed his eyes shut, understanding for the first time why men swung or cursed at him when he came to collect their debts. He forced them to face their mistakes and the consequences just like Laura was forcing him to face his.

'Life is about risk, Philip, you can't hide away from it.' Weakness sat hard in the pull of her fingers against his neck and the faint struggle between breathing and speaking. Her bravery shamed him. She was stronger than he. 'It was a risk to accept you when you proposed to me, to give you my future, my happiness, my body. I had to trust you would be a man worthy of them all and you have been. You've been kind and good, even when I doubted you. You stood by your word, even when I thought so low of you. I wouldn't have blamed you for giving me over to Halcyon House. Instead you took me as your wife, showed me your heart and your soul.'

He jerked up straight. She didn't understand. The Philip she wanted was dead, crushed by dread. He was ugly and hard and damaged, incapable of loving her, his sister, maybe even his son. 'The man you want never existed.'

'No, he's right in here in front of me. He always has been.' Warm hands slid along the sides of his face, drawing him in, comforting, tender. Her belief in him was more powerful than his doubts, the whisper of her touch stronger than anything he'd ever done to maintain the cairn of stones crushing his heart. Like water, she slipped between the cracks, penetrating him until the stones began to tumble and light filled the darkness. 'I love you, Philip, and I know you love me, too.'

'I do.' He opened his eyes and took her by the waist, pulling her into the arch of his body, his strength supporting her in her weakness. 'I have since the night you first barged in here.'

He brought his lips down hard to cover hers. They dropped to their knees together, clinging to one another, life, love, happiness in every mingled breath. He couldn't push her away or live without the deep connection of their embrace. She believed in him, loved him, even when he hated himself. He couldn't deny her his belief and love in return, nor did he want to.

Laura broke from him, leaning into his chest and clutching his jacket. He hugged her tight, supporting her. For the first time, her exhaustion didn't frighten him. Eventually her weakness would fade like the nasty stain on the floor of their bedroom and the horrid events of the other night.

'I guess I wasn't as strong as I thought,' she stated without submission to her listlessness but in jest of it, defying it. She wasn't afraid of her injuries, wouldn't surrender her life or their future together. Neither would he.

'No, you're so much stronger.' Philip laid his forehead against hers, gently so as not to cause her pain, his body aching to be close to hers. In time, when she was recovered, they would be as one once again, and from it would come children and a future that he'd almost surrendered to his fear. 'But now, you must rest.'

He bundled her into his arms and lifted her up. The firmness of her against him was a reminder of her life, her strength and her love. He'd been so wrong to think he could close himself off to the woman he'd known from the first was meant to be his.

He carried her out of the room, past Mr Charton and Justin.

Mr Charton nudged Justin with his elbow. 'It's a beautiful thing.'

'Yes, it is,' Philip murmured to Laura, kissing the soft hair framing her face. She didn't look away as he carried her upstairs, her love for him as sure as her arms around his neck, her slender form in his hands.

At the top of the stairs, Jane and Mrs Townsend stood outside the nursery. Jane gaped at the sight of them. Mrs Townsend's hands flew to her heart, her besotted expression almost as sweet as Jane's.

'Isn't it romantic?' Jane sighed, her childish excitement feeding Philip's.

'Hush now, Jane,' Mrs Townsend chided with a laugh, taking her by the shoulders and drawing her back into the nursery.

'But it is, isn't it?' Jane insisted.

'Yes, it is.'

Thomas's happy coos joined their conversation as Mrs Townsend closed the door behind them.

Philip carried Laura into his room, the place which encompassed their first meeting and the first trial they'd been forced to overcome. He knew there would be more difficult times ahead as well as good, life never flowed so simply, but they would face them all together, without fear of the future.

'Will you stay with me this afternoon?' Laura asked, as he laid her gently on the bed, kneeling beside it to keep her arms around his neck, unwilling to let go.

'I will stay with you. Always.'

## Epilogue

⁓⁓⁓⁓⁓

'May I have your attention, everyone.' The ring of a knife against crystal faded into the clear, late summer air. Mr Charton stood with a full glass of punch near the fountain, his nose a little red from one too many glasses.

Everyone mingling through the Rathbone garden stopped their conversation and turned to him. Philip watched him raise his glass, wondering what he was about. Overhead, paper lanterns glowed brightly, the candles inside flickering like the stars in the evening breeze.

'I want to offer my congratulations to Jane on her fourteenth birthday. She's becoming quite the charming young lady.' Mr Charton pointed at his lanky son, who stood beside Jane. The young man was clearly besotted with her. 'You mind your manners with her, Milton, or you'll have Mr Rathbone to answer to.

He's quite the boxer. Why, I remember once when we were near Portsmouth, preparing to inspect some collateral. My, what collateral it was. I've never seen statues in such positions. They were—'

'I think we should save your story for another time, darling,' Mrs Charton interrupted, tugging her husband's arm just hard enough to make her point.

'But I—' he began to protest before a stern look from his wife finally sobered him. 'Yes, of course, another time. To Jane.'

Everyone raised their glasses and chimed in unison. 'To Jane.'

Philip nodded at his sister, who glowed under both the guests' attention and that of the young Mr Charton. Dressed in a pale-blue gown with an appropriately high neckline, she appeared the confident young lady she was quickly becoming under Mrs Townsend's tutelage. Young Mr Charton whispered something to her. Her eyes sparkled as she listened, then a hearty laugh escaped her. In the past few months she'd shed much of her seriousness. As had Philip.

'Jane looks very lovely tonight, my compliments to you and Mrs Fairley,' he said to Laura.

She stood beside him, dressed in a silk gown in a shade of green as rich as the leaves of the rose bushes. 'Oh, I had nothing to do with it. She chose the pattern all on her own.'

'She selected a modest dress without a fight?'

'She did.'

'You and your mother have worked a miracle.' Though the miracle was more in the change in Jane's temperament than her attire. He couldn't remember when she'd last stood in front of his desk, hands balled at her side, punctuating each demand with the stomp of her left foot. He vaguely remembered enduring such a tantrum during Laura's first night in his house, before Laura's love had brought him back to everyone who surrounded him.

Mr and Mrs Charton passed Philip and Laura as the wife drew her husband from more libations. Mr Charton paused, almost swaying into Philip. 'Portsmouth was one strange evening, wasn't it, Rathbone?'

'Indeed it was,' Philip agreed, before arching a knowing eyebrow at Laura. 'Though we've had stranger, haven't we, my dear?'

'Indeed we have.'

'Though nothing can top the printer's shop. You remember him, the one who use to sell all those portraits of women—'

'Another time, Henry,' Mrs Charton insisted,

twining her arm in his and leading him off to where the Moseleys stood.

Laura crossed her arms beneath her breasts, drawing the silk tight over their roundness and stirring Philip's interest. 'Why haven't I heard the story of the statues or the prints before?'

He caressed her elbow just above the glove, making her shiver. 'Because they're quite stunning.'

'Then I look forward to hearing them tonight.' She squeezed his arm, making it clear the story was not all she expected from him that evening.

Philip returned the silent hint with a wink, wondering if they'd be missed if they disappeared upstairs for a while. With Jane ensconced by the fountain with the two Felton girls and young Charton, she wouldn't likely search out her brother or sister-in-law. Mrs Townsend could serve as chaperon, though she was too much involved in a discussion with Dr Hale to take much notice of her young charge.

Laura rose up on her toes, resting her hands on Philip's shoulder to whisper in his ear. 'Come with me, I have something to tell you.'

He turned, finding her lips temptingly close to his. 'Does it have anything to do with clocked stockings?'

With a devilish smile she lowered herself from his shoulder. 'It might.'

'Then lead the way.'

She took his hand and pulled him into the shadows of the portico, seeking out the darkest corner near the study where the rose bushes were highest. Orange light from inside the house spilled over the stone still warm from the late afternoon sun.

'Are we to abandon our guests?' Heat settled low in his body, the idea of creeping away enticing.

'Not just yet.' She wrapped her arms around his waist, leaning her body into his until it was all he could do not to press her against the wall and shock anyone who might happen by.

'Then what surprise do you have for me?' He touched his cheek to hers, her gardenia perfume intoxicating.

'Quite a large one,' she whispered, her breath teasing his hair. 'I'm with child.'

His fingers tightened on her waist, crinkling the silk. He leaned back, studying her eager eyes. 'You're certain?'

'Dr Hale confirmed it this afternoon.' She arched back, a wide smile making her glow as bright as the lanterns. 'In a few months' time, we will be keeping Thomas's new nurse quite busy with another charge.'

Philip stroked her forehead and the faint red line that streaked over her eyebrow. It was the only thing which remained of the terrible night last spring. Philip tightened his arms around her, bringing her in closer to him. The darkness of the past was far behind him. All there existed now was a future with Laura and their child. He wanted both more than anything he'd ever wanted before.

'Are you happy?' she pressed at his silence, nervously biting her lower lip.

He met her eyes, the hazel depths which had first caught his notice, capturing him again. Elation rose from deep inside him, welling up until the sternness of his cheeks eased and a smile wider than any he'd ever experience spread across his lips and through his entire being. 'It's the most wonderful news I could receive.'

Her mouth fell open at the sight of his grin before her pretty lips turned up into a radiant smile to match his. 'Philip, I've never seen you like this!'

'And you will again, and again and again!' He picked her up and whirled her around, his deep laugh filling the evening air. It was joined by Laura's as the two of them twirled together, heedless of their guests and anything but each other and their joy.

\* \* \* \* \*

# MILLS & BOON®

## Two superb collections!

**40% OFF!**

Would you rather spend the night with a seduct[ive]
sheikh or be whisked away to a tropical Hawaii[an]
island? Well, now you don't have to choose!
Get your hands on both collections today
and get 40% off the RRP!

*Hurry, order yours today at*
**www.millsandboon.co.uk/TheOneCollecti[on]**

0215_INSHIP1

# MILLS & BOON®

## The Chatsfield Collection!

### 2 BOOKS FREE!

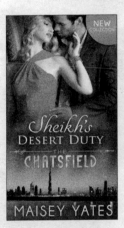

*Style, spectacle, scandal...!*

With the eight Chatsfield siblings happily married and settling down, it's time for a new generation of Chatsfields to shine, in this brand-new 8-book collection! The prospect of a merger with the Harrington family's boutique hotels will shape the future forever. But who will come out on top?

**Find out at**
**www.millsandboon.co.uk/TheChatsfield2**

LD_PROMO_BK

# MILLS & BOON®

**Classic romances from your favourite authors!**

Whether you love tycoon billionaires, rugged ranchers or dashing doctors, this collection has something to suit everyone this New Year. Plus, we're giving you a huge 40% off the RRP!

Hurry, order yours today at
**www.millsandboon.co.uk/NYCollection**

0215_INSHIP2

# MILLS & BOON®

## Seven Sexy Sins!

CATHY WILLIAMS
To Sin with the Tycoon

DANI COLLINS
The Sheikh's Sinful Seduction

### *The true taste of temptation!*

m greed to gluttony, lust to envy, these fabulous
stories explore what seven sexy sins mean in
the twenty-first century!

ether pride goes before a fall, or wrath leads to a
sion that consumes entirely, one thing is certain:
road to true love has never been more enticing.

**Collect all seven at
www.millsandboon.co.uk/SexySins**

# MILLS & BOON®

## &HISTORICAL

**AWAKEN THE ROMANCE OF THE PAST**

## A sneak peek at next month's titles...

### In stores from 3rd April 2015:

- **A Ring from a Marquess** – Christine Merrill
- **Bound by Duty** – Diane Gaston
- **From Wallflower to Countess** – Janice Preston
- **Stolen by the Highlander** – Terri Brisbin
- **Enslaved by the Viking** – Harper St. George
- **Promised by Post** – Katy Madison

Available at WHSmith, Tesco, Asda, Eason, Amazon and Ap

*Just can't wait?*
Buy our books online a month before they hit the shop
**visit www.millsandboon.co.uk**

**These books are also available in eBook forma**